BBC
# DOCTOR WHO

# MYTHS & LEGENDS

BBC

# DOCTOR WHO

# MYTHS & LEGENDS

## EPIC TALES FROM ALIEN WORLDS

RICHARD DINNICK

ILLUSTRATIONS BY ADRIAN SALMON

BBC
BOOKS

*To my beloved Clare, for everything.*

1 3 5 7 9 10 8 6 4 2

BBC Books, an imprint of Ebury Publishing
20 Vauxhall Bridge Road,
London SW1V 2SA

BBC Books is part of the Penguin Random House group of companies
whose addresses can be found at global.penguinrandomhouse.com

Penguin
Random House
UK

Doctor Who is a BBC Wales production for BBC One.

Executive producers: Steven Moffat and Brian Minchin

First published by BBC Books in 2017

www.eburypublishing.co.uk

Illustrator: Adrian Salmon
Editorial Director: Albert DePetrillo
Copyeditor: Steve Tribe
Cover design: Two Associates Ltd
Production: Alex Merrett

A CIP catalogue record for this book is available from the British Library

ISBN 9781785942495

Typeset in India by Integra Software Services Pvt. Ltd, Pondicherry

Printed and bound in Great Britain by Clays Ltd, St Ives PLC

Penguin Random House is committed to a sustainable future for our business, our readers
and our planet. This book is made from Forest Stewardship Council® certified paper.

MIX
Paper from
responsible sources
FSC
www.fsc.org    FSC® C018179

# CONTENTS

# INTRODUCTION

Many of the stories in this collection come from our own early history – a period sometimes referred to as the Dark Time. As such, it can be difficult to establish whether everything that is contained within these pages is unequivocally true or simply embellished myth. Many of these tales, however, do help shed light on periods of our history that are otherwise shrouded in uncertainty.

You may be unaware of the colonies Gallifrey once had in our expansionist past, before time travel had been fully developed. We had both civilians and soldiers on the front line and often the greatest bravery or shrewdest stratagem came not from a General or Colony Leader, but from the lowliest echelons of their command.

We are given insight into these rarely seen levels in tales of military campaigns and even missions undertaken by a fledgling Celestial Intervention Agency. In the latter's case this account has either been fabricated or declassified, we cannot be certain which.

Whether it is the lofty spires of the Capitol or the lowliest farm in the hills really does not matter. What is important here is not the setting, but the characters we find there.

Maybe that is the enduring nature of these myths. No matter which planet you're from, we are presented with situations that we may all recognise. The familial bonds – mother and son, father and daughter, brothers, sisters, comrades in arms or simply those whose nature it is always to try to do the right thing, no matter the odds. They hold a mirror up to us and we recognise what we see in the reflection. Perhaps we even aspire to *be* that reflection.

While we may not face a giant red spider killing our friends or face the loss of our offspring at the hands of an evil race, we all face decisions that are universal in their nature. For life is a series of choices and the path we choose defines us. That fundamental truth is seen across the universe.

Some of these myths have come to us through our own storytelling tradition, while others have their origins either with established races or ancient worlds. There even seems to be a cautionary tale about a scheming member of our own Time Lord race. I am tempted to say that this character must be an amalgam of several other figures. However, we cannot be sure for the individual is never given his or her Gallifreyan name.

In reading these tales, there do seem to be occasions on which a mysterious character appears almost from nowhere to interfere and help things along. He could easily be dismissed as nothing more than a *deus ex machina* – a convenient plot device that is often employed in such legendary fare. However, I suspect there is more to this character – or archetype – than meets the eye. Despite the fact that we only have three or four instances of his appearing in this volume, he can be found woven through the tapestry of Time Lord myth and legend.

He is never given the same name twice and always seems to wear a different face. This has given me cause to wonder if he could even be a member of our own species – a Time Lord wandering his own history. Or perhaps he is a shape-shifting figure of help and guidance, or even a mischievous new-born god.

His purpose is clear: to aid those he finds in need. As is often the case in real life, we find ourselves faced with decisions and choices. Difficult ones. Ones we find easy to ignore because they are so complex or have far-reaching consequences. The status quo is easy. Change is difficult and it is at this juncture that this character can often be found. He is a catalyst of action and change. Something, I suspect, we could all do with on occasion.

This then is the cornucopia of myth and legend that awaits the reader but I must issue my warning once more: myths and legends are complex – if not in the telling then certainly in their history and derivation. Like me, you must pluck what bones of truth you may find within their bodies.

*Chancellor Drakirið*
*Historian to the Bureau of Ancient Records on Gallifrey*

# THE MONDAS TOUCH

The twin planets of Dinasis and Bagoss were infamous. Dinasis, the smaller of the two, orbited its larger sister at such velocity it created gravity wells lethal to starships decelerating from hyper-light speeds.

This would not have mattered quite so much if Bagoss was not celebrated across the quadrant as the best place to get your hands on anything your heart desired. While its sister was renowned for the danger it posed, Bagoss earned its infamy by asking no questions about where the goods it traded came from or for what purpose they would be used.

The sleek dartship belonging to Seeker Sylen had come of out hyper-light some distance from these terrible twins. It had taken four days for the ship to reach orbit, but Sylen had not wasted her time. She had pored over maps of the fabulous market that spread across one-fifth of the planet's landmass. She had read scout reports of the best traders with the most exotic technology. She had amassed a wealth of information about local customs liable to offend the market vendors or fellow buyers.

Now, after three weeks living and breathing the amazing, shocking and sometimes dangerous market life, her search was at an end. A VR chip dealer had told her – after many bottles of horudo – that he had seen the gauntlet in the possession of a merchant named Ki.

She'd first heard of a mythical glove on Pyro Shika, a fascinating planet in the Claudian cluster. The gauntlet was said to possess magical powers: to heal, to give eternal life, to repair sailing ships or ancient weapons. It was the glove of a god, they said.

Following a sizeable donation to the religious order's coffers, Sylen had been allowed to read holy texts in which it appeared.

Mythic it may have been, but Sylen was almost certain the gauntlet was real. That had been confirmed when she'd found the desecrated tomb of priest-king Xanthos in the ruined city of Sagli-Ghent. It was here that the gauntlet had once been buried. But along with a lot of other religious artefacts from the time, it was no longer there. The trail – albeit temporarily – had gone cold.

Then, several months later, on the trail of an ancient soldier supposedly driven by malfunctioning tech she met a women in a bar who offered some new information. She was an archaeologist – feisty and unconventional – who, over a sumptuous dinner Sylen bought her, mentioned that one of her more impoverished associates had been persuaded to join a shady tomb-robbing expedition to Pyro Shika.

Sylen had immediately asked the Professor what had happened to the team and its findings. She had laughed and given a sarcastic reply. Last she'd heard, the impoverished colleague – a rogue by the name of Cedo – was a rich playboy on some space station with a lurid name.

It hadn't taken Sylen long to track down the station; not with a name like *The Pink Monoid*. It catered to the most imaginative appetites when it came to matters of the flesh. Sylen had travelled extensively, but even she had been shocked by what she witnessed there before she found the ex-archaeologist.

Cedo was a shadow of a human, haggard and sunken-eyed. He had all but spent his fortune on indulgencies of every fashion. So, for a price that would last him until the remainder of his life was done, he told the Seeker that the expedition leader had handled the sale of the artefacts. Sylen, seeing he was into his last days, risked asking specifically about the gauntlet. He'd grinned. 'That gauntlet made me an even richer man.'

It was only after she'd found the expedition leader's widow that she learned what he meant by that. A metal virus had killed many of the crew on the return journey from Pyro Shika. It was this that had increased Cedo's cut.

Of course, now the treasure was cursed, and if anything drives the price up on stolen archaeological items it's a good horror story. However, hardened thieves do not listen to such nonsense, and after the Solarium Panatica acquired the gauntlet it was stolen in a raid less than a year later.

From planet to planet Sylen had followed the trail; from private collector to thief and back again until the gauntlet had ended up on a freighter that had been lost. No insurance claim was made for the vessel as it hadn't exactly been space-legal and its owner was keen to avoid the investigation. Only the owner's assistant, a pathetic member of the Tovolian race, knew that the ship had crashed on Dinasis; he was only too happy to tell Seeker Sylen, once she had given him safe passage back to his occupied home world.

Knowing that the ship carrying the gauntlet had crashed on Dinasis, Sylen guessed that the planet's native scavengers would have stripped it bare. They would have then sold the contents to a trader on Bagoss who would put it up for sale in the market.

If the drunken VR chip dealer was to be believed, that trader was called Ki and she was standing before his emporium now.

The sky overhead was a crisp light blue, criss-crossed with jet plumes from the trade skimmers and taxis that braved the chilly atmosphere. Here, beneath the dome, the temperature was kept constant and the sometimes overpowering odours were extracted by hovering fan-drones.

The emporium itself was the standard three-storey building, a little more battered than most. This didn't surprise Sylen. She'd heard that Ki was down on his luck. That would make the deal all the easier. Sylen had located the gauntlet and her Queen would be very happy.

✢

'What an exciting tale!'

The woman who spoke was seated at the head of the table. She was poised and elegant, a slender neck leading to a noble, chiselled face; long, lustrous black hair fell below her shoulder, kept in place at the top by an angular crown that looked like both a sunburst and a mechanical cog.

Halfway down the metal table sat Sylen. She was surrounded by the other Seekers, all of whom had returned for the Ceremony of Giving. She was now wearing an emerald green cloak that marked her as an elite member of the Seekers of Catrigan Nova. The woman at the head of the table was her Queen, Lydia.

'You have the gauntlet with you?' the Queen asked. She was excited and nervous, like a child on its nameday.

'Of course, Majesty.'

Sylen stood and tapped the touchscreen surface of the table. Immediately the doors that gave onto the Hall of Seeking opened with a slight hydraulic hiss. Two members of the Royal Companions – the palace guard – entered, resplendent in their bronze armour and helmets. Between them they carried a green velvet cushion. On this sat the gauntlet.

It did not look like much when seen in such surroundings. It appeared to be what it was: a piece of scrap, purchased from a dubious shopkeeper in a faraway place. But Sylen knew it was also so much more.

Queen Lydia regarded the gift with a fixed smile. Sylen could see she was trying not to hide the fact she was a little nonplussed.

'Do not be unduly disappointed, Majesty. The gauntlet is ancient. But its powers are legendary.'

'*Legendary?*' Lydia asked, with a slight laugh.

'Being legendary does not make them untrue,' Sylen said. 'I assure you. You need only don the mitt to discover its power.'

Lydia reached out her favoured left hand and ran it down the length of the glove. It was constructed from a grey metal that had long since ceased to shine; it was almost matte now. But, as the Queen's fingers caressed the gauntlet, it seemed to shine where they passed, turning silvery.

Everyone saw and a collective gasp of approval came from around the table. The Queen seemed captivated. She picked it up and held the gauntlet to the glittering chandelier above to better see its construction.

It seemed almost like a perfect facsimile of a humanoid hand. Metal knuckles and fingertips, sinews and muscles that stretched from the back of the hand almost to the elbow. Queen Lydia hesitated but then with the encouragement of all the Seekers around the table, she slipped her slender hand and forearm into the metal glove.

She gasped as the metal inside the gauntlet felt almost alive. A pleasant tingling sensation spread from her fingertips all the way up her arm, way past the end of the mitt.

Lydia held up her arm before her, marvelling at the feeling she was receiving from it and the fact that it now looked almost new.

'Can it be true?' she asked, almost to herself. 'The glove of a god?'

'I think that unlikely, Majesty,' Sylen said. 'But I thought the one element of truth might be its ability to repair mechanical devices.'

The Queen smiled. 'I would like to try out *that* theory,' she said. Her eyes lit on the two Companions, now standing to either side of the Hall of Seeking's main door. She beckoned one forward. 'You!'

The armoured man stopped before Lydia, standing to attention. 'Yes, my Queen?'

'I just want to try something,' she said. 'Stay still ...'

The Queen slowly reached out her gloved hand, the silvery mitt contrasting with the bronze of the Royal Companion's armour. As the two metals made contact, there was a sizzling sound and the smell of soldering ozone filled the air.

At first the guard did nothing, but then he arched his back and stumbled away from the Queen, roaring in pain. The Seekers leapt to their feet as he doubled over and fell to the floor.

The Royal Companions had long been equipped with the best, bleeding-edge technology. Their body-armour could usually withstand all manner of projectiles and even some energy weapons, they could activate personal protection shields and had built-in communications devices and secondary weapons systems such as smart-darts and flash-bang stun pellets.

The other Royal Companion was reacting to his comrade's situation now, speaking into the communicator housed in his right forearm armour. 'Medical Emergency! Hall of Seeking!'

The Queen watched wide-eyed. A handful of the Seekers had drawn their weapons in case the man now posed a threat to Lydia. Sylen was one of them. She needed to appear most loyal – especially as she was thinking that perhaps her gift had not been the success she had hoped for. She could see a few other Seekers giving her sideways glances that confirmed they were thinking along similar lines. Especially old Gordias, the Seeker-in-Chief.

At last the man lay still and the second guard knelt by his side. The Queen and her Seekers gathered around, craning to see his face. The Companion's eyes flickered for a moment and then opened. He started directly at Lydia.

'Your Majesty,' he breathed.

Several Seekers helped him up and, as he stood, Sylen could see that the golden armour on his chest had not only turned to a dull silver, but that it had changed shape. Instead of the smooth, beaten gold breastplate there was now a crude facsimile of his musculature: a series of ridged metal plates.

The Companion smiled and the Seekers gave a loud cheer.

Just then, a Court clinician rushed in flanked by two nurses, each with mobile infirmary packs over their shoulders. Behind them came a young woman. She was dressed as a noblewoman of Catrigan Nova: a simple, graceful dress of night-sky blue. You could see in her face that she closely resembled the Queen.

The clinician bowed and rushed past her to examine the Royal Companion.

The young woman ran towards the Queen. 'Thank Catrigan!' she said. 'I thought they were talking about you!'

The Queen kissed her lightly on each cheek. 'Mida, my darling. How could anything happen to me? I have the Royal Companions, the Seekers are here. I have seldom been better protected!' She waved the gauntlet at those gathered around the table.

Mida bowed her head. 'Yes, Mummy,' she said. Then she spotted the metallic glove. 'What is that?'

'A gift from one of the Seekers. The cause of this alarm!'

Mida looked over to the fallen palace guard, now being tended to by the clinician and the two nurses. She watched as they scanned his life signs, and took samples of tissue and fluid, passing them through the mobile infirmary packs. A moment or two later, the clinician stood up to face the Queen once more.

'I can report that Companion Litarsas seems to be in good health,' he said. 'May I ask what happened?'

The Queen told him about the gauntlet and that she had touched his armour with it.

'I see,' he said, nodding. 'That does conform with my findings.'

'Which are?' Mida asked.

'Litarsas's medical function has been ... *improved* by the most sophisticated nanotechnology I have ever seen. For example, according to Palace medical records his blood pressure was slightly elevated, possibly due we believed to an overindulgence in high-cholesterol foodstuffs.'

'I do like my pies,' Litarsas said. Everyone laughed.

'That is true,' the clinician said. 'But, your Majesty, that condition has been corrected. Indeed, any slight medical weaknesses he might have had before – which weren't too many as a Royal Companion – have vanished.'

'So, it does heal!' Lydia gasped, marvelling once more at the gauntlet.

'There's more, Highness,' the clinician added. 'His body has been fused with his armour around the abdomen.'

The smile faded from everyone's lips. The Queen turned to her guard.

'How do you feel, Companion Litarsas?'

'Fine, your Majesty,' he replied. 'Better than that, even.' He smiled. 'The armour feels ... natural. Part of me. It doesn't hurt.'

He hit his stomach and chest with his fists to prove his point.

'But you were in pain?' the Queen asked.

Litarsas cocked his head. 'I know I was wriggling about on the floor liked a landed fish,' he said. 'But I don't think you'd call it pain, Majesty.'

The Queen nodded and smiled. Everyone was suddenly talking at once, babbling about what had happened like tournament fans after a team victory. Lydia sought out Sylen.

'You are to be congratulated, Seeker Sylen,' she said, almost purring. 'This is, with little doubt, the best find I have ever been presented with.'

Sylen grinned then and her eyes flicked over to old Gordias. He was speaking with Mida, smiling like everyone else. But only with his mouth. His eyes told a different story. Perhaps it was time for a retirement ceremony. The Queen noticed her staring at the old man.

'Gordias has served us well,' Lydia said. 'And he is a favourite of my daughter's. It occurs to me he should be rewarded with elevation.'

Sylen turned back to her Liege Lady. So, the Queen was thinking the same thing she was! Promotion from the Seekers meant a seat on the Guiding Council, which everyone knew the Queen took no guidance from. She loved technology above all else and so, if she listened to anyone, it was the Seekers and especially the Seeker-in-Chief.

'Yes, Majesty,' Sylen managed to say, a broad grin forming.

'But let us keep that as a surprise for now.'

The Queen turned and swept the Seekers with her. 'Come, I want to try this marvel on a datapad! Mida, join us!'

❖

The Queen was delighted with her new toy. She used it on as much technology as she could. When she used it on the datapad, it enhanced the machine beyond recognition, giving it a much wider signal range, faster processing speed and even larger memory. It was truly astounding.

Each new piece of technology she touched with the gauntlet was upgraded beyond her wildest dreams and the society on Catrigan Nova was one that almost saw technology as a religion.

News of the amazing gauntlet spread across the nearby systems, and the planet's fabulous wealth found a new revenue stream to match its gold panning at the famous gilded whirlpools:

tourism. At first it was dignitaries from local governments and first families. They requested audiences with the Queen to see the fabled glove.

Realising there was interest not only from outsiders, but from the population of Catrigan Nova itself, Lydia ordered that a permanent display be built in the Palace Museum. Once that had been created, it was itself enhanced when the Queen opened the exhibit and touched all the interactive displays.

Meanwhile, the Queen had instigated a voluntary upgrade programme for the Royal Companions. The changes to Litarsas had continued. He had become faster: capable of running at almost twice the speed of Catrigan Nova's fastest athlete. He could go without food and water for prolonged periods, stay awake for days and he could lift three times his own bodyweight. He had become a superhuman in less than a week. He now bore what had become known as the Lamp of the Royal Companions – a circular blue light on his chest unit – that everyone saw very much as a badge of honour.

By the time the first tourists arrived, Queen Lydia had used the gauntlet to upgrade every mechanical, electronic and computerised machine, instrument and device in the Nova Palace. The ranks of the Royal Companions had swollen from the elite 48-strong force to over 100 and of those, nearly 30 had joined the august ranks of what the Queen had dubbed the Royal Champions – those who had been touched by the gauntlet.

At the suggestion of Litarsas, new armour for the Companions was constructed that was not made of gold. He had become the first Champion Commander and now held the most senior military position Catrigan Nova had ever had. The planet had long based its economy and culture on the fabulous wealth afforded it by the whirlpools. No monarch had ever had military pretensions or even ambitions. Until now.

One night as she sat in her bedchamber, a servant combing her hair, Mida came in to see her.

'Why are you expanding the Companions?' she demanded.

'Because this is our time, my darling,' Lydia replied. She turned to face her daughter and the maid moved round with her, gingerly keeping her distance from the gloved hand that rested in her Queen's lap. 'Don't you see?'

'No, I don't!' Mida said and flopped on the bed. She was not long out of childhood and could still behave with some petulance if she did not get her own way. Which, the Queen reflected, was no bad thing for a future monarch.

'Mida, we have been given this technological marvel. So far it has given a small number of the palace guard great speed, strength and health. Should that really be the limit of our ambition?'

'Ambition?' Mida stared at her. 'What "ambition"?'

'You know there are jealous powers out there,' Lydia said. 'Aliens who would snatch our wealth from us if we permitted it.' She sighed. 'Perhaps you don't understand because you are still so close to your schooldays.'

'It's because I'm close to my schooldays that I totally understand,' Mida said, standing up. 'I learnt my lessons very well. Top grades. Especially in Politics and History. That's why I know that our wealth would never be "snatched from us" because while some might want to, others would prevent it. We've kept that balance of power for centuries because we've always been neutral and fair.'

'That is the trouble with status quos,' Lydia snapped. 'They often become broken by those we least expect at times we are least prepared for them.'

'Nonsense.' Mida turned on her heel and stalked from the room, leaving the door ajar.

'Your daughter is right,' said a voice. It was hard, yet softened by a pleasing lilt.

The maid gave a little shriek and dropped the hairbrush. The owner of the voice was across the room and picking it up before either woman could react. He was skinny with a lined face and hair the colour of pewter, swept up away from his forehead. He smiled and handed the brush back to the servant.

'Who are you?' the Queen demanded, a slight nervousness showing in her voice.

'No need for alarm. Or guards for that matter, I don't really like guards. They're always locking me up. And I'm always escaping. Perhaps we could bypass that, eh? It's a bit boring in the long run. And I've had a very long run.'

'We are sure you'll agree we would be a foolish Queen if we did not summon security when a strange man breaks into our bedroom.'

Lydia indicated the maid should do so, and the mousey woman bobbed her head before scurrying across to a communicator on the bedside table.

'Well, I'm no Michael Fagan, but perhaps you should. They're the reason I'm here. Well, them and that gauntlet of yours.' The man thrust his hands into the pockets of his trousers, whipping out the wings of his jacket in a flash of scarlet lining.

'Who ...' the Queen tried to ask again.

'A friend. Indeed. And you're in need.'

Just then, the doors burst open and Litarsas burst in with two other Champions and a four-man squad of her regular Companions behind them. They fanned out, surrounding the new arrival.

'See?' said the man. 'What did I say about guards? They just get in the way!'

'Majesty?' Litarsas said.

'This man has entered our bedchamber. Is this the level of competence we can expect from our Companions? Our Champions, even?'

'Hold him,' Litarsas said. He sounded totally unfazed by either the strange nature of the interloper or the harsh words of his monarch.

Two of the Companions marched forward and grabbed the man, pinning his arms behind his back.

'My apologies, Highness,' Litarsas said. Again his voice sounded as if had been drugged. Not slurred, just a monotone.

The new arrival pulled his arms away from the Companions and strode across the room to stare at Litarsas, face to face. He even tapped the blue lamp in his chest.

'Yes,' he said. 'Primitive. But undeniable.' He spun quickly and approached the Queen. 'You're in terrible danger!'

Lydia looked at him. He seemed in earnest, but he was clearly deranged.

Litarsas flung out a silvery arm and now the two Champions moved forward. They took the stranger's arms and he winced.

'All right! All right!' he growled. 'Just mind the tailoring. I'm fond of this red lining.'

'To the dungeon level,' Litarsas said.

'Perfect,' the pewter-haired man said. 'Take me *away* from your leader.'

✳

Lydia remained troubled by the intruder's words, but she thought it was probably the fact that news of her super-soldiers was spreading across the quadrant. It was natural such information would rouse fears in some people – especially those of an unhinged nature.

Mida didn't see it that way at all. She thought the man had been speaking sense. She still failed to see why Catrigan Nova had to put itself on what amounted to a war footing.

Then came that morning, a few days later. It was that period of the year when the chill of winter creeps up to play at the edges of the still-summery day. The Queen was at the Making Ceremony for a squad of new Champions.

By now, the implants and upgrades on those she had already touched with the gauntlet were very widespread. Few of the Champions slept any more. They drew up plans for ships and weapons that Litarsas assured her would be necessary in ensuring their wealth was not taken from them. And yet he was also advocating the sale of their gold at an unprecedented rate. He claimed it was to finance the building of these new marvels. But it was lowering the price on the markets in three quadrants.

Lydia stood on a raised dais, her breath forming in the cool morning air. The suns were creeping over the pointed apex of the Companion barracks, slowly diminishing the shadows. Before her stood six of her subjects wearing the new, burnished steel armour of the Companions. She herself wore a steel scarf that hung from her neck and was decorated with a stylised circuit board.

The gauntlet was on her left hand – as it always was these days. Lydia did not want to admit to anyone, but she had been unable to remove the glove since before the intruder in the bedchamber arrived. She looked at it now and frowned. Had it grown? Her hand and forearm seemed much larger: like a powerful man's – or, indeed, one of the Champions.

As the Anthem of Catrigan Nova began to play, the Queen stepped down from her platform and approached the line of Companions. She was pleased to see that one was a woman. Lydia moved to the first man and, as was now the custom, he took one smart step forward. She placed the palm of the gauntlet on his chest plate – where the Champion's lamp would form.

It took a few seconds, but then the man gasped. He managed to step back before he bowed his head in what seemed like pain – even though after the event everyone claimed that the process did not hurt them. The process of upgrading seemed to take more time now. The Queen had no idea why. Perhaps the gauntlet was running out of power. Still, by the time she reached the only woman on parade, the first man's chest armour had all but changed.

When fully converted, the armour resembled the muscles and ligaments of the body cast in metal. Each limb was striated with lines and some form of ex-skeletal tube ran very closely down each leg and arm from shoulder to elbow and from thigh to knee. Standing to one side was Litarsas. Lydia had noted that his neck was now covered in a metal brace and the metallic spine of his armour extended up over the back of his head, almost to the crown.

Under his arm he held a helmet. Lydia raised an eyebrow. That was new. Like the armour, it was a dull silver in tone with a slot for a mouthpiece and round holes for eyes. Oddly, there seemed to be a second, much smaller circle at the bottom of each one, facing to the side of the helmet. At the apex, was a wedge-shaped attachment for which the Queen could not see a use.

She made a mental note to ask Litarsas about it at their next audience and then, with the ceremony completed, the Queen left the chilly square and made her way back through the Palace. As she reached the familial apartments, Mida was waiting for her dressed in a simple, short-sleeved dress. Lydia could tell by the way she was standing that her daughter was upset.

'How many does *that* make?' Mida asked gruffly.

'The Champions are now at Company strength,' Lydia replied and swept past her daughter into the hallway. 'Just over 70 or so.' She looked at herself in the mirror. She looked pale, drawn even. 'But I'm tired, darling,' she added, watching her daughter in the reflection. 'Can we have this fight another time?'

'No,' Mida said. She had her hands on her hips. 'You've changed, Mother. That gauntlet thing. That's what's done it.'

'Darling, I just need to rest.' Lydia went to move to the next room to sit down, but Mida blocked her.

'That man was right,' she said. 'I think that thing's dangerous. When did you last take it off?'

Lydia balked at answering the question. How could she tell her daughter she hadn't been able to? This made her realise that there might be some truth to her words.

'I haven't,' she said, finally.

'What?' Mida shook her head. 'Unbelievable. And you don't think it's dangerous. And you don't want to talk about it. And you're always tired!'

She turned to leave but Lydia went after her, stretching out a hand to stop her, pacify her. 'Please wait, darling.' But then it happened. Her hand gripped Mida's arm. But it was her gloved hand.

Her daughter screamed as her shoulder seemed to break out in a rash of silver that covered her upper arm in seconds. Mida snatched her hand away from Lydia's grip and looked in fear and loathing at her mother.

'What have you done?' she breathed.

'No!' Lydia moved forward to help her daughter, but Mida cowered. 'No, please. Mida, darling.'

She didn't know what to do. For the first time in many months – years even – there was nothing she *could* do.

Lydia watched, unable to move, as the silver spread down Mida's arm and across her hand. Her eyes wide in horror, the Queen watched as her daughter's arm quickly became a copy of her own. Another gauntlet.

Her daughter looked at her, tears in her eyes, a hatred in her voice that had never been there before. 'I told you!' she shrieked. 'I told you it was dangerous!'

She looked at the floor as Lydia stood, her own cyborg hand to her mouth.

❊

'Dungeons,' the man said. He looked as if he had been staying in one of the Palace's luxury bedrooms, not a cell two metres square and furnished only with a bed, wash basin and toilet. 'Wooden doors.'

Lydia was standing before him, the other side of the heavily barred cell door.

'Bit of a miscalculation on my part, otherwise I'd have been there to help.'

'Can you help now?' the Queen asked quietly.

'I can try,' the man said. He came up to the cell door and peered through, trying to see what was beyond the outer door. 'Let me guess. No "Champions" down here. Prison guard duty is far too lowly for your new super-soldiers. And besides they're probably off building space ships and ray guns and planners and controllers.'

Lydia nodded. 'We are planning a new fleet with new weapons,' she said. She was looking at the ground and then she choked, starting to cry. 'I feel so ashamed.'

'So you should,' the man said. 'But it's no good crying over spilt Cyber-technology.'

The Queen looked up at him, wiping away the tears with her right hand – her normal hand. 'You know the origins of this gauntlet?'

'I do. A nasty species of cyborgs. You might have heard of them.' He smiled humourlessly. 'Cybermen.'

The word did sound familiar. Lydia pulled a face as she tried to dredge the memory to the surface. 'Cybermen,' she repeated.

'That's it. You can do it! Your schooling was a long time ago, wasn't it?' He smiled, this time with genuine warmth. 'No offence.'

'But …' The Queen could remember it now. 'They died out. The … hibernation galaxy blew up. Or something. No, it can't have been a galaxy.'

'It was. The Tiberian spiral galaxy. I've been hunting that thing for a long time,' he said pointing at her left arm. 'And they never die out. They always survive. It's their prime motivator. No matter what. You could almost admire them if they weren't so unutterably inhuman. And now you have the Mondas touch!'

The stranger quickly outlined a plan. She needed to speak to her most trusted guards – those Champions who had not yet volunteered for the upgrading process. Any of the original Companions, too. Those totally loyal to her and not in awe of or in debt to Litarsas. He asked her if there were any other force she could call upon and she smiled as it hit her: the Seekers. Sylen, especially.

'Good,' the man said. 'They're just a precaution. Hopefully we won't need them, but you never know. Now! Your daughter. Bring her down here. We'll set up base in the dungeons. They'll never think to look here for trouble. I can treat her and then I need to kidnap you.'

He smiled again, his eyes wrinkling at the corners. The Queen managed a faint smile in reply.

19

Thank you,' she said. 'What should I call you?'

'Oh,' the man laughed. 'Let's not give them any clues. Just call me "Mr Clever".'

Then she turned to go and make the arrangements.

'One last thing?' he asked.

Lydia stopped in her tracks. 'Anything,' she said.

'Open the cell door?'

❈

The Queen's secret recruits quickly moved about the palace, bringing Mr Clever medical supplies and an upgraded infirmary kit, persuading the princess to attend the dungeons and trying to keep out of the Champions' way.

The Champions themselves were now wearing the new helmets. Lydia came across three of them in the throne room. They were standing in a row, motionless. She walked right up to one of them and tried to peer through the eyeholes. She could see nothing beyond the black mesh that covered them. She asked one of them what they were doing there, but he didn't answer.

She was about to give them an angry dressing down when she saw that small metal tubes were growing upwards steadily from the sides of the helmet where the ears should be. Similar pipes were protruding from the top of the head where the wedge-shaped crown was. Lydia watched, transfixed as the two ends curved towards each other and finally met, giving the helmets the appearance of having handles. She rushed to the dungeons to tell Mr Clever about them.

He was standing over her daughter who was lying on the cell bunk. The bed had been stripped of its grey blanket and had been replaced by a pristine white medical sheet. He had his sleeves rolled up and was wearing surgical gloves.

'Handles,' he said. 'He was a good companion.'

The Queen had decided not to question him further about it but asked after her daughter instead.

'She's in a coma,' he said. 'I thought it best. The reversal process is very painful and while the Cybermen don't care about that sort of thing, I do.'

She watched him working for a few minutes. He was gentle and assured. Every movement and action filled her with confidence that she had done the right thing coming to him.

'Please,' she whispered under her breath. 'Save my daughter. I beg you.'

Without looking up and despite being on the other side of the open cell door he said: 'I will.'

The Queen slept fitfully that night and when she awoke she was greeted by news that the Champions had started rounding up members of the public – even visitors to the planet. They called it conscription. She dressed and hurried to the dungeons.

A miracle greeted her. Mida was sitting up in bed, her arm completely back to normal, save for a few scratches on her shoulder.

'No permanent damage,' Mr Clever confirmed. 'But I recommend a period of rest. I'll leave you two alone.'

After an emotional reunion and promises made on both sides, the Queen found Mr Clever in the passageway outside the dungeons. He was eating a pasty on a wooden plate. She stared at him as if somehow she never imagined him eating.

'Always have a hearty breakfast before a battle,' he said.

'Battle?'

'Yes. Now Mida is cured, I need to take you prisoner and deal with the Cybermen.'

Again, he outlined his plan to her. If he was right, it would be simple. It only required one of the Champions who was best known to Litarsas to tell him that the Queen had been taken by a group of rebels led by an alien. In fact, Mr Clever would take Lydia to the gilded whirlpools on his own. The troops loyal to the Queen would only head there once all the Cybermen had left the Palace.

The plan was set in motion. In order to reach the whirlpools quickly, Mr Clever was persuaded to let Seeker Sylen pilot them there in her Hyperdart. They reached the amazing geographical structure in less than an hour.

Sylen explained to the newcomer that the area was a vast indentation in the ground – a mile deep and almost a hundred miles wide, covered almost entirely by naturally occurring pools. These pools were filled by water forced from the ground by volcanic activity beneath the planet's surface. The liquid was forced through narrow vents at such high velocity that they became whirlpools. They were dangerous for two reasons: the speed of their currents and the fact that they could pull a person down without warning, through larger vents that acted to empty the basins as soon as they were filled.

'Just like pulling the plug from a bath!' Mr Clever said. 'I love the idea of giving the Cybermen a bath, don't you? Make sure they clean behind those ears of theirs!'

As they circled overhead prior to landing, the sun caught the valley and the pools glinted and flashed in the sun. Lydia had not been out there for a long time and had forgotten its natural beauty.

'But that's why we're really here,' the man said.

This was the source of Catrigan Nova's fabulous wealth. Along with water, tiny nuggets of gold were also forced through the vents. They were swirled around by the current at very high speeds, but they also tended to settle on the bottom of the pools, too.

'Gold,' said Mr Clever, rubbing his temple. 'I know for a fact that the Cyberiad still suffers from a weakness to it. I presume you use a suppressor to keep the speed of the water in check so that you can extract the gold?'

Lydia nodded. 'But I don't know where the control is.'

'No matter,' the man said. He pulled out a strange blue tool that had a light at the end. 'Got this. All we need to do is wait for the Cybermen to come and rescue you and then we switch off the suppressors. Bathing the Cybermen in a suspension of gold will, I hope, be like putting them in a blender.'

'But why will they save me?' Lydia asked.

'Because you are necessary,' he said. 'You are a figurehead. Although they have started conscription, they still need you to ensure the people don't rise up. If they killed you too early, they would face resistance – however futile it might be.'

He put his hand around the Queen's shoulders and led her away. 'There is one other thing. This will be difficult,' he said. 'Both for you to hear and for you to do.'

Lydia nodded. 'Whatever you say ...'

'When the time comes, you'll need to put the gauntlet into one of the whirlpools, too. The gold will have the same effect on your arm as it hopefully will on the Cybermen. The *same* effect.'

The Queen looked puzzled for a second and then painful realisation spread on her face.

'My arm,' she said.

'I'm afraid you will lose it. Below the elbow. It will be painful. I'm sorry.'

Lydia nodded, a grimly determined expression on her face. 'So be it,' she said.

They did not have to wait long for the enemy. The company of Cybermen came over the ridge of the depression, like a herd of silvery wildebeest. Their speed was breathtaking as they approached.

They stopped a short distance off. At the front of the ranks was what used to be Litarsas. His helmet was slightly different to the others; it had black handles rather than the same silvery colour the others had.

Mr Clever stepped forward. 'Leader,' he said, greeting Litarsas. The man furrowed his brow at the Cybermen, glowering from beneath his eyebrows in a manner no one alive would argue with.

'You are known and recorded as an enemy of the Cybermen.'

'Yes, yes. I'm sure I am.' He put on a strange twanging accent. 'But the question you need to ask yourself tonight is: sink or swim!'

He turned to the Queen and Sylen. 'Whaddya say, folks? *Sink* or *Swim*?' He pointed to the sky and everyone looked up, even the Cybermen. But there was nothing to see. Then Lydia noticed he wasn't pointing. He had the blue tool in his hand and it was buzzing like a nest of angry wasps.

'I hope your troops are here, your Highness,' Mr Clever said.

Sylen nodded. 'I received their signal just before they arrived,' she said.

'Tell them to open fire!'

Suddenly the water in the whirlpools became wilder and louder, thrashing over the sides, splashing the glittering suspension over Mr Clever, the Queen and Sylen as well as several Cybermen.

'Fire!' yelled Sylen into her wrist communicator.

'Kill him,' intoned the Cyber-Leader.

Everything became a blur then. Before the Cybermen could operate their weapons, the laser fire from the ridge hit them. This threw them back, but did no permanent damage. By now the flow of liquid gold was a torrent and it quickly rose to waist height and as the cyborgs stumbled backwards under the impact of the gunfire, some of them fell into the deeper pools.

Immediately the tiny grains of gold ripped into the Cybermen's enhancements. Lydia watched as one had its helmet torn away piece by piece to reveal a horrible visage beneath: the woman who had been on parade only days before. Her eyes were gone and a silvery material that clung close to the undulations of her skull had replaced most of her skin. Wires and circuits stuck out from the cranial area and she raised a hand – whether as a gesture of defiance or as a signal for help was impossible to tell – as she slipped beneath the waves.

There were now only a handful of Cybermen left above the surface and even those that were, collapsed as their legs and knees were worn away. But still the Cyber-Leader stood. In fact, he was wading forward, his hands outstretched for the Queen.

His silver hands grasped at Lydia's throat, but she, too, had a strong Cyber arm and managed to hold him off. But the thing that had once been Litarsas was stronger. Then the Queen recalled her personal protection training. If ever she was attacked, her old teacher had said, she should use the assailant's strength and momentum against them.

So she did.

Lydia rolled backwards, which took the Cyber-Leader by surprise. He fell forward, stumbling into a nearby whirlpool of the deadly liquid. He struggled to remain above the waterline, but the Queen not only had the strength of a cyborg but that of an enraged mother. She pushed down on the metallic ear handles and the face of the Cyberman disappeared beneath the surface.

So did her arm. Lydia screamed in agony as the metallic part of her arm was flushed with the golden suspension. But she clung on.

It was Mr Clever who gently lifted her from the water, pointing to a metal body as it was carried away by the golden rapids and eventually sucked down into one of the pools. Then he once more lifted his whirring device into the sky. Almost as suddenly as it had burst forth, the water receded. He ran a hand through his soaking pewter hair and smiled at Lydia.

'Like a blender,' he said.

'Mummy!' They all turned to see Mida running across the sodden ground. She was about to throw herself into an embrace with her mother when she saw that her mother's arm had vanished below the elbow. She came to an abrupt stop and started crying.

Lydia gently pulled her daughter to her and they embraced for a long time. She had given up the magic gauntlet; the one that had promised technological salvation and delivered the exact opposite.

Mida looked up at her mother and smiled. 'You were so brave,' she said.

Lydia smiled and thought it was due to Mr Clever. She turned to look for him. But the mysterious stranger wasn't there. He had vanished. The Queen smiled and tasted a tear that had trickled down her face. It was one of happiness, and they owed it all to him.

# THE TERRIBLE MANUSSA

When she was eight years old, Persisalevatolla had looked into the Untempered Schism and seen one thing: the possibility of adventure. The trouble was, she was from the Patrexes chapter and for them adventure did not come easily. That is why she had made it her business to find out everything she could about the Celestials.

She had first heard of the Celestial Intervention Agency in connection with the Shakri. But few spoke of the interventionists, and when they did it was in hushed voices. Persis had tracked down small references to the CIA's activities in the library, but they were oblique at best. Every other enquiry for information was blocked or brought up zero results.

As she approached her graduation, Persis became convinced that the life she sought was beyond her and a career at Space-Time Control beckoned, logging TARDISes on and off Gallifrey. Then, something incredible happened. On her last day – hours before the graduation ceremony – her temporal classics master, a Prydonian cardinal called Kroshen, sidled up to her in the Rothe Tower library and whispered in her ear.

'You're interested in the Celestial Intervention Agency, aren't you, Persis?'

When she graduated with a double first, she went straight into training with the CIA. And while the staser ranges were exciting, it was mostly more lectures and study. Reading about alien planets and strange creatures was certainly more lively than the dry times of the Academy but she wanted to see them for herself.

And now her moment had come.

The briefing room was a plain, white cell with two white chairs designed for discomfort and a white desk with no discernible function. Persis had never seen a briefing room before and had no idea what she should do.

Without Persis noticing, a Time Lord dressed in black appeared behind her. A clipped, male voice told her to sit down so she sat.

The Time Lord moved around the table as if floating. He wore the tight black hood and elongated collar that marked him out as a former member of the ST-ST: the Special Time-Space Troopers. His face was calm but weather-beaten. Not the usual pudgy, pasty complexion older Time Lords had. Persis found herself automatically respecting him.

He sat down on the adjacent side of the table and smiled. 'Welcome, Persis,' he said. 'Please pay attention to the screen.'

Straight away an image appeared on the wall opposite her. It was a beautiful young woman: lustrous dark hair, hazel-flecked eyes and a poise that told Persis the woman was extremely comfortable in her own skin. Around her neck was a red crystal pendant.

Information flowed to the left and right of the image, as the man in black gave some biographical details.

'The woman you are looking at is an alien princess called Manussa, a native of the planet G139901KB – the fourth planet of the Scrampus system. For several decades now, she has become increasingly powerful through the use of special crystals.'

The image changed again and Persis sat back, frowning. It was only just possible to see that the face belonged to the same woman. Gone were the glowing complexion, dark chocolate hair and soft brown eyes. In their place, Manussa now had her face tattooed with the scales of a reptile. Her hair had been plaited and painted to look like snakes, and her eyes had become as red as the pendant she had worn in the previous photo.

'Through guile, a singular determination and a distinct lack of morals, she has now become queen of her people and channelled all their resources into creating these great crystals using the most powerful telepaths the species has ever developed.'

The image changed again to show a five-sided blue crystal. Then another in red and a third in orange. The screen reverted to the image of Manussa.

'If you look closer at the ornate armour she wears, you'll see that it is actually made up of the orange and red type of crystals. We believe each colour reflects a different use but we are not certain. They are manufactured off world on the moon of Grey-Eye in anti-grav environments.'

Persis stared at the screen, rapt by the exotic and alien images it was showing. She tried not to let the thrill show in her body language. If he noticed, the man in black did not comment.

'These crystals can be used for many things. But we now know they have also been used by an interstitial creature known as the Mara to cross over to our reality. Manussa is now not only queen of her planet – and a ranged empire beyond – but also her species' religious leader. At first she was simply the head of a cult called the Union of the Snake, but now hers is the only religion on G139901KB. This took place after she outlawed all other creeds and converted their temples to Mara worship.'

Persis nodded. She had heard of the Mara. 'The Mara itself is a huge snake-like creature of legend,' she said. 'A powerful being of temptation, fear and hatred that is said to live in the dark places of the mind.'

The man in black looked at her like a proud father would look at his favourite daughter. 'Your interest in the more esoteric aspects of your training clearly stand you in good stead.'

'The crystals are impressive,' Persis said. 'But what is the CIA's interest in this woman and her snake myth?'

Her fellow agent bobbed his head and waved a hand over the table. Immediately it lit up and a holographic display of a throne room appeared in miniature on its surface. The crystal-armoured figure of Manussa sat raised above a group of viziers and advisers.

' … and the workforce needed for the Grey-Eye weapon is being transported to the moon now,' said one of the viziers – a woman with a sight-visor.

'Good.' Manussa looked down from her throne. She licked her lips and Persis clearly saw a fork tongue. 'But I also hear that there has been a problem with the crystal growth vats.'

The visored woman's face fell. 'Majesty,' she began, but Manussa silenced her with a lifted finger. The other viziers moved away from her discreetly.

'Were you trying to hide this from me?' Her voice became a hiss as she rose from the throne and advanced across the floor.

'Great Manussa, I would never …'

Before the woman could concoct an excuse, Manussa stood and her hair became alive. These were not braided facsimiles. These were real snakes. They hissed and snapped as Manussa's eyes glowed red. Suddenly the vizier was lifted from the ground, caught in a red glow of time energy.

Persis nodded. 'Temporal stasis,' she said. She had studied the subject during her second year at the Academy. It was rudimentary. But then the woman vanished completely. The hologram faded.

'Time looped?' Persis gasped.

'That is our belief,' the man in black said. 'The indigenous people have dubbed the power "tempetrification".'

Stasis was one thing, but this ... 'How? With her mind?'

'Again, we are uncertain, but it is clear that the focus afforded by the crystals has given Manussa an ability to control temporal energy to an astounding degree.'

So far, the ability to properly time-loop an object had eluded the Time Lords. It was a little difficult for Persis to fathom how a relatively backward, quasi-religious civilisation had done so.

'I'm afraid there is worse to come,' the man said. 'The power of the time-loop is developed as a much larger weapon on the moon of Grey-Eye.'

The image on the wall changed to show a lunar base with several soldiers in snakeskin uniforms marching through a hangar bay.

'We foresee a time when this weapon will be fitted with a planetary propulsion unit.'

Persis gasped. That posed a significant threat to the supremacy of Gallifrey.

'Manussa intends to use the weapon to freeze entire planets, thus demonstrating her power and forcing countless new worlds to worship her. You can understand that unchecked not only would her empire spread across the galaxy, but that such a weapon would cause incalculable damage to the time-space continuum.'

Persis looked at the man briefing her. 'I understand.'

'We would like you to travel to the Scrampus system at a point in time before the weapon is fully developed. First, you will need to gain access to the moon of Grey-Eye. You are to destroy

the weapon or render it inoperable permanently. Alternatively, if you learn of some key component in its operation, you are to return it to Gallifrey for examination.'

Persis smiled. Cunning.

'Once that is achieved you are to bring Manussa herself to justice.'

'You mean kill her?' Persis asked.

She wasn't a child; she knew that assassination was sometimes a necessity. And she certainly saw the threat that Manussa posed. She just wasn't sure it merited the ultimate sanction.

'I will leave that to you,' the man in black said as he rose from the uncomfortable chair. He brought a metal object from a hidden pocket in his robes. 'I will also leave this with you. A Time Ring. It will return you to Gallifrey once you have finished.'

Persis took it. She knew it worked in a similar – if more primitive manner – to a TARDIS in that it locked onto suitable environments for materialisation. She'd also heard they could be unreliable.

'Be careful not to lose it. Persis. That Time Ring is your lifeline. Good luck!'

And he was gone.

Persis stood and activated the wardrobe circuit on her personal camouflage device. Her own simple black robe and skullcap became the snakeskin uniform and hood of a Manussan Strike Force officer.

Then she slipped the metal bracelet onto her arm and disappeared into the time vortex.

※

The metallic corridor stretched away in both directions, disappearing as it curved round in an arc. Persis turned first one way and then the other. It made no difference which way she went as both ways seemed identical. She shrugged and set off to her left.

She could feel the gravity was artificial and as there were no windows, she wondered if her Time Ring had deposited her on a space station or ship rather than the moon of Grey-Eye.

Before she could process this, she heard something unusual just around the curve of the corridor. It was a deep, mellifluous voice reciting poetry. Cautiously, Persis moved forward and saw that a large access hatch had been removed and a man was lying with his legs protruding from the panel.

As she watched, the man became aware of her presence and slowly disentangled himself from the workings. He had a mop of unruly blond hair and was dressed like a colourful jester. His gaze was clear and burned with intelligence. He looked at her, blinked and then smiled, jumping to his feet. Before Persis knew what had happened the man had grasped her hand.

'Hello!' he said. 'What brings you down this remote corridor?'

Persis was about to give a plausible answer when she remembered her disguise. She was an officer in the Manussan Strike Force.

'I might ask you the same question!'

'You might,' he said. 'But I think you have bigger fish to fry?'

This threw the Time Lord agent somewhat. 'Fish?'

'Yes. It's a saying.' He paused to put his hands in his pockets and lean forward. 'I don't think my tinkering here is of that much concern to you.'

Persis eyed the man suspiciously. Could he see through her disguise? Did he have some form of psychic ability? Was he a mischievous deity? Whatever his power, Persis felt her suspicion fade. There was something about his demeanour that made her ... trust him.

'That remains to be seen,' she said finally. 'What are you "tinkering" with?'

'Aha! Now that is an interesting question. Pertinent even.'

He took his right hand from his pocket.

'I think you can help me, actually.'

He opened his hand to reveal a mechanism that looked not dissimilar to an old dematerialisation circuit.

'This is how she does it, you see.'

Persis couldn't help but smile. 'She? You mean Manussa.'

'Yes. Very interesting isn't it? How things get started. Or concluded. That's what I'm trying to do, really. Tie up some loose ends.'

He took her hand and placed the small instrument in her palm now, before closing her fingers.

'All yours. The key to the weapon. You can dispose of it just as well as me.'

Persis took a step back. 'I thought we were on a space station.'

The man scoffed. 'This is no space station. It's a moon!'

Persis nodded and placed the tiny component in one of her combat pouches.

'Thank you for your help,' she said. 'I don't know who sent you ...'

'No one sent me!' The man smiled a tight-lipped smile. 'I am the cat who walked by himself and all places are alike to me!'

'Another saying?' Persis asked, arching an eyebrow.

'Touché.' The man smiled broadly now. Then he turned and began to replace the hatch. 'But tell me, there is more to your mission. Isn't there?'

Persis hesitated. 'Yes.'

The multicoloured jester turned back to her, realisation and concern on his face. 'The Manussa herself?'

Persis nodded. 'I must bring her to justice.'

'You know she has the power to time-loop you?'

'Those are my orders.'

'Orders!' The man blew out his cheeks. 'Well, you won't be able to carry out those orders without a little sonic technology. Come on. There's a lab back this way.'

He strode off down the corridor as if he lived in one, hands clasped behind his back. He was almost out of sight before Persis realised she should be following him.

His head bobbed back around the corner. 'Come on!'

A mad dash later, Persis was standing in the centre of a tech lab. There were items of machinery and computer circuit boards scattered about, a hologram projector in one corner and a sonic lance on a nearby bench. The man picked up this last object.

'Excellent! I need to replace mine!' He turned to her and grinned sheepishly. 'A little encounter in the sewers did for the last one.'

'What exactly are we doing here?'

The man was already examining pieces of technology; either piling them on his arms, or discarding them with childlike grimaces.

'Sonic technology,' he repeated. 'It can bend temporal energy at the correct frequencies.'

Persis smiled. She'd never heard of these abilities, and sonic technology was native to the Time Lords.

'Discovered it from some Ice Warriors. Quite by chance.'

She had no idea what he was talking about now, but he had proved to be a valuable imp of a collaborator and she was just grateful he was on her side.

'I would help you myself,' he said, as if reading her thoughts. 'But my life seems to have become rather complicated of late.' He looked up from his collection of equipment and smiled again. 'You know how it is?'

Persis still had no idea what he was talking about but she indulged the gaudy angel with a bob of the head. 'Of course.'

'Very perspicacious of you, my dear.' He dumped the pile of components on a nearby table. 'Now. What you need is a sonic shield. Come on, you can help me!'

Together they put together a rudimentary sonic shield. She'd made similar devices at the Academy, but the flamboyant man had added some modifications and tweaks she had never thought of.

It looked like a metal plus sign with a strap for a handle right on the centre. When operated, the four ends extended and a permanent wave of sound was generated from each crosspiece, giving the appearance of a translucent blue circle.

When Persis had finished testing the shield, her protector moved towards the door. 'Best be going. As I say – and without wishing to sound like an Ogron – there are complications …'

As he left, Persis thought of running after him, of asking his name, thanking him again. But she knew it would be no good. If he'd wanted to share his name, he would have done. And it seemed he needed no one's thanks or permission for anything!

Instead, she prepared the Time Ring on her wrist. She was about to operate it when she noticed a handwritten note on the shield.

It read: 'Two final things! Don't materialise inside the palace and don't let the Mara tempt you. D'

She marvelled at this rogue's abilities and then adjusted the Time Ring for the citadel rather than the palace. As she disappeared, she thought she heard a wind rising and falling in a familiar pattern …

❊

Sarpenton was the capital city of the Manussan Empire: an extensive megalopolis of traders and temples, ornate priests' houses and squalid dwellings belonging to the workers. It was as bright and gaudy as the clothes worn by the man who had just helped her. Even in the shanty towns the cloth roofs were orange and deep red. But this colourful wall was a façade that hid a dirty and unloved reality.

Persis had materialised in a wide, dark access road between tall, sandy buildings. She moved quickly into the shadows and edged to the end of the street where it joined with a much busier thoroughfare.

Two law enforcers of the Hooded Guard approached Persis as she stepped out from the access road. Their helmets had a hooded snake rising from the nose section, and their body armour was patterned like snakeskin. They were looking at the cross-like device she held: the shield. However, they paused when they realised the uniform she wore was of an agency that outranked their own. They gave a two-armed salute – hands clasped across their chest – and quickly turned to walk away. Fear. It pervaded everything.

As did the overpowering smell. Persis had never experienced anything like it. Alien, exotic spices mingled with perspiration and the masculine aroma of wood fires. She smiled, despite herself. Adventure. This is what she'd wanted. She'd never even considered the fact that adventure could have a perfume. But if it did, this was certainly it.

She gathered herself and looked down the street, past the stalls and emporia, to a large expanse of well-tended and incongruous lawn. Rising from the earth beyond that was an astoundingly high palace, ringed by impossibly tall pillars, each one seemingly fashioned from one piece of red-veined marble.

As she stood marvelling at this, two women passed her, each wearing a green-brown serpent mask and with hoods made to resemble open snake mouths. Persis recognised them from the holovid she'd seen on Gallifrey. They were two of the advisers she had seen when the Manussa time-looped her vizier.

She started to follow them. If they had been in the throne room before, it was reasonable to think they might well return there. As she dogged their footsteps, Persis marvelled at how much the image of the snake had permeated this society – especially with regard to those in positions of power and authority. She supposed it was all to frighten the 'profane'; and Persis guessed this meant anyone who defied Manussa. There was that fear again.

The two viziers approached the huge, gated entrance to the palace, but the guards did not move. Persis had expected them to check credentials or at least acknowledge them. So, she strode forward purposefully. As part of her training she had learned that getting into anywhere you weren't supposed to was mainly down to walking in as if you owned the place.

'Halt!' The two guards were suddenly coming towards her. So much for owning the place. 'State your business.'

Persis regarded them with what she hoped looked like utter contempt. 'You dare question me?' she hissed. 'I will have you tempetrified for this!'

The nearest guard quailed at this. He turned to the other, now not so certain.

Persis took this opportunity to continue on her way once more.

'Although as you are merely doing your job, I may convince Manussa to spare you,' she said over her shoulder. And leaving the two artless soldiers in her wake, Persis pressed on deeper into the palace.

It was late in the afternoon and the corridors were buzzing with activity. Servants moved quickly and efficiently up and down the wide hallways, always sticking to the sides avoiding the important courtiers who moved in ambling groups.

There was no trace of the two viziers so Persis had to find her own way to the throne room. It wasn't too difficult. She soon realised that most of the traffic was headed in that direction. She just fell in behind a group of courtiers and soon emerged into a huge vestibule.

It reminded Persis of the atrium that led to the Panopticon on Gallifrey. The buzz of conversation was the same as was the charged atmosphere of excitement. The difference was here there was an added level of apprehension. These people were scared despite – or maybe because of – their familiarity with Manussa.

The vestibule was the shape of a diamond with two great doors where two of the marbled walls met. Before these were a line of Manussan Strike Force soldiers – the Queen's personal guard. It was their uniform that the personal camouflage device was projecting.

The doors, however, were firmly closed and anyone approaching the line of soldiers was being turned away. Manussa was not holding court at the moment. Persis smiled. This might make things easier. No crowd; no one getting in the way.

She had decided that her orders to bring Manussa to justice were not a euphemism for assassination and that she would do exactly as directed. She would capture the alien and use the Time Ring to transport them both to Shada. Of course, Manussa would attempt to use her temporal powers, but Persis still had the sonic shield that the colourful stranger had given her on Grey-Eye.

As she monitored the crowd outside the throne room, Persis began to see a pattern to the ebb and flow of people. Just as had happened with the palace corridors, the vestibule became a puzzle to be solved. She soon had the solution.

The walls of the vestibule were lined with exotic plants with large, bright leaves, variegated with dark greens and reds. It took a while to notice, but every now and again servants would enter and, keeping to the side of the chamber, make their way towards the main door. As they reached the halfway point they seemed to vanish.

Persis edged across the room, as if calmly patrolling the room – an action that befitted her uniform. No one looked at her. Or if they did, they hardly noticed and never thought to question.

When she reached the far side of the vestibule she saw that there was a small side door hidden among the alien vegetation. There was a soldier here, but he was standing off to the side so as not to draw attention to what he was guarding.

Persis waited.

After a short while, she spied a small man dressed in cream clothes making his way along the side of the room. He was not making eye contact with anyone and he held in his hands a salver of gaudy-looking fruit.

Persis made her way across the floor, manoeuvring so she was now behind the servant. As he approached the door, Persis made her move.

'Halt!' she said loudly. The servant froze. A couple of courtiers looked round but hurriedly moved away sensing trouble.

The guard's hand moved to his pistol belt, looking at Persis, the expression on his face posing an unvoiced question: What's going on?

'We suspect this man is an infidel,' Persis said calmly. 'The fruit may be poisoned.'

The servant said nothing. His fear was palpable. He looked like he was going to cry.

'Take him for questioning,' Persis said. 'Test the fruit. I will report this incident to the Manussa herself.'

The guard gave Persis a double-handed salute and grabbed the servant in one hand, snatching the bowl with the other. Then he marched the man away quietly toward another corridor.

Persis hoped that once the fruit had been tested and found clean, the man would be released. She frowned. That hope may have been in vain, but at least she had tried.

Without hesitation, she darted forward and opened the small door, passing through it while everyone was watching the prisoner and escort.

She found herself in a dark, narrow passageway with tapered slits on one side. Persis peered through one of the tiny windows. She was staring into the throne room. She recognised it from the holovid. It was empty.

Continuing down the cramped passage, she found that it coiled around behind the throne room. She realised it must lead to an antechamber, part of Manussa's private quarters; perhaps where she rested between audiences and time-looping her subjects.

Sure enough, Persis found a door that gave out onto a wide room with high windows lining one wall. Translucent curtains shimmered in the late afternoon sunlight, undulating in the gentle breeze.

At the centre of the room was a huge bed. It was covered in soft, shiny cushions – clearly made from the most expensive fabrics. And on the bed lay her quarry, asleep.

Persis could not believe her luck. Perhaps she would be able to capture the alien without ever waking her. She moved forward silently now, steadying her breathing to almost nothing.

As she approached the woman, Persis examined Manussa for the first time. In sleep, there was something of the beautiful girl she had once been. Despite the cosmetic surgery or whatever procedures she had performed to make her more snake-like, she still had a wonderful bone structure and the parts of her body that were not covered in the crystalline armour were supple and muscled.

Persis readied the Time Ring and reached out to take hold of the alien's wrist.

'Sumara?' Manussa stirred, her voice soft and low.

Persis froze. Totally still. Had she heard her?

Then Manussa's eyes snapped open. She was staring straight at Persis.

The Time Lord grabbed at the snake-woman's arm, but Manussa was alert now and flew from the bed.

'Sumara! Guards!' shouted Manussa.

She lowered her head and her hair now came alive, too, writing and coiling as she hissed at Persis.

Persis stared at this, mesmerised. Adventure suddenly seemed a thousand light years away. On the far side of the room a petite brunette appeared in wine-coloured robes.

'Majesty!' The woman moved forward, uncertain.

'Stay back, Sumara,' Manussa said. 'I do not want to catch you in my gaze!'

And with that, she took a deep breath, summoning the power of her suit. The crystals began to glow and Persis realised she was about to be time-looped.

She snatched the metal cross of the sonic shield from her belt and quickly operated it. There was a high-pitched buzz and a circle of almost invisible blue light covered the cross, forming a circle.

'Foolish girl,' Manussa roared, her voice now echoing and sizzling with power. 'You cannot defeat me with sonic technology. I am not just Manussa. I am the vessel of the Mara!'

She rotated slowly on the spot, her hair lifting. The spin became faster and faster, her hair now whipping round as her face snapped round every second to stare at Persis.

Again the Time Lord felt transfixed. It was the gyration of a practised dancer, amazingly fast. But it was not this that held

Persis in place. It was the being that was manifesting in the room, coiling round and round, mimicking the movement of the creature it possessed.

It was a huge snake, an evil red colour tinged with scales of dirty green and yellow. Two vast fangs protruded from the top of its mouth, dripping with venom and a pair of hideous emerald eyes, thin slits of deep black for pupils, stared at Persis.

This was the Mara.

It circled her once and then stared unblinkingly at Persis, its tongue tasting the air around her.

Persis felt her mind invaded. She had been taught about psychic assaults during training but nothing prepared her for the sudden and overwhelming feeling of violation.

In her head she heard a silky voice. 'Time Lord,' it said. 'You are an interesting individual. An interesting race.'

Persis tried to block the mental intrusion.

'Please, child,' the voice said. 'Don't throw me out before you have heard what I have to say. Surely we can be reasonable?'

'I know what you are,' Persis thought. 'The Mara. I know your supposed origins and abilities.'

'Then you will know what I have to offer.' There was a lightness to this statement as if the Mara was pleased with itself. 'Take me back with you. We can accomplish so much more there than I can here.'

'You are evil,' Persis thought. She was concentrating hard, focusing on the conversation in her mind and what was happening in the real world. The Mara was still positioned right in front of her. Manussa was simply standing to one side, but curiously with one arm outstretched. 'I could not bring you to Gallifrey.'

'Could not?' the Mara teased. 'I am sure you could. If you desired it.'

'I do not desire it.'

'You desire many things. You crave adventure, yes. But also ... advancement. Ambition is a clay I can help you mould. Why be a simple tool of the Time Lords when you could be their Empress?'

Persis hesitated. She had never really thought about what she might do with her near-eternal life. The CIA. Promotion? Maybe, in time, taking up a senior position? Perhaps rising to head the agency as Director?

'See?' the Mara whispered. 'You do crave power. Everyone does. Given the opportunity.'

The offer was tempting ...

*Don't be tempted by the Mara.*

The words of her colourful guardian angel came back to her, writ large.

'No,' Persis said. It was emphatic, and the Mara could feel that.

The snake spat and hissed in fury as the room came back into full focus. She could see that Manussa's arms bore a tattoo: a representation of a snake – almost childlike in its simplicity. But the image was moving, slithering down her arm so its head was on the back of her hand, its fork tongue extended down her index finger. Persis realised that it was the mark of the Mara, the physical manifestation of the being's control. It had been ready to take her in Manussa's stead.

'Kill her!' snarled the Mara.

Manussa turned her gaze on the Time Lord and the red beam of temporal energy began to form around her eyes. Persis raised the shield, ducking behind its protective sonic barrier.

The crimson rays shot from Manussa and struck the shield. But it had no effect on Persis. Instead, the beams were deflected away from her, striking the Mara's body just below the jawline.

The vast snake writhed in agony for a moment before its head fell to the floor, neatly severed. The rest of its body thrashed around for a few seconds before both it and the lifeless head vanished in a blur of white light.

Manussa collapsed to the ground and Persis lowered the sonic shield. Before the Time Lord could move to check if Manussa was alive, Sumara came rushing forward. She knelt down beside the prone form of her mistress and took her hand. Manussa's eyelids fluttered briefly and then remained open, her eyes staring lifelessly at the canopy over her bed.

Sumara turned to look at Persis. Her face was twisted with sorrow and anger. 'You killed her,' she whispered. Then she turned, looking towards the door. 'Guards!' she shouted. 'The Queen has been murdered!'

The sound of heavy boots outside told Persis that Strike Force guards were about to pour into the room. She went to operate the Time Ring.

Just before she vanished from the antechamber, Persis saw the tattoo on Manussa's arm become alive once more, this time sliding all the way down the arm of the dead Queen onto the arm of her faithful servant.

# THE UNWANTED GIFT
# OF PROPHECY

Honourable. That was the label she was entitled to use on her wedding invitations. Entitled. She let herself stare at the reflection in the dressing table mirror. But she saw no one there. Not really. Not any more. He had broken her.

With hollow eyes, she looked down at the ornate pillbox before her. The one he had given her: the one with the image of a foxhunt led by the Master of Hounds. Her delicate hand hovered over the china pot, quaking slightly. Why not? She thought. One more would make no difference.

She prised the lid off the pillbox open between thumb and forefinger. Lifting it on its tiny gold hinges, she revealed a sweet shop array within: green and white capsules of fluoxetine, pink citalopram tablets, the white innocence of escitalopram. The serotonin Smarty box she called it.

How had it come to this? What would her father have said? She was never a political person. So how had she ended up here? Married to him? She plucked a blue and white capsule from the mass and popped it in her mouth. Then she reached for the crystal tumbler beside it to wash down the pill.

Suddenly he was behind her. She hadn't heard him come in; she hadn't even seen him in the mirror. He came right up behind her, now using the reflection to look her in the eye. He stroked her long blonde hair with a black-gloved hand.

'That mission we spoke of? I think we're ready. Finally.' He sounded like an excited child. She managed a wan smile and rose to follow him from the room.

Two guards snapped to attention as they passed through the double doors of their private chambers. She reprimanded herself. How could she think of them as 'their' chambers? He had not come to her at night once since that day. The day of madness. The day he assassinated the President and brought the children pouring down from the sky.

'Come, Lucy. Don't dawdle, my darling.'

He held open a blue door and ushered her through. The room beyond was bathed in red light. Its circular walls almost seemed to be painted in blood – dark in places where it had dried. But she knew it was just the energy from the central pillar – a dark metallic mesh around a mushroom of modern computer screens, antiquated handles, oversized buttons and bizarre pieces of junk.

Her husband moved around this technological terror he had created, almost dancing with glee. Then he abruptly came to a halt and collapsed into a battered cream chair on the far side of the pillar. Lucy had to follow him around it to see his face. He was smiling, eyebrows raised.

'Are you ready?' he asked.

'I think so,' she replied.

He laughed. It had a manic tinge to it. 'How could you be? You're about to travel in time. It's fraught with danger. That's why I can't go.'

He rose from the chair and came over to cup her chin in his gloved hand. She couldn't recall when she had last felt his skin. For this, at least, she was grateful.

'You wouldn't want anything to happen to me, would you?' he asked, putting on a *faux* sad tone, his lips pouting.

Lucy hesitated. His grip tightened. 'Would you?' This last through angry, clenched teeth.

Lucy tried to look him in the eye and shook her head, forcing a smile onto her lips.

'Of course not, Harry.' She felt the tear role down her cheek.

'So it's "Harry" today, is it?' he asked, letting her face drop as he snatched his hand away. 'And of course I can't go because I'll be recognised.'

Lucy was confused. He'd said he was sending her into the past – or at least another time zone. 'By who?'

He laughed again, a brief manic outburst. 'You mean "whom".' He paused and came up to her again. 'By myself, of course!'

She shook her head. 'I'm sorry. I forgot.'

'Marry a Time Lord and you forget we can have different bodies.' He held up a datapad and pointed to a spot on the floor. 'Never mind. Just stand there.'

She moved into position. He came forward once more, but this time he was handing her something.

'Matrix Data Slices,' he said. 'Please remember them. It's vital to the future of us all.' He gave her a package. 'Nine to be precise. Detailing every single past encounter with my friend out there. The one in the cage. Make sure you call him my "best enemy".'

Lucy frowned. 'You mean the ...'

Harry put a leather finger to her lips. 'Don't say his name. There's no need for that.' He came forward and took Lucy's left hand. He toyed with her wedding ring. 'Remember,' he said. 'Activate this when you have what I want. The projector will reverse and you'll be back here. I'll be waiting.'

He stood back from her now, his expression neutral. Then he blew out his cheeks. 'Good luck!' He drummed his fingers on the rail that circled the pillar – that peculiar four-tone tippity-tap. Then he lifted one hand to the datapad and waved with the other. 'Byeee!'

The circular room faded from view.

✻

The man on the rowing machine was older than the man she knew. He was wearing an odd, off-white ensemble that looked more suitable for sleeping than exercising. He had also been laughing, pleased with himself. That she recognised well enough.

His laugh died when he saw her standing there. His eyebrows knitted, giving his already devilish face a deadly quality.

'Who are you?' he asked, standing up.

'My name is Lucy. I've been sent with a proposition for you.' She moved across the room to greet him. She had no idea whether to embrace the man or simply shake hands. Either seemed odd. He solved this conundrum by moving away from her, wary but not scared.

'A proposition!'

He grabbed a multicoloured towel from its hook, dabbing at his neck. 'You do realise this is a prison? A guard could come in at any moment. And then where would we be?'

Lucy smiled. He was certainly more charming than the man she had taken as her husband. But he looked old enough to be her father – his neatly clipped beard flecked with white at the corners of his mouth and his hair streaked with silver and grey.

He smiled back and took a seat at a long table, indicating she should do the same. 'Why don't you tell me what it is you want?'

'First, I want to show you what I have.' This was what Harry had told her to say. This man would only be interested in giving up his most prized possession if the counter offer was something equally valuable.

The bearded man gave a short laugh. 'Very well, *Lucy*. Tell me all!'

'My employer has nine Matrix Data Slices.' She showed him the package with the Gallifreyan technology within. The smile had not exactly frozen on the man's face but it had faded somewhat. However, his eyes had become hard, one eyebrow arched.

'May I?'

She passed him the package. He quickly examined it and passed it back.

'Where did you get these?'

'My employer.'

'Who is?'

'He wishes to remain anonymous.'

The man sat back. 'I see. Well, you can tell your employer that I have no need of Time Lord technology at the moment.'

'It's what's on them that will be of interest.'

'Dark scrolls – the electronic book version?' He smiled beatifically.

Lucy had no idea what he was talking about. She shook her head. 'My employer believes you will be pleased with the offer.'

'Do tell!'

'They contain information about every future encounter with your ... "best enemy".'

The man leant forward. 'My best enemy?'

'That is what he told me to say.'

'I see.' He stood up now and paced the room before turning back to her. 'And what does your employer ask in return for such riches?'

'Again, these are his words: access to your TARDIS while you are not using it. Not a permanent situation. He just wants to borrow it. He said it would be the ultimate time share!'

The man laughed. 'Well your employer certainly has a sense of humour!'

Lucy smiled.

'But I'm afraid it's out of the question.' He sat down again. 'You must think me a fool! Do you really expect me to believe this tale? You just want to *borrow* my TARDIS!'

'It's true,' Lucy replied. She was nervous now. What if the man did not agree to this? Harry would be angry. And that never ended well. 'Please, you must believe me.'

'Must I?' the man sighed. 'You may not realise this, but we Time Lords are highly attuned to time travel. The only way you could have come here is using a very limited osmic projector jury-rigged from a TARDIS console – probably one that isn't working properly.'

Lucy's face fell.

'So if you have a TARDIS, why do you need mine?' he continued. 'Shall I tell you? Because you want to find its location. This is plainly a ruse employed by my "best enemy" who – as you know – has only just left here having asked me the whereabouts of my TARDIS!'

Lucy tried to explain again but he held his hand up.

'Knowing I would never tell him this, he has used his worn-out old excuse for a TARDIS to send you here with a cock and bull story about deals I cannot refuse seeking to extract the same information.'

'No. That isn't it. I swear.' Lucy was desperate. 'He'll be furious with me.'

'I dare say he will,' the man said. 'It's a very clever little plan, but not today, thank you.' He stood and moved over to the door. 'I'm going to summon the governor of this prison now, so I suggest you leave!' He knocked on the door with two double-taps. 'Guard!'

Lucy twisted her wedding ring and the room blurred as she travelled back to the future.

✻

She thought he'd be angry. But Harry seemed more philosophical, blaming himself rather than her. He actually smiled and then paced the round chamber, shaking his head.

'He was always obsessed,' he muttered. 'Obsessed!' Harry turned back to her now. 'I was always convinced it was him, every setback, every issue. The devil's in the detail.'

He came back to the leather chair and picked up the datapad.

'I was wrong to send you to him, but I only have three time-traces so we're pretty limited on options!'

Lucy bit her lip. She fully expected him to lose it any second. She almost flinched just thinking about it.

'Of course he was never going to give up the location of his TARDIS. I wouldn't! Perhaps we'll have better luck with this one.'

He went to operate the datapad but then stopped.

'Tell you what, if this is a future incarnation, he should recall the encounter he just had with you. I think I can ...' Harry's eyes swivelled upward at the ceiling for a moment. 'Yes ... yes! I really did believe it was a wily plan from the old fox!' He laughed loudly for a moment or two. 'So let's add some pressure!'

He removed three data slices from the package and threw them on the floor. 'Our most recent encounters ...'

His foot ground them into the metallic floor, twisting and shattering them beyond use or saving. Then he looked up at Lucy once more. 'What are you waiting for? Off you go!' His fist hit the datapad and she felt a lurch in her stomach as she entered the time vortex.

❉

The huge radio telescope was tilted at 90 degrees, its antenna pointing across the landscape. Beneath it, Lucy found herself in an area of heathland – all gorse bushes and rough grass tufts. It seemed most unlikely she would find her husband anywhere near such a place, but she knew he wouldn't be wrong about this.

She walked towards the telescope, reasoning it was far more probable that he would be tampering with this vast contraption rather than wandering the countryside.

Suddenly, an annoying warble filled the air – obviously, some sort of alarm.

Lucy took cover in the undergrowth and watched as a group of four people half-ran, half-staggered across the grass. Three security guards with white hats pursued them. They easily caught the group, which Lucy could now see consisted of two women, a man and a boy. She didn't think either of the males looked like her husband – or what she thought he might look like given her previous encounter.

Suddenly, an ambulance pulled up and the man – who was dressed from top to toe in burgundy – was put in the back by two grey uniformed orderlies. While the boy was pointing at something in the sky, the two women jumped into the driver's cab and sped off across the heath. Lucy almost laughed. It was like watching a comedy programme from her youth: lots of people running about, escaping, being caught, and causing mayhem.

But then she heard the sound she'd been told to listen for: the asthmatic wheeze of a TARDIS. It had materialised by the ambulance, which now stood abandoned. This was her chance. She darted forward, flattening herself against the side of the vehicle. The guards, the ambulance men and the boy were all too astonished by the arrival of the time ship to notice her. Suddenly, colourful bolts of lightning flashed from the ship's exterior, stunning all the men, who fell to the ground.

With no witnesses, Lucy ran to the ship and stumbled inside, the clopping sound of her shoes alerting the man in the console room to her presence. He finished what he was doing at the controls and turned to face her. In his hand he had a small black weapon that looked like a plastic pepper grinder.

'Not a step closer, my dear,' he said.

He was a handsome man with a clipped beard – younger, Lucy thought, than the regeneration she'd visited before, but not too dissimilar really. He was squinting at her as if he were short-sighted and couldn't quite make out who she was.

'I know you,' he said, edging around the console. His grin was perhaps even more frightening than Harry's.

'Help me!' A weakened cry came from beyond a small door that led off the console room. Now Lucy knew she had the right man.

'Yes,' she said. We met once before. When you were in prison.'

He laughed. 'Yes. I recall it very well. You had a bargain to make, yes?'

She nodded.

'And now?'

'The same bargain.'

'From your mysterious employer.' He squinted again. He clearly did it when he was strategising. 'Last time, I made an assumption about where you came from. I am not sure I was right about that.'

'You weren't.'

'And you can tell me no more about who your employer is?'

'His name is Harry.'

The man cackled. 'Ooh, this is delicious. You still have the data slices?'

'Some of them.' She held out the six remaining packages.

'How interesting! You've lost three.'

'My employer wants to impress on you the urgency of the offer. He destroyed the other three.'

The man stroked his beard. 'Oh my dear, you have been naive! I might have agreed had the collection had been complete. But only six? I'm afraid not.'

'Please!' wailed the voice from the next room.

'And as you can see I am occupied at the moment.'

Lucy stepped forward. 'Please.'

The man was suddenly serious. He aimed the weapon at her chest. 'I am armed,' he said. 'I could kill you.'

'Must escape …' the voice moaned.

'I have to go,' the man said, backing away. 'As you can hear: I have a … guest. But you first.'

Lucy sighed but nodded. She felt a tear on her cheek. Was it frustration or dread?

'Goodbye, Lucy,' he said. 'Or is it *au revoir*?'

He laughed again and Lucy gave her wedding ring a violent twist.

✳

'He said *what*?' Harry was angry this time.

'He might have agreed if I'd still had nine.'

Harry smashed his fist into the mesh that surrounded the console. Then he slowly turned to face her. 'You're not trying hard enough.'

'I am, Harry! I swear.' She choked on the last word. No matter what he looked like, her husband could not be reasoned with. 'You … *they* just won't listen.'

He froze, cocking his head. 'Yes. I remember.'

He walked around the mesh, stroking it now. 'Recursive occlusions. Paradoxes. What a mind. What a mind!'

Harry completed his circle of the room and came up to Lucy, his breath catching her hair. 'One last chance then,' he spat. Then he was reeling away across the round chamber. 'One last spin of the wheel. One last throw of the dice.'

He stopped, facing away from her.

'Make sure, this time. Now, please attend carefully …'

✳

When Lucy arrived, she was almost relieved. It was London. Her London. The way she remembered it before Harry came along: frenetic – but in a good way – humming, full of life. She even knew where she was. Paternoster Row on Ludgate Hill. Right in front of St Paul's, surrounded by tourists and cafés.

To one side were a group of schoolchildren in naval uniform and a crowd of teachers and parents. A couple of policemen walked past, clutching guns closely to their chest. This gave her pause, but perhaps there was some security alert?

Lucy frowned. This was not where Harry had said he would send her. He had said it would be the same man as last time. He'd said that it was important. He'd also said she would arrive in some far-flung outer borough of London she'd literally never heard of and that she'd have to go to Horsenden Hill.

Something had gone wrong.

Lucy was just beginning to contemplate staying there – never going back – when she noticed a woman watching her from a nearby table. She was dressed unusually for the twenty-first century. The hat for starters. A purple and black number that matched her dress. She was peering at Lucy over the rim of a tea cup. Lucy felt uncomfortable and turned to walk away.

'Lucy?' The voice was sing-song but precise.

Lucy wondered if she was someone she'd met at a Downing Street do. Or perhaps a friend of her mother's? This was not the time, but Lucy felt drawn to the voice somehow. She turned.

The woman was smiling a very thin smile, her eyes equally thin.

'It is you! As I live and breathe!' She made a dramatic gesture to her forehead to show she might faint and then rose to greet Lucy as she would a long-lost friend. She kissed her on both cheeks and took her arm, gently leading her back to the table. 'Long time, no see!'

Lucy sat down. She had no idea what to do. Perhaps she should return to Harry. He'd made a mistake. He'd see that. It wasn't her fault.

The woman raised an arm and snapped her fingers. 'Waiter!'

Lucy gawked at her. No one did that any more. And if they did, they'd certainly not get served any time that year.

A waiter came running over. 'Yes, madam?'

'Mistress, actually, but close enough,' the woman said. 'My ... *friend* here looks like she could do with a cuppa and my Lapsang needs a top-up. Tea OK with you?'

Lucy nodded. 'Forgive me,' she began. 'But I don't ...'

The woman waved away her concerns. 'That's OK. Wife of the Prime Minister. Busy, busy, busy! Weeeeee!' She wobbled her head. 'Must make your head spin.'

'I suppose.'

'And that husband of yours!' She leant in. 'Quite the ladies' man. Handsome. Strong. Masterful.' She smiled. 'I could quite go for him maself.'

Lucy looked at the woman; was that a tinge of Scottish? The woman smiled back at her and picked up an odd-looking smartphone – or was it a tablet? The women gazed at her over the top of it.

'We should take a selfie! Commemorate the moment,' she said. Then she dropped the smile and the device. 'Maybe later.'

The waiter arrived with the tea.

'Ooh! Goody! Shall I be mother?' The woman took the pot and poured two cups, passing one to Lucy who lifted it to her lips.

'Let's talk about men!'

Lucy choked on the liquid, spilling it down her front. The woman passed her a napkin to clean herself up.

'I say men, I mean man. Just one. Your husband.' She winked.

'Harry?'

'That's the one.' The woman took a sip of tea. Then she put the cup back in its saucer very precisely and looked at Lucy with steely eyes. 'You hate him, don't you?'

Lucy hesitated. She smiled. Then she looked at the woman's eyes. They were like swirling galaxies. They almost felt familiar; compelling her to do what she didn't want to do.

'Yes,' she whispered.

The woman sat forward and took Lucy's hands in hers. 'You. Are. Not. Alone,' she said.

Lucy stared at her in astonishment.

The woman smiled. 'You've got a friend in me!'

The woman leant back in her chair, carefully removing her hat.

'Now, don't ask me how I know. Just listen. You have three Gallifreyan data slices in your possession. I would very much like to have them. You see I have plans! They won't affect you, I promise.'

Lucy shook her head. 'How ...'

The woman scowled. 'I said: just listen. He gave them to you to get something he wants. Yes?'

'Yes.'

'What I'm suggesting is you use them to get something *you* want.'

'What I want?'

The woman smiled. 'I appreciate your husband's predicament. *Really*, I do. But I think you should think about you for once. Have some "me" time. Do a "me" thing. We both know you want to leave him and we both know that's not possible.'

Lucy looked at the ground. 'I should go,' she said and stood up.

The woman pulled her back into the chair. 'Hush now. That's silly talk! I know what he's done to you; what he's *been doing* to you. What he's *still* doing to you. Even now. Manipulation. Abuse. Scorn. Rejection. If I were you, I'd kill him!'

She smiled sweetly and took another sip of tea.

Lucy pulled her chair closer to the table, making a horrible scraping sound on the pavement. 'I can't.'

The woman sneered. 'No such word as "can't", Lucy. Isn't that what your father used to say?'

'You know him?'

'Uh-uh-uh! No questions. I won't answer.' She rolled her eyes. 'OK. Just one. Yes, I know him. I know he has many businesses. Industrial, chemical, medical. He's a Lord, isn't he?'

Lucy brightened. 'Yes.'

'But the trouble is, your husband is a Lord, too. A Time Lord. And if you kill him, he'll just change and come after you.'

Lucy's happy expression wilted. 'There is no escape. I thought about staying here. Not going back.'

The woman shook her head. 'You need to Lady Macbeth up! And here's how. Soon he will become vulnerable. An opportunity will present itself. A 9mm opportunity, if you catch my drift.'

'A gun.'

'Top of the class! That Roedean education did pay off after all. Who says blondes are dumb? They have all the fun, right? Not like dull old brunettes.'

Lucy examined the women while she spoke. She was animated, clearly very clever, and she knew things she couldn't possibly know without the benefit of time travel. She must be a Time Lord, too, Lucy thought. The woman winked.

'That's me!'

If she was a Time Lord, she could be an enemy of Harry's. She might just be Lucy's best way of escaping. Hell, she was Lucy's *only* way of escaping.

'You want me to shoot Harry?'

'Trust me. He won't regenerate. He'll have his reasons. But I'm afraid you will go to prison. Ironic, really.'

Lucy agreed. How could she go to prison for ridding the world of the worst dictator it had ever seen? But then she realised: she had played her part. Too well, in fact. She'd even ... *liked* some of it. The power. The ability to do whatever she wanted. But what price had she paid?

'It won't be easy,' the woman said gently. 'Trust me, I know. But that won't be the end of it. He'll try to come back, to resurrect himself. And he'll use you. But this will be his big mistake. Huge!'

Lucy couldn't believe it. Use her? 'Why?'

'Because I'm going to tell you what you need to do. What chemicals you need to get your father to make. Who to bribe at the prison to become your friend.'

Lucy stared at the woman. She seemed earnest. Was this the only way Lucy had of escaping the hold Harry exerted on her? She nodded. She supposed it was. She reached into her coat and pulled out the data slices. She slid them across the table and the woman took them with a gleeful laugh.

'Now, say something nice.'

'Thank you,' Lucy said. She smiled and meant it. 'For telling me this. For helping me.'

The woman's eyes slid to the side and she gave a little choke of laughter. 'Well, I couldn't very well keep it to maself, now, could I?'

# THE EVIL AND THE DEEP
# BLACK SKY

Despite travelling at a velocity of more than 700 kilometres per second, the space station never seemed to move. Its engines were fighting the most massive gravitational forces, straining just to stay in one place. The engines' performance and the station's relative position were monitored constantly, not only by the most powerful computers but by the best engineers the Time Lord race had ever produced. These were the criteria for survival when you lived on the precipice of a black hole.

In the vehement periods of insomnia, Omega would find a modicum of peace by visiting the observation chamber to stare at the vast ball of nothing they were orbiting. He found it calmed his mind to see the object of their study, to look it in the face and try to take its measure.

The black hole was called the Heart of Messina because of the blood-red nebula that ringed the stellar collapse some distance out, a circular shape caused by lensing. What had once been the planetary system around the Messinian sun had long since been swallowed by the whirlpool of spatial forces. The area around the Heart of Messina was devoid of any life now, although the huge powers of attraction were already pulling in more distant objects such as debris fields, asteroids and even exoplanets.

Omega was determined to succeed this time. Despite the fact he and Rassilon were friends – good friends – the stellar engineer was jealous of the soldier-politician. As Lord President, Rassilon commanded the respect of all Gallifreyans; his successes in building Time Lord society and in combatting the massive threats they encountered as they expanded their empire were well documented and celebrated publicly. Omega's work was long and laborious. Most of it was kept secret from the rest of society, so no parades and feasts for him. No plaudits. That had to change. Omega was tired of living in the shadows – especially the one cast by his friend.

'Lord Omega?'

He turned away from the huge window. It was Lady Karidice. She was standing in the doorway as if it was she that had been caught off guard not him. He attempted a smile, but it was half-formed.

'I did not realise others came here,' she said.

'No,' Omega said. 'Nor I. That is, I have never seen anyone else here.'

The Time Lady came forward now to stand beside him and they both turned to look at the view.

'It is curious,' Omega said, 'that the very object we know can power our future is in actuality an absence of anything. Does that portend an empty future for us?'

Karidice laughed politely. 'I believe the expression you use is: "time will tell",' she said.

'It always does ...' Omega replied.

'Especially today.'

Omega nodded. Today was the day. After all the theorising, measuring, rechecking, modelling, experimentation and preparation, today he would make history. And Karidice would be by his side. Although he disliked the term assistant, she was certainly a trusted colleague and a high-ranking one. She had a brilliant mind, amazingly quick and adept at the type of calculation that – if all their work proved correct – would keep Omega alive in the next few hours.

'Shall we go?' he asked.

She looked at him and nodded, suddenly silent at what lay ahead. He took her arm and babbled some anecdote about how he had recently got the better of Rassilon in some childish debate about something trivial.

The main control room was circular, with an energy spire at the centre that extended up from the floor through the ceiling to the void outside. There was a simple, curved door in the structure at floor level that led into the small dematerialisation chamber. Around this were arrayed control desks at which sat technicians and scientists, all pouring over the data one last time.

On one side of this area was another door that led to an antechamber – a dressing room in which hung the suit. It was in itself a marvel of Time Lord engineering. It was made of special isomorphic plating that protected the specific wearer from the powerful forces of the time vortex and the Heart of Messina itself.

Omega gave a brief greeting to his team and went into the dressing room, closing the door. He took a moment to savour the momentous nature of the occasion. This would be the one, he knew. After this, he would be adored and revered as Rassilon was. He would make their research public and his race could finally take their position as the true Lords of Time and earn the right to dub themselves thus.

The suit was magnificent. It was cast in a metal alloy that was almost bronze in appearance and consisted of a suit, boots, gauntlet and helmet. Over the suit, Omega wore a robe made from a green-blue synthetic material that served as an additional level of protection – similar to the chainmail worn by ancient warriors. The idea that this was armour pleased him and had played no small part in its design. Rassilon was always portrayed as a great warrior, and Omega wanted to emulate that. Over his head and the robes, he pulled on the chest piece. This added a third layer of protection to the vital organs, and its geometric design reflected that of the helmet – each a triangular shape.

When he stepped from the changing room, the crew were on their feet and started applauding as he made his way towards the dematerialisation chamber. He smiled at them all, especially Karidice who operated the door control, sending a portion of the curved wall sliding open. Omega put his helmet on and, with a brief wave, stepped through. He turned around as the door closed behind him.

'Omega? Can you hear me?' It was Karidice. Her voice was entering the chamber via a speaker, giving it a slightly deeper tone.

'Yes!' Omega called. 'Proceed to system checks.'

Karidice started calling out the name of each station that had a control position on the Internal Vortex Activity experiment. The Time Lord at those stations then gave a confirmation of their mission readiness: black hole power drain, event horizon flight control, dematerialisation and rematerialisation regulators, vortex monitoring – everything had to function perfectly or the undertaking would be aborted. Omega listened with mounting excitement and a little trepidation as each Time Lord confirmed the functionality of their stations: 'Go for IVA.'

Finally, it all came down to one switch. Emsical, the young Time Lady at dematerialisation regulation looked at Karidice eagerly.

'Go Demat!' she called.

Emsical nodded and pulled down the large lever.

In the chamber, there was a strange sound almost like gusts of wind, rising and falling. Omega faded in and out from the rest of reality. This was the first occasion a Time Lord had entered the time vortex in any capacity: a pioneering moment and one Omega tried to live in the moment, soaking in the magnitude of what he was doing. And then he was gone.

Karidice watched the internal monitors carefully as he disappeared.

'Switch to vortex monitoring,' she said.

A Time Lord technician called Ralics duly operated the controls, and a screen at the back of the room lit up. They all turned to stare at the strange swirling eddies of the time vortex. While this was not the first time they had seen the vortex – they had been examining it for years – it was the first time they had ever seen a living thing within it. Omega was floating in the centre of the screen, like a diver in the ocean, an almost imperceptible stasis halo in place around him.

'Can you hear me?' Karidice asked.

There was a moment of silence, and a few anxious glances were exchanged across the control room. Then, with a slight reverb on his voice, they heard Omega.

'Receiving you at 100 per cent!'

A few of the Time Lords cheered.

'How is the reciprocal?' Omega asked.

'Reciprocal seems steady at 93,' Karidice replied. She leant forward to the microphone. 'What's it like?' she asked. 'Subjectively, I mean.'

In the vortex, Omega looked around him. 'Magnificent,' he said. 'Nothing can prepare you for the majesty of the environment.'

Karidice turned to the vortex monitoring station. 'All good?' she asked.

'IVA is stable,' reported Ralics. He smiled. 'Readings could not be more perfect.'

Immediately, an alarm sounded on one of the panels. It was event horizon flight control.

'What's going on?' asked Karidice urgently.

'Orbit is deteriorating by 0.01. Reason unknown,' the engineer said.

Omega's voice cut across the control room. 'What is the status there?'

Karidice ignored her superior for a moment. 'Unknown?' she said. 'What readings do we have?'

Before the Time Lord could answer, another alarm started to buzz at vortex monitoring. Ralics was staring intently at his monitor.

'Well?' There was a definite note of alarm in Karidice's voice now.

'Status!' Omega repeated gruffly.

Ralics shook his head. 'Unknown, but it's a large space-time event.'

This represented just too many unknowns. 'Cease the IVA, bring him back!'

She turned to the vortex screen and spoke into her throat mike: 'There's something in the vortex with you,' she said. 'It's destabilising our orbit. I'm pulling you back!'

'Negative! Negative! What is the orbit differential?'

'It is 0.01 but we are deteriorating,' she said.

'Safety parameters are at least 0.05!' Omega said crossly. 'You are not to terminate the IVA. Do you understand, Karidice?'

'But Omega, the crew! The station! You yourself are in danger. We do not know what the cause of the instability is.'

'Monitor it, then!' he shouted. 'The readings I am collecting are invaluable! If the orbit decays by more than 0.03, then terminate. But not until then. Do I make myself clear?'

Now it was Karidice's turn for silence.

'Deterioration now 0.02,' reported the engineer.

Karidice shook her head. She was about to argue with Omega when she saw something on the screen. They all saw it: a huge distortion in the vortex. It was twisting the swirling patterns to give itself shape and form. At first it was difficult to see in its entirety but then it showed itself: a vast winged being – almost like a bird of prey.

'Remat! Now!' shouted Karidice.

The rematerialisation process was operated and Omega was pulled back aboard the space station. He threw open the door of the chamber and emerged, wrenching his helmet off in fury.

'How dare you!' he screamed at Karidice.

She simply pointed at the screen. 'Look,' she said.

Omega was about to loose a tirade against his assistant but then noticed the screen. He stared for a few seconds. 'What is that?'

'We don't know,' Karidice said icily. 'That is why we pulled you out of the vortex!'

Omega was crestfallen. 'I'm sorry,' he said quietly. 'Of course you are right.' He looked around the Time Lords at their stations. 'I apologise,' he said.

Everyone was looking at him except the engineer, who was gazing steadfastly at his monitors. Omega noticed and moved across.

'My Lord, our orbit is still worsening. It has reached 0.04 now.'

'We need full power to engines,' Omega said. 'Redirect power from the Heart of Messina!'

The space station began to vibrate. They had been maintaining a very precarious orbit as close to the black hole as possible to draw energy from it without falling into it. Now that orbit was destabilising, they were falling towards it. They had a safety margin of 0.05 but no more.

A high-pitched whine let them know the black hole power was now online.

A nervous few seconds passed and the engineer looked up from his console. 'Stable at 0.04.'

Omega nodded in satisfaction but before he could say anything, the ship began to shake violently.

'Space-time disturbance!' reported Ralics.

'We're not interested in the vortex now,' Omega growled.

'My Lord, it isn't in the vortex,' Ralics said and operated the screen. 'It is off the port bow!'

They all looked at the screen. The star field outside looked normal at first but then everyone began to see the shape of the creature against the pinpricks of light. It was huge – almost the same size as the space station itself. Now it looked like the being was wearing some form of helmet, its eye slots glowing white.

As they watched, transfixed by the mysterious organism, it reached out an arm towards the hull of the Time Lord craft.

Karidice asked for the status of the shields and was told they were fully operational, but the creature's feathery digits came through the force field as if it wasn't there. The huge transparent hand then penetrated the ship itself, reaching inside all the way to the control room.

Omega was now standing between Ralics and Karidice, stunned and outraged by the events transpiring. It was clear this creature was extremely powerful, but they had no idea of what its intentions were. The Time Lord tried talking to it, but the translucent digits simply continued their exploration of the control room, coming to a halt over the engineer.

Karidice started to move towards him, but the creature squeezed its fingers together, closing over the top of the engineer's head. There was a blinding implosion of light and the engineer lay dead, his ability to regenerate clearly stopped by whatever method the being had used to kill him.

'No!' Karidice shouted and was at the fallen Time Lord's side in seconds. The creature snatched its hand away from the control room and then seemed satisfied to just float in space close to the station, watching.

'We leave,' Omega said. 'Now.'

One of the respected Healers rushed into the room in her white tunic and red jerkin, examining the dead engineer. She shook her head at Karidice. Omega immediately began issuing orders to the crew to plot a course past the monster outside. Then Ralics pointed out that they were already at full power and were barely maintaining a stationary orbit. The creature seemed to be preventing them from leaving.

'And our only option for escape is over the event horizon towards the black hole,' Karidice said.

Omega looked at the dematerialisation chamber and passed a gauntleted hand across his chin. 'Not our only option,' he said. 'We can use the chamber.'

'But only you have the suit, my Lord,' Karidice said.

'You misunderstand,' Omega said with a slight smile. 'I do not intend for us as individuals to enter the vortex. I am proposing we reverse the vortex chamber's alignment, radiating the stasis halo outwards not inwards.'

'You mean to take the station into the vortex?' Karidice asked.

'I do,' Omega said. 'And we need to do so with haste.'

So the Time Lords hurriedly worked to alter the chamber and the computer programs so that the same mechanism that had sent Omega into the vortex would do the same for the entire ship. It took them several hours and all that time Omega helped with the most menial of tasks and the hardest calculations, coaxing the best from his crew with one goal in mind: to save his ship, his experiments and his crew from the alien intelligence that had already claimed one life.

As the different stations reported ready once more, Omega stood in the engineer's place, operating his control panel. He needed Karidice doing what she did best – control in-flight operations.

She looked at him, forced a reluctant smile and then gave the order: 'Go for IVA.'

Again, the young Time Lady called Emsical took hold of the large handle and looked at Karidice. This time, though, her enthusiasm had been washed away by fear and uncertainty.

'Go Demat,' Karidice said quietly.

The strange wheezing, groaning sounds that had earlier filled the dematerialisation chamber now filled the entire control room, echoing through the station. The Time Lord craft began to fade in and out of reality and finally disappeared.

The creature now roared in anger and faded from view.

'Space station stable,' Omega said. 'The stasis halo is protecting it admirably.'

He was about to issue orders for the navigational team to begin their manoeuvring when the station shook once more. The vibration was accompanied by a sickening twist of the vessel's internal dimensions. Everything seemed elongated for a brief moment and then snapped back to reality. Omega knew it was the creature. This time, however, it was not a translucent giant that appeared or a feathered hand. A white figure the same size as Omega now stood in the control room.

'You cannot escape,' it said in a deep, booming voice.

'You killed one of my crew,' Omega said angrily. 'For no reason.'

'How can a being as small as you in power and intellect possibly understand my reasoning?'

'What do you want?'

'I feast on time,' the being said. 'For I am a Chronovore. Anything touched by the vortex is a delicacy to my palate and you are something new!' It laughed.

Omega turned and walked to the only weapons locker on board. It contained two staser pistols. He removed one and turned, pointing it directly at the alien.

'Leave my ship,' he ordered.

'Threats?' the Chronovore sneered and began walking across the chamber. He was making for Karidice.

'Stop!'

The creature ignored him and Omega squeezed the trigger. The bolt of energy hit the Chronovore in the back, but the weapon had no effect.

The creature turned back to Omega. 'You would kill me?' it asked. 'Then I will repay the compliment.'

With no further warning, the Chronovore reached out and snatched at Karidice, catching her a blow to the head. Now she too fell to the floor.

'No!' Omega rushed across the room and lifted the head of his fallen friend. Her pale blue eyes were still open, staring blindly up at him. Omega looked at the Chronovore.

'Please,' he said. 'This is senseless.'

The creature regarded the Time Lord for a moment and then turned, taking on the form of a female humanoid. 'You brought this on yourself,' she said. 'And I will feed for I am hungry.'

'If you need sustenance from time, you are overlooking the best source on this station. It is not the crew. See for yourself.' Omega walked over to the dematerialisation chamber. 'It is in here.' He opened the door, and stood back. A white void pulsed within.

The Chronovore approached and sniffed the air. 'You know you cannot destroy me.'

'I just want to give you what you want so you will leave us.'

The humanoid nodded and stepped forward. Omega threw himself at its back, thrusting the creature into the chamber and slamming the door.

'Safety controls off!' he shouted 'Black hole power now!'

In the chamber, the Chronovore was immersed in the raw radiation from the black hole and cried out in sudden in agony. 'You will die!' it screamed and then vanished.

Straight away Omega put his plan into operation. Entering the time vortex allowed the station to move in space without being on the spatial plane. The pilots navigated the space station towards the space-time event of the black hole and then across the maelstrom to the far side. Only then, when they were several million miles from the event horizon, did Omega order their rematerialisation. They had escaped both the monster and the cosmic whirlpool of the Heart of Messina. But the cost had been too high.

Before they returned to Gallifrey, they had services for the engineer and Karidice. Omega gave his friend's eulogy, extolling her virtues but also vowing to his fellow Time Lords that he would never again place their lives in danger in order to pursue his dream of time travel. He would rather sacrifice himself than lose any more friends.

# JORUS AND THE
# VOGANAUTS

Jorus stood proudly on the bridge of the *Vogo*. The ship was the finest his race had ever built; an interstellar craft possessed of such beauty it had captivated the entire planet of Voga. An elegant and streamlined hull, twin spatial-torpedo launchers, a pair of huge solar sails, and on the stern a carving of their god of wealth and good fortune, after whom the ship was named. Around the captain, the golden surfaces of computer panels hummed and glowed as the pilots and navigators guided the ship through the void of space.

'We are approaching the farthest point, captain,' said Collig. He was the senior pilot, his silvery hair cut short to reveal the dome of his grey-brown head – as was the fashion. His deep-set eyes and large, protruding features were the same as the rest of the crew: all good, Vogan qualities.

Jorus was staring at the holoscreen that displayed a three-dimensional image of their environs into mid air at the centre of the bridge. 'Very good, Collig,' he replied. He returned to

the captain's chair, positioned above and behind the rest of the command deck, allowing a smile to flicker on his face. This was indeed a landmark, he mused – if such a statement could be used to describe a breakthrough in space travel.

The farthest point Collig was referring to was the outer asteroid belt of the Voga system. No Vogan space ship or probe had ever been beyond it. That was part of the reason why tens of thousands had attended the launch of the *Vogo*, cheering the brave crew off on their mission of exploration and discovery. The 'Voganauts' the media had dubbed them.

'We are about to make history,' Jorus said. 'Ready on intra-space engines.'

Collig reached forward. His hand hovered over the lever that would take the *Vogo* from speeds measured in familiar distances to those that were almost unfathomable.

'Now!'

Collig operated the engines and the ship seemed to blur slightly. Jorus was pinned back in his seat momentarily before the inertia inhibitors kicked in. As the greyish-white blur of intra-space reflected from the holoscreen on his face, Jorus finally allowed his smile to show.

Almost immediately, a two-tone alarm sounded, sending the bridge crew into a panic. Jorus recognised it straight away but the junior pilot, Mishar, confirmed its designation.

'Intra-space misalignment! Dephase collision!' she said.

The *Vogo* was swinging dangerously off course. If it deviated too much, the ship would hit the side of the artificial wormhole that the engines had created, and that would be catastrophic. The *Vogo* might even be destroyed. Jorus rose quickly from his chair and came down to the pilots. He placed a hand on Collig's shoulder.

'Cut in standard power,' he ordered, raising his voice to be heard over the sound of the vibrating hull.

Collig looked across at Mishar and a tacit understanding passed between them. Acting in unison now, they performed a perfect deceleration procedure.

Nothing happened.

Jorus read the surprise on his pilots' faces. 'What's wrong?'

'Negative response, Jorus!' Mishar screeched.

'We're out of control!' shouted Collig. 'We're going to dephase!'

✴

'Did the experiment work?'

The humanoid had a head like a white kingfisher, with a very long pointed beak. It was a rainbow of yellows fading into greens and teal-like blues. Her body was covered in beautiful snowy feathers – like a swan – but with a pattern that looked like flames running down her back. As she spoke, the elaborate feathered crest on her head shook. This was Euxine.

The man she addressed was hunched over a large computer bank, LEDs flashing in sync with the program it was running. He wore a simple one-piece suit, which bore a handful of unstitched tears, and his beard was a little ragged and untrimmed.

'Are you going to be silent again, Rassilon?' Euxine asked, a hint of a sneer in her voice. 'You know that annoys me.'

The Time Lord turned to face his captor. 'No,' he said. 'I was merely trying to concentrate on the readings.'

'And ...?'

'It does not appear that the time experiment worked,' Rassilon said raising his eyebrows. 'I will have to fine-tune the mechanism. Check the program again. This is unchartered territory.'

'Yes. "Uncharted territory",' Euxine mimicked her prisoner. 'I know. You have said that every time the experiment has failed.' She came forward, waving a winged arm at the Time Lord. 'I need this to work. The Ra'ra'vis will have time travel. You will see to that.'

'You're a scientist,' Rassilon implored, spreading his arms. 'You know that breakthroughs do not come all at once but with, well, time . . .'

'Time,' said Euxine. 'I would choose your next words very carefully, *Lord President*. They may be your last!' She turned and waved her wing at a Ra'ra'vis guard that stood the other side of a grilled door. The soldier released the lock and hurriedly opened the door for his leader to pass.

Rassilon returned to the computer. A small tickertape read-out was spilling from a slot in the machine's side. The Time Lord took it in his hands and read the information once more. This time, though, he allowed himself a discreet smile.

He had been reckless, that was true. He should never have left the safety of the main fleet to check on the rumours of a Vampire nest in this quadrant. But the bickering politicians had told him that they were fighting on so many fronts already that a new one could not be opened up. Besides, there were no troops available. So, he had come himself. Alone. He was a warrior, after all; capable of taking care of himself. Or so he thought.

Then he'd run into what he assumed was simple engine trouble and had been forced to put down on a conveniently placed asteroid. Of course, he'd sent a message to the fleet giving his coordinates. As soon as he'd done that, his communications had been blocked and an energy dome had formed over his one-man craft. An electro-magnetic pulse had hit his ship, and all its circuits had been blown. Before he had even time to fish out a staser, the asteroid had suddenly – and unexpectedly – gone to warp.

The Ra'ra'vis did not appear until they arrived at the planet on which he was now imprisoned. He'd recognised the bird-like aliens as they appeared in the dome shortly before they pumped his ship full of a very strong knockout gas. Even he could not filter it out of his system, and when he awoke he was in a large cell. It was well furnished and actually comfortable. He'd certainly been in worse military accommodation during his many centuries of warfare.

What surprised him was that the cell was simply an antechamber to a large laboratory. It was not as well equipped as the ones he was used to working in on Gallifrey, but what was there was a very good approximation of the apparatus required for rudimentary time travel experiments. Rassilon had marvelled at this and expressed his admiration to Euxine when he met her for the first time.

The sly Ra'ra'vis had accepted Rassilon's praise and then informed him that they had been intercepting the Time Lords communiqués about their temporal experiments for many years. Their best scientists – including Euxine herself – had been trying to emulate them in their own laboratories, but without success. Their military had then hit on the idea of kidnapping Time Lord scientists and forcing them to work for the Ra'ra'vis.

Of course, they had had no idea when they set their asteroid traps that they would catch Rassilon. A stroke of luck, Euxine claimed. Rassilon wondered if this was a lie and they had been after him all along: tracking his movements and springing their trap as soon as he'd left the protection of his forces.

He had no proof this was the case and, with no other option, Rassilon had started to work for the Ra'ra'vis using their rather basic technology. From what they had told him about their own test results, he knew that, although they were close to the Time Lords in their quest for true mastery of time, the aliens were missing core parts of the research.

This allowed Rassilon to add in extra components that he told Euxine were necessary. He could not send a distress signal with the machinery he had; it was not meant for communication. It would have been like trying to light a fire with an ice cube. Indeed, he could not use it to do anything extraordinary, and certainly not to travel in time. However, the technology was advanced and did allow him to set up warp fields and interfere with the hyperspace dimensions.

When Euxine had demanded progress and wanted to see a demonstration, Rassilon had showed the Ra'ra'vis scientist his hypothesis about using hyperspace as a means of entering the time vortex. He knew it was a dead end because it had already been tried on Gallifrey. Crucially, Euxine did not know this. The 'experiment' had gone ahead and, while it seemed to have failed, Rassilon had succeeded.

He had pulled a ship in warp drive to him.

❁

It had been a rough journey. The *Vogo* had been buffeted and spun, testing the inertia inhibitors to their full limits. It had survived, however, and so had the crew.

'Damage report?' Jorus asked groggily.

'No damage to systems or structural integrity,' Collig said.

'But we're not where we should be,' Mishar added.

Jorus stood and his legs managed not to buckle under him as he walked across the pilots' pit. 'Where are we, then?' he asked.

Mishar shook his head. 'The computer's trying to get a fix, but none of the stars or constellations match those we know.'

'That means ...' Jorus sighed and rubbed his eyes. 'We're a long way from home.'

'A very long way,' confirmed Mishar.

'I want an analysis of our intra-space warp field,' Jorus said. 'We should only be a couple of light years from Voga. That was the plan. What went wrong?'

He retired to his cabin to think, but it wasn't long before he was interrupted. Collig entered and told him that they had picked up something very odd in their analysis of the intra-space accident. Together they went down to the engine bay.

Here the only Vogan who really knew the ship's engine back-wards was cleaning his ears with a conduit sponge, his feet up on a bank of instruments as he reclined in a battered, high-back chair.

'Keston!' Jorus said, bringing the engineer from his chair with a jolt.

'Captain!' Keston jumped up, sending his long white locks into a mess around his face. He tidied the stray strands of hair and threw the sloppiest salute any Vogan had ever given, before moving across to a holoprojector mounted on the wall.

'We use this for monitoring the engines, checking the integrity of the intra-space field, that sort of thing,' he explained and then hit a button. The room darkened and a cross section of the *Vogo* appeared. Around it was an oval of swirling patterns.

'So this is the ship,' he pointed to the *Vogo*.

Jorus gave an exaggerated sigh. 'Thank you, Keston. I know what my ship looks like.'

'Right. Sorry,' Keston flustered. 'But ... but this is the field our engines generate at intra-space speed.' He waved roughly at the oval pattern. 'Now, this is an exact rendition of what happened after we entered intra-space.'

The oval pattern began to fluctuate and suddenly it shrank so that the prow of the ship almost protruded from it.

'That was the worst point,' Keston said. 'The misalignment.' He turned to Collig. 'The one you thought was gonna cause a dephase collision. And it shoulda done, too.'

The oval then grew again – this time to much larger proportions – before flaring and then dissipating entirely.

'And then we came out of intra-space ... here. Wherever "here" is.' Keston laughed.

'Collig tells me there was something odd?' Jorus prompted the older man.

'Yes! The flare. Did you see it?' Keston rewound the projection. Again they watched as the oval grew and then just as the light increased, he paused the image. 'There!'

Jorus peered at the image, and then something made him take a sharp intake of breath. He moved forward to check what he was seeing.

'Give it a moment,' Keston said, grinning as if he was introducing a new-born to the family.

What Jorus had seen was a pattern of circles. Some were concentric and others interlacing. But as he started at them, they formed a single word that he could actually read.

'"Help"?' he asked.

'Exactly!' Keston said.

'We believe it is a psychic message,' Collig said. 'It's not in our language, but it contains within it a psychic impulse that, when read, translates the message.'

'A distress call.'

'Precisely, captain!' Keston was holding a spanner of some kind now and jabbed it at Jorus as he spoke. 'We need to respond.'

'And it was this distress call that pulled us off course?'

'No,' Collig said 'But the message and the navigational deviation bear the same intra-space signature. It's the same person. Or people.'

'A distress signal sent by someone who has universal translation at their fingertips and can pull a ship across half the galaxy?' Jorus asked. 'Who could exert that kind of power and yet need assistance?'

❃

'Rassilon!'

Euxine stormed into his cell and held up a data-tablet. The Time Lord was lying on his bed.

'We analysed your last experiment.'

'Ah,' Rassilon said swinging his legs onto the floor and sitting up.

'*Ah*, indeed!' the Ra'ra'vis said. 'We found your little message.'

'I'm your prisoner, Euxine. You cannot blame me for wanting to escape. I have a war to fight. One that affects your people, too.'

'Do not bring the Vampires into this,' she said, exasperated. 'Please. You're obsessed. And how many times have I told you? Hellion is too far away from this conflict of yours for it have *any* bearing on us.'

Rassilon shrugged.

'You will have to be punished,' she said.

'What?' Now he was standing. 'You have treated me well, Euxine. I understand your thirst for time travel. Believe me. But I *will* escape your gilded cage and *fly* home.' He parodied the wing movement the Ra'ra'vis made when she moved her arms. 'I was thinking of not wiping your race from existence. But if you treat me badly ...'

Euxine smiled at him, her eyes twinkling. She had come to know this Lord of Time since he had been incarcerated in her care. She understood that he truly was a great man. She also knew he was only half serious – as she was about the punishment.

'You have resorted to playground impersonations,' she said. 'Tut. Tut!' She turned and walked out of the cell. 'We will be monitoring you even more closely now,' she added over her shoulder. 'And no supper tonight!'

✸

The *Vogo* sailed through the strange, new planetary system. It was on silent running protocol. While the ship did not possess a cloaking device as such, it did have an adaptive camouflage shield: taking the visual data gathered from the port bow array and projecting it from the starboard array, and vice versa.

On the bridge, the illumination from control panels and computer screens was dimmed, the main lighting switched to a dull yellow, almost like moonlight. Jorus was leaning forward in his command chair as the pilots manoeuvred them at low speed from planet to planet. The logic was that whoever was holding this high-tech alien prisoner would be scanning for approaching ships and they had no idea which planet the captive was on.

'Sir, I think we have something,' Mishar said. 'There are some strange readings coming from an asteroid field around the fourth planet.'

'Strange?'

'Our instruments are picking up complex alloys, Jorus,' the junior pilot said. 'They don't occur naturally.'

'Change course to intercept the largest asteroid,' Jorus said. 'Bring us to a full stop a safe distance from it. And ready a DOVE.'

The DOVE was a small, self-propelled probe that was designed for Defensive Observation, Verification and Examination. It would be able to get in closer than the *Vogo* could without alerting anyone to its presence. The DOVE had enough equipment to give the Voganauts a very good idea of what was hiding among the asteroids.

As they neared, the field of spinning rocks, a port opened on the *Vogo*'s hull. It had a twin on the opposite side of the ship. More normally they fired varied types of spatial torpedo, but this time it was a probe that was propelled from the firing tube. The DOVE flew steadily towards its target, slowing as it came nearer to the large asteroid. Behind it the *Vogo* came to a halt much further out.

On the bridge, Jorus and the command crew watched as the DOVE manoeuvred between two smaller asteroids, getting closer to the large one. Suddenly the two rocks – about the size of one-man skimmers – sprang together, crushing the probe and sending small components spinning away to rebound off smaller rocks.

'Warning! This is a Symple-Guardz asteroid field. The planet beyond is under quarantine due to space plague. Any attempt to pass through the asteroids will result in your destruction.'

The transmission that had been playing throughout the ship ceased. The crew looked uncertainly at one another. Then they all turned to Jorus.

'Sentient asteroids?' he asked.

'Not sentient, captain. Autonomous.' Keston was leaning in the doorway, smiling.

*

The Ra'ra'vis maintained a very small staff at the base: a squad of eight guards and one officer, three technicians who monitored the planet's defences as well as any stray communications

94

they might pick up and a 'backroom' team of three scientists. This was Euxine's full contingent. She didn't need it to be larger due to the automation. One of the technicians was approaching her now across the control room. He told her in hushed tones that he had detected an infringement in the asteroid field. When she asked for clarification, he told her that it was a small space probe of unknown origin. Euxine checked it wasn't Gallifreyan and then dismissed it. If there were hostiles out there, they would be in for quite a ride.

❄

It was perilous, but Jorus was willing to risk it. He ordered the *Vogo* in closer to the asteroid field. As he suspected, the rocks had rearranged themselves so that the two largest ones were now spinning less than a thousand metres off the prow. Keston had explained that the asteroids were probably controlled by a computer system. Whatever sized object it detected, the system sent two rocks large enough to crush it. They didn't do so immediately; only once the object closed on the planet.

Jorus knew that to pass beyond the asteroid field and reach whoever it was that needed the Voganauts' help, he would need to buck the system in some way. He ordered the launch of a second DOVE. This time, he'd ordered Collig to remote pilot it so that the probe passed between the two largest spinning boulders. He figured that the system would use those rocks as they were nearest and capable of the job rather than assign the job to two smaller ones.

As the DOVE sped towards its doom, he had Mishar monitoring the asteroids very carefully because they would only have one chance.

'DOVE closing on nearest target,' Collig confirmed. '300 metres.'

'No other large asteroids in the vicinity?' asked Jorus.

'200 metres.'

'None that could cause us any real damage,' Keston said. Jorus had assigned him the seat usually reserved for his second officer, but as Collig was the second officer, he already had a seat in the pilot pit.

'100 metres.'

Jorus bit his lip.

'Asteroid moving!' Mishar called.

On the screen, the two huge boulders closed on the DOVE and then suddenly accelerated, crushing the device.

'Retract solar sails! Engines to full!' Jorus said. 'Head straight for those asteroids!'

The *Vogo* sped forward, just as the asteroids parted once more. They kept moving apart as the Vogan ship flew towards them, their image increasing in size alarmingly on the holo-display. Just as the two vast rocks reached the peak of their separation, the *Vogo* was already sailing between them. The asteroids raced to crush the ship, but they missed the main section, sliding across the stern of the vessel with a stomach-turning grating sound.

'We're through!' Collig said.

'Scan the planet surface for life signs.'

The report came back that there were minimal life signs – sixteen or seventeen – all clustered on one small area on the eastern continent of the northern hemisphere.

'Prepare the guards for a landing party,' Jorus said. 'Collig, Keston – you're with me. And if anyone contacts the ship, act tough!'

*

Meda was a moral Ra'ra'vis. She had never really liked her job. She didn't like being away from her family; she hated missing the solstice of Pajaro and the celebratory meal that always accompanied it with four generations of her brood.

She thought she'd been posted to Chilsos complex as a punishment. She had just come on duty, replacing the quiet Calcatori. She disliked him, too. He'd told her about the probe in excited yet hushed tones and then disappeared to his rest quarters.

Now the control panel was lit up like a Pajaro garland. Something much bigger than a probe had somehow managed to pass through the Symple-Guardz protection system. Meda looked over her shoulder at the empty control room. Due to the skeleton crew, only one technician was on duty at any time and Director Euxine was never there to report to.

Remembering her training, Meda decided to take the initiative and opened a communications channel. It was extremely weak but that was to be expected.

'Unknown ship, this is Chilsos control,' Meda said, trying to sound as official as she could. 'Be advised, this planet is under quarantine. We are the only survivors. Please, stay away.'

'This is the battleship *Vogo*,' came the gruff reply. 'We believe you are holding an alien ally against their will. *You* be advised that we have a large commando force landing in your area to mount a rescue mission.'

The communication cut off. After four attempts to raise them again, Meda gave up and hit the emergency evacuation alarm.

In the laboratory, Euxine was sitting with Rassilon, examining a modification he wanted to make to their computer systems. She jerked her head up and ran to the door.

'What's happening?' Rassilon asked.

'They must've come for you!'

'Who?'

'Your people, of course!' she tapped impatiently on the grille. 'Guard! Open this door!'

The Ra'ra'vis soldier hurried over and unlocked the door. Rassilon made to follow Euxine, but she slammed it behind her. The Time Lord rested his hands on the crossbars.

'I'm afraid this is where we part company.' She turned and brushed his fingers ever so slightly with her feathers. 'I have enjoyed working with you,' she said. 'Stay with him,' she ordered the guard and then rushed away.

'Even under duress, it was a pleasure,' called Rassilon, smiling. He was taking this remarkably well, but his primary concern was to return to the front and now he could.

The guard eyed him nervously.

'Don't worry,' Rassilon said. 'I'm locked securely in a cell. You should go.'

Before the Ra'ra'vis could move, there was the sound of blaster fire in the corridor behind him. He was unarmed and stood ready to attack whoever entered the cellblock with his three claw-like fingers.

Suddenly Jorus stood framed in the doorway. The guard went to attack him, using his wings to intimidate the enemy. Keston appeared behind him, Vogan rifle in hand.

'Don't even think about it,' he said and managed an imperious stare. 'Unless you want to be served up as roast fowl!'

Jorus strode forward, approaching the cell door. 'You are the prisoner?' he asked.

'And you must be the rescuer,' Rassilon said.

The two bearded men regarded one another for a moment and then smiled.

❄

Aboard the *Vogo*, Rassilon was treated very well. The Vogans had never heard of the Time Lords before and were very happy to learn they had rescued someone of such galactic importance.

As recompense for their heroic rescue, Rassilon gave the Vogans technology and knowledge beyond their understanding. He told them it would help in the wars they had to come.

Jorus did not understand this, but he was in awe of the Time Lord President. As they transported him back to Time Lord space, he spoke with Rassilon often about politics on Gallifrey and about the way their government was organised.

Rassilon showed Jorus his Seal – the Presidential one – that was used as a symbol of authority and honour. Of all the things Jorus marvelled at, this was the thing that most seemed to affect him: that a pictogram could be so powerful a tool. This did not go unnoticed and so when they reached the Gallifreyan lines and Rassilon returned to his people and his seemingly endless battle with the Vampires, he gave the Voganauts his Seal in a grand ceremony of thanks.

When the Time Lords used their technology – which seemed like the power of gods to the Vogans – to return the *Vogo* back to its home system, Jorus was determined that he would adopt the spiral pattern as their own and that they would set about creating a government based on the chapters and councils Rassilon had told him of in their many discussions.

# THE VARDON HORSE

*The Precinct of Anitroilia, Citadel of the Assembly*
*Dessinday 34th Alpus*

The war edges ever closer.

Last night the light of battle reached us from the five conjoined worlds of Trallinhoe. This is less than one parsec. Subspace communication is awash with news of the Kosnak horde and how they plundered the five worlds and then detonated its host star to prevent their enemy from gaining any strategic advantage. I would call them base, but they have such technology! Truly, it is amazing what the simple mind can conceive when forced to by threat of death.

The Kosnak may be three light years away, but they could be here tomorrow. They possess ships of such size and speed I just don't know if our planetary defences would hold out against their onslaught.

Today, I met with the other Senators to discuss our plans. There is division among them: stay, flee, fight, hide. And we could do any of these things. I don't fear the weaponry of the Kosnak. Nor the Vardon. It is losing the fundamental values of our civilisation that terrifies me.

A case in point.

When was the last time we sought a military confrontation with any other species? For thousands of millennia we have lived in harmony with our neighbour and our environment. Yet Senator Minzak would have us utilise our psychic abilities, 'weaponise them', he said. Naturally I advocated for a peaceful solution. Of the four options, I would rather flee or hide than unleash our destructive capability on any race.

The council chamber was in uproar after Furis suggested using our reconnaissance and intelligence potential to gather as much information as possible about both races. Perhaps, she suggested, there would be something we could offer the Vardon and the Kosnak to leave us alone.

Minzak was on his feet, incandescent that we should 'sell our principles to appease embryonic invaders'! His was a good speech, I must say, but then he called Furis a coward and a lowly trader in morals and ethics.

I remember, when I first came to the Citadel, I was amazed by the stunning crystal decoration, the walls built from natural geodes. The Augmented Reality set had dubbed it 'a bastion of reason where considered discussions had built our civilisation and maintained it for countless generations'. Ha! If the writer of that work could have seen the behaviour of the Senators today. No unanimous desire for reason here. Just disarray and mud-slinging.

Of course, Senate Principal Orfak sought to placate everyone no matter his or her viewpoint. His vacillations will probably kill us all. 'Senators,' he said in that annoying, nasal tone of his. 'We have a hard decision ahead of us. Let us contemplate all the options and choose the one that is right for Xeriphas.'

Platitudes!

'No matter what foe we face, the Xeraphin will be the Xeraphin.'

And soundbites.

After the session, I consulted with the other members of the Core Scientific. Epeyak has been working on a focus for our powers. He has an interesting theory on how we might use what he called the collective application to make the aggressors simply leave without ever firing a shot. I must confess I like this idea, but prefer to use the focus to hide us from our enemies, rather than confuse or intimidate them. He berated me, even tapping my silver tunic!

'Odyson! You must be prepared to leave the cocoon of your own standards and understand that sometimes the rasher course is the most beneficial.'

I can see why he's a scientist and not a politician! When has recklessness ever been the best course of action? I said as much, but will let him continue his work.

*The Precinct of Anitroilia, Citadel of the Assembly*
*Essenday 35th Alpus*

The month draws to a close with horrendous news. We woke on the day of peace with the warlike Vardon already in our solar system.

We know the Vardon of old. Their race and ours signed a peace treaty not 300 years ago. The great appeaser, Jayentas, negotiated with the dimpled warriors that they should consider our system an exclusion zone. In return for this, we promised that no matter what action they took against the Kosnak – or anyone else for that matter – we would not interfere.

It is not hard to understand why appeasement is not a popular option in the Senate. Jayentas has been reviled ever since.

It is said he lived out the twilight of his years in solitude on the sombre moon. No one would actually want to live there. Due to its unique rotation, it's almost constantly in the shadow of Xeriphas, and there's no breathable atmosphere. I doubt it's true.

What is true is that Senator Furis has stepped down. A great loss. She was capable and a strong voice against Minzak. With one less of our number, I fear we will end up doing something unspeakable.

*The Precinct of Anitroilia, Senate Principal's Quarters*
*Abanday 1st Belagaw*

This morning there she was on the Assembly Way. Furis. She stopped me as I walked. I must confess to being a little taken aback by this. She, on the other hand, looked very composed for a recently deposed member of the Senate.

'I know you don't agree with Minzak and his crude policies, Fellow Odyson,' she said.

I inclined my head in respect. 'I am only an adviser on science, Senator. I have no ballot to cast.'

She smiled generously. 'Thank you for still using my political title. Your diplomacy and wise manner are why I believe you can help me.'

Now, I am not one for conspiracies. Indeed, I don't think there has been one on Xeriphas for decades. That said, perhaps Epeyak's words concerning rashness of action had affected me! 'Help you?' I asked.

She indicated we should walk, and so we did – away from the Assembly towards the Senate Gardens. No matter what the machinations brewing in the Senate, nature always continues its endless cycle and, in seeming defiance at our current situations, the kukir trees were in late blossom, orange and pink petals drifting up from the boughs on the spring thermals.

'Something has happened,' Furis told me now we were away from the crowds.

I frowned. Did she mean the Vardon? I asked her.

'No,' she said. 'Someone has arrived on Xeriphas – quite by chance he claims.'

Again I was confused. 'Arrived? You mean from the moons?'

She shook her head, gazing steadily in front of her as she sauntered away as if she were one of the debauched 'hedonistas' out walking with a favourite cousin. 'He's an alien.'

'How did he penetrate the defence barriers?'

She smiled at a winged burrel as it fluttered by. 'I have no idea. He just did. The important thing is that after his capture by the heralds, they took him to Orfak.'

This stopped me in my tracks. 'Why did they do that? Orfak is a xenophobe. Always has been. That's why he'd never meet with the Vardon or the Kosnak.'

'Well, quite.' She took my arm and started walking again. 'But this being is old. His hair is the same colour as our skin. And he demanded to be taken to our leader!'

'Hair?' This was incredible. 'The Silver Soothsayer,' I breathed. 'Exactly!'

'This must be a coincidence! Surely even Orfak cannot believe this is true. It's a folk tale! It's older then these buildings! And they're what? Ten millennia?'

'Whether Orfak believes this man is actually the Silver Soothsayer or not, he is dining with him at this very moment.'

I now turned and propelled us back towards the gardens' entrance. 'How do you know all this?'

Furis regarded me with a twinkle in her eye. 'I have many sources in the Citadel,' she said. 'I am, after all, Senator of the Watch.'

As if I could forget! With the power of both the heralds and the far more secretive emissaries, her resignation had struck me as odd.

'And what does Orfak intend to do with him?'

'Shall we go and find out?' she said.

When we reached the Senate Principal's chambers, there were two Plasmavores outside his door. Another of Epeyak's creations. Despite their rather primitive appearance these creatures could ensnare an intruder and transport them away or hold them in place. They rendered their victims unable to move and could be used to communicate telepathically.

They wobbled forward, but Furis dismissed them with a wave of her hand. She swept past them as if she were Senate Principal and not Orfak. Indeed, the heralds guarding the inner doors saluted and let her pass without a word. Was I to be witness to a coup?

Orfak's personal study was an ornate affair. There were several cases of old books to make him look worldly. I doubt he'd read a single one. The furnishings were all from his home province of Teven – a backwater in the southern hemisphere that had only ever produced one Senator.

He was sitting in one of the padded, high-back chairs with a crystal goblet lolling in his right hand. He was gently swilling the yellow ferment within round and round as he spoke to the occupant of another identical chair less than a body-height away.

Incredibly, Orfak did not seem surprised by our sudden arrival. He finished his sentence and stood to greet us. I tried to hide my amazement at his generous and uncharacteristic behaviour, but I must have betrayed myself in some way.

'No need to look so startled, Odyson,' he said. 'You are most welcome here on this auspicious day.'

The alien that had been sitting opposite Orfak also rose, albeit more slowly and with a certain stiffness. He did indeed have silvery hair and wore a coat of black. The Senate Principal smiled as he started to introduce the stranger:

'May I present —'

Furis cut him off. 'Of course! You need no introduction here. You are most welcome.'

'Really, my dear?' he asked, and his hand moved to the neck of his upper clothing, gripping a flap that folded back from the rest of the black garment. 'Most kind. Most kind!'

'I am Furis, and this is Odyson, the leader of our Core Scientific,' she continued.

He turned to me and offered a broad smile revealing aged teeth within his mouth. 'I am delighted to meet you, Odyson, was it?'

As we spoke, it transpired that he was a traveller. He had been captured by heralds in the lower levels of the Citadel and turned over almost immediately to the emissaries. This is where Furis had heard of the alien arrival.

The next piece of news left me more speechless than anything else today.

Furis had recognised the stranger as the Silver Soothsayer and moved him to the most secure accommodation on the planet – within the Senate Principal's quarters! With the complete cooperation of Orfak, mark you.

The silver-haired man preferred not to say how he travelled but had proposed a trade. He would help with what he called our 'predicament' in return for the Xeraphin simply letting him go once he had aided in the creation of a strategy.

'What you need,' he said, 'is a solution that both satisfies the desires of the races threatening your world and allows you to maintain your existence in a peaceful manner.'

He seemed very at home holding politicians in the palm of his hand.

'You have amassed the greatest collection of knowledge in the known universe,' he said. 'That must endure.'

We all agreed. But how?

So many options had been debated and explored by the Senate that actually we had very little that all our people could agree on. The old man had smiled at this, wily like an experienced hunter. 'Well, that makes our deliberations all the more straightforward, hmm?'

As we worked, news reached us that the Kosnak had been detected in the outer reaches of the system. They had always lagged behind the Vardon. Of course, now they were so close at hand, the news could not be contained within the corridors of power.

The general populace is now aware of just how precarious – nay, desperate – our situation is. Naturally they are scared and had started gathering at public buildings around the planet to demand answers.

I write this as night falls. I doubt I will have time later. We have been working all day and I think we have the glimmerings of a plan. The Soothsayer is indeed very wise and possessed of a fierce intellect. I hope that by tomorrow, we will be in a position to save our people.

*The Precinct of Anitroilia, Citadel Crisis Shelters*
*Borenday 2nd Belagaw*

A terrible day in our history.

Using the abilities of the best psychics the emissaries had at their disposal, we watched as the two warmongers met over our planet. Images of their ships were projected into the centre of the Senate Chamber. The Soothsayer and I watched from the gallery, unseen by the others. Orfak did not want to scare the others unduly, although I think the time had long passed for being scared.

As we probed deeper, the image changed and suddenly we were on the bridge of a Vardon ship. They were unmistakeable: pale, almost white, skin dimpled with hexagons; eyes and mouths of jarring blackness. Their heads were crowned with a sort of bone halo that ringed their scalps, joining up with the base of their necks.

At the front of their group stood their current leader, Admiral H2-L0. For the usually composed Vardon, he looked furious. Indeed, they were all staring at a screen, fists clenched, angry expressions painted on their monochrome faces. The reason for this was clear when we saw what was on that screen: the Kosnak.

In comparison to the almost clinical appearance of their mortal enemies, the Kosnak were brutish and tribal. They were much larger humanoids with an abundance of facial hair and ferocious-looking teeth bared in insult. Each one wore bulky clothing of rich, deep colours and bore a topknot on its head that denoted rank or status. I'd read a report on them several years ago, but cannot recall the details. However, it was clear that the Kosnak in the foreground – with a white topknot and matching beard – was their leader, Ur.

'We have rrright to this worrrld,' the Kosnak leader growled. 'You, go!'

'You have entered an exclusion zone,' the Vardon Admiral replied. 'We signed a treaty with the Xeraphin. This system is under our protection.'

'You have worrrds?' Ur spat. 'We have arrrms!'

The Vardon ship shook violently as it was bombarded by Kosnak weapons fire.

'Our shields can easily withstand your pathetic attack,' H2-L0 replied.

'We arrre matched,' Ur said.

'So, will you leave or must we destroy this planet to prevent you from seizing its knowledge?'

'Morrre worrrds!' The Kosnak looked as if he might almost be smiling, but he could easily have simply been baring his teeth. 'We destrrroy Xerrriphas!'

The screen went blank. There was silence both in the Senate chamber and on board the Vardon ship.

Then H2-L0 spoke. 'Start landing troops. The Kosnak will not claim the prize!'

At that point Orfak ordered the telepathic transmission cut.

'Prepare for invasion,' he ordered. 'All power to the planetary shield. We must have time!'

'Time for what?' called a Senator.

Before the words had died on his lips, the doors to the chamber flew open and dozens of heralds marched in, heavily armed.

'The Senate is dissolved,' Orfak said. His voice trembled at the enormity of his words. 'I am imposing martial law.'

At that point Furis strode into the chamber.

'General Furis will be in command of the planet's military and civil defence,' Orfak announced. General! When did the Xeraphin last have a *general*?

The Soothsayer actually placed a hand on my shoulder. 'All will be well. We must believe that.'

No matter what he said, they could not detract from the reality of the bombardments that started almost immediately. At first their impacts on the shields appeared like pretty decorations in the sky, but after many hours the Kosnak managed to break the harmonic code and the first radioactive beams penetrated through to the surface.

As night falls, we are in the crisis shelters beneath the Citadel. They have not been used for decades and are rudimentary and cold. News came in almost by the minute of more devastation and death. Already, the population has literally been decimated.

We must act before extinction becomes our destiny.

*The Precinct of Anitroilia, Academy of the Core Scientific*
*Capulenday 3rd Belagaw*

We decamped from the crisis shelter very early, under cover of darkness, and relocated to the Academy of the Core Scientific and set up our base of operations in my office.

Epeyak was duly roused from his rest period and brought before us. He looked saddened and groggy as he was introduced to the Soothsayer. Considering the silver-haired man was the first alien on Xeriphas for a dozen generations, my old friend took it very much in his stride.

Orfak put it to Epeyak that we might be able to use the technology he was developing to hide ourselves.

'All I have been working on is a way to harness our abilities,' he said.

'Let me see if I understand your research properly,' I said. 'The "focus" you have been working on combines the psychic essence of our people.'

'It does.'

'How?' asked the Soothsayer.

Epeyak explained that in essence the device was like a transformer: taking the minds of the Xeraphin and altering them, fusing them into energy that could then be directed however we saw fit. His idea was to use mental projection to show our planet laid waste; something that would fool the Vardon and the Kosnak, sending them away from us forever.

'A nice idea,' the Soothsayer said. 'But not practical.'

He pointed out that only those on the ships now in our solar system would be affected. Those using long-range scanners would see that this was a ruse and invade anyway.

'Besides,' he said, 'that won't stop the radiation bombardment.' He walked around the room with his head cocked to one side and bony finger to his lips. His pale, intense eyes seemed to burn with an intelligence that made even ours look stunted.

'This reminds me of another conflict I encountered not so long ago,' he mused. 'That was only two warring factions, mind you. But I don't see why the solution shouldn't be similar! No indeed. If a little less horse-shaped, hmm?'

He was clearly being humorous but we had not the faintest idea what he was talking about. We just inclined our heads politely.

'As we know,' I said, 'evacuation is not an option either as we will simply be pursued wherever we go.'

'So,' he said, 'tell me, ah, Epeyak, what would happen if you were to attune your device to transform not just mental energies, but the entire essence of your people?'

There was silence.

'You mean absorption?' I asked. 'The entire race?'

'Precisely, my boy!' the Soothsayer said loudly.

Epeyak confirmed this would – in theory – be possible.

'But would it be desirable?' Orfak asked. Furis nodded.

'Compared to your destruction? And the destruction of your amassed knowledge?' the Soothsayer asked angrily. 'I would say it is!'

We all exchanged glances.

'I fail to see what the benefit would be,' Furis said. 'We hide from the Vardon and the Kosnak. How do we regenerate?'

'You don't hide,' the Soothsayer said. 'You present yourself as a gift!'

*The Precinct of Anitroilia, Academy of the Core Scientific*
*Dessinday 4th Belagaw*

A week since the war reached Trallinhoe.

Heralds have been marshalling the populace to what have been dubbed 'liberator stations' across the planet. As many Xeraphin as possible are being transformed by Epeyak's technology into beings of pure energy.

Naturally, some are refusing. Some do not even bother to come to the stations. They are trapped in their outmoded beliefs or desperately hiding from the truth behind a curtain of false hope.

What we have achieved in such a short time is nothing short of astounding. It is almost impossible to believe how the Scientific Core have pulled together, using the myriad Archivists – the repository of all our accumulated knowledge – to find methods of doing what needs to be done.

The Xeraphin that have transcended their physical forms were transmitted from the liberation stations to the Citadel for storage in what Epeyak is calling his sarcophagus. No one is very keen on the term as it makes us sound like a dead race, but the Soothsayer tells us it will serve very well; the conjuror's art of misdirection, he called it.

Meanwhile General Furis has her heralds and emissaries battling the Vardon and the Kosnak on almost every front. When the planetary shield failed, she had the foresight to use smaller versions around the major conurbations, altering the frequencies so the Vardon did not break through immediately.

The Kosnak are actually helping us in all this. Unintentionally. They are hindering the Vardon in their efforts to reach us. Of course, a great many Xeraphin are being caught in their cross-fire – a microcosm for the whole situation.

The Soothsayer is saying that he has one part to play before he departs. He must wait for the last of us to join the Xeraphin gestalt in the sarcophagus. He will then tinker with the last of the defence shields so that whichever side it is can break through and believe they have won. He will then leave in whatever way he arrived, I suppose. This trap of his will be sprung and his work done. The rest will be up to us.

I am still nervous about this idea of becoming one with the whole of my species: amalgamated into one organism with one immense personality. We are all individuals who must have our privacy – partly in order to process how we deal with one another.

It is indeed fortunate that we do not rely on archaic technology like computers to store our data. Our minds are developed enough that, with the right training, we can retain vast amounts of data. The Archivists are selected at a very early age for their unique assignment. The intelligence quotient of all Xeraphin is measured and those with the highest who also possess the sort of eidetic memory necessary to the task are given special training.

This was the prize that both the Vardon and the Kosnak sought to take from us. A prize worth fighting for and over. This was the crux of the Silver Soothsayer's plan.

Instead of being a collection of individuals who might resist giving up the information they possessed, the gestalt offered a much more attractive proposition. The nucleus of the sarcophagus will present a tempting 'gift' for whichever side claims it: an immeasurable intelligence at the centre of a psychic vortex. This not only represented the most comprehensive database in the universe but also a weapon or power source equal to that of a galaxy of supernovae. It would be more than capable of destroying the other's enemy.

Orfak let this be known by contacting both fleets and speaking directly with Ur and with H2-L0. He told them that instead of letting ourselves be conquered and killed we had decided to ascend to a higher plane where their petty disputes could not touch us. He also let it be known that with our knowledge we could easily have destroyed them a thousand times over. But we were a civilised species – perhaps the most civilised in existence.

Orfak ordered that the sarcophagus be placed in the largest arena in the Citadel; the Arena of Inauguration. Around it were stockpiled all the weapons belonging to the heralds and the emissaries. Every last piece of food and drink was brought in, too, and piled high.

Even I helped. It felt good to be carrying out this last act of defiance. It was agreed that we four – myself, Epeyak, Furis and Orfak – would have one last night of physical existence before we became one in the morning.

These may be the last words I dictate. Who know what will happen when our personal archivists are consumed by the gestalt?

*Essenday 5th Belagaw*

We are one. Odyson, the leader of our Core Scientific, joined us on this morning. He stood before the sarcophagus and bathed in the agonising golden light before becoming part of the nucleus. Every atom of his existence was converted to pure energy.

Then we waited.

As we suspected it was the Vardon who entered the Arena of Inauguration. Our plan to give the impression of our total surrender appeared to work. They wandered, marvelling, among the stockpiles of weapons, the crates of food and tankers of water and other consumables. They shook their heads in disbelief and they felt melancholy at our demise.

This did not stop them from taking the nucleus back with them aboard their ship. It did not stop them from using it to send out an energy wave that turned the Kosnak vessels to dust in an instant. It did not stop them celebrating their victory. How could they know that the powerful radiation they used also permeated their own ship?

Now was our time to persuade them to surrender to us. No. Now was our time to strike.

We are one mind. We must regenerate. Take back our physical form.

*Aboard the Vardon Flagship*
*Deep Space*
*Abanday 6th Belagaw*

Those of us who regenerated today were confused by what we found. As one, we had witnessed the destruction of the Kosnak fleet. What happened after that was clouded. When I try to recall, it is as if two pieces of music are playing at the same time. I cannot concentrate on one for the notes of the other become entangled.

What we found on board were the dead bodies of the Vardon. Epeyak and his assistant, Anithon, both expressed confusion. We knew the dimpled aliens should be suffering from radioactive poisoning, but they should not have been dead.

Epeyak came up to me on the bridge of the ship, away from the earshot of the heralds that had been brought back to individual life alongside their leader, *General* Furis.

'Plasmavores,' he whispered.

I looked at him and the inference was clear. Plasmavores had been sent to kill the crew.

'But who sent them?' I asked.

Epeyak looked at me. 'You fool,' he said. 'We did!'

I was so taken aback I could not reprimand him for his insolence. But I realised at once what he meant. A fool I may, be but an idiot I am not.

As one mind we had many voices. That is why I seemed to recall multiple versions of events. They were not memories they were arguments for what we wanted to happen. Clearly the majority – the mob! – had elected to deliver vengeance on the Vardon.

I found myself collapsed in the captain's chair. Staring at the screen we had watched days before. But now it was blank. There was nothing out there. I then became aware I was being watched. I looked over at the door. Furis was standing there, regarding me with a cool gaze.

'I will need that, Odyson,' she said, moving forward. Then she smiled at my expression. 'The chair!'

I stood up. 'Of course.'

A few emissaries then trooped in and took up positions at stations that had once been manned by the Vardon crew.

'We need to escape the radiation,' Furis said, taking the captain's chair.

'Of course,' I repeated. I was suddenly very nervous in her presence. 'Where is the Senate Principal?'

She waved a hand. 'I believe he is in the kitchens. You know how fond he was of his ferment ...'

I took my leave and stole through the ship like a spy. Orfak must be made aware of this. I could not prove it, but I was convinced Furis had taken over the gestalt. I could scarcely credit it. Furis! I had trusted her. I had *liked* her. Had she engineered this whole thing? Impossible. She must have seen an opportunity and taken it. But she could not go unpunished.

I spoke with Orfak and told him of my concerns. He was deeply shocked but admitted to having the same fugue state when it came to the events of last night following the use of the sarcophagus by the Vardon.

'Epeyak brought this to your attention?' he asked.

'Yes, Senate Principal.'

'Do you think he can be trusted?'

'I believe so.'

'And no one else has this information?'

I told him I did not know. He nodded sagely and then summoned an emissary I had not met before. His name was Zarak. He was, Orfak assured me, totally loyal to the Senate and would gather similarly dependable heralds to arrest the General.

Before this could happen, however, Epeyak called an emergency meeting in one of the communal chambers aboard. As we had emerged as the architects of the Xeraphin's survival, only the four of us were in attendance. I noted Zarak on guard at the door and nodded to him as I entered. He totally ignored me. At first I felt slighted but realised he was a clandestine operative whose nature was not to show his hand.

Epeyak was standing at the centre of the room looking more sombre than I had seen him – even in the past week.

'I have analysed the radiation poisoning suffered by the crew,' he said. He bowed his head then. 'It is very powerful and has affected the regenerated Xeraphin.'

Orfak grabbed him 'Affected? You mean we've been poisoned?'

'I'm afraid so, Senate Principal.'

Orfak clenched his fists and turned away. With his back still towards us he said: 'This is your fault, Furis.'

Furis reacted as if she had been slapped. 'Mine?'

'Zarak!'

The door burst open and Zarak entered with several heralds.

'Arrest General Furis.'

'On what charge?'

'Treason!'

Zarak had already gripped the former Senator and pinned her arms behind her back.

'This is an outrage! Who was it that brought you the Silver Soothsayer? I could have used that to my advantage, but I have too high a regard for the Senate, for the rule of Xeraphin law!'

I stepped forward. 'I believe Orfak is right. The evidence is that the Plasmavores killed the crew of this ship. I believe that General Furis was behind the order.'

'You believe?' Furis shouted. 'Belief is not a body of evidence!'

'Execute her!' Orfak said.

'What?' I stepped forward. 'There has not been an execution on Xeriphas for several millennia!'

'We are not on Xeriphas,' Orfak hissed.

'I agree with Orfak,' Epeyak said. 'And anyone who doesn't is also guilty of treason.'

I looked into the eyes of Furis as she pleaded with me silently.

It was clear to me now what was happening. It *was* a coup. But not by Furis. Orfak had taken over with Epeyak's help. He controlled the Plasmavores after all. At least, that is what I thought. Until another Xeraphin stepped forward.

'I think you are all guilty of treason,' said Zarak. 'You will be taken to a cell and held there until the radiation for which you are responsible ends your lives. The Xeraphin will endure. We will return to the sarcophagus to outwait the sickness.'

Zarak! He must have seen his opportunity for power and seized it, betraying his Senate and his superiors.

Now trapped in this cell, I record these words for you, my brothers and sisters. So that when you wake, you will know that we escaped through a ruse of fiendish devising. Further, that we were trapped once more by our own stupidity and lust for power. And last that we must change if we are to ever return from the quagmire of mob rule that this gestalt has enforced upon us.

# DEFIANCE OF THE
# NEW BLOODS

This was to be his finest victory. His troops had fought
hard on the battlefields of planets and in space across five
systems to reach this point. Countless Sontaran warriors had
died, but each one had done so in the certain knowledge that his
death was glorious because it would not be in vain.

The Sontarans hated one race above all others. They especially hated them for their cowardice in battle. There was no
honour in taking on the appearance of others. That was what
the Rutans did. Amorphous and green in their natural state,
Rutans adopted the form and technology of any race or species
that would serve its battle against the Sontarans.

Due to their amoeba-like physiology, they preferred dank,
watery worlds on which to breed. While many planets had been
adopted as Rutan breeding grounds, the Sontarans had identified them and wiped them out, one by one.

They called Group Marshal Sten the 'Breed Slayer'. For under his command the 12th Sontaran Battle Group had succeeded where so many had failed. He was on the verge of winning the war that had been raging so long, they had forgotten when it started.

The main screen on the bridge of his Mothership showed a yellow-green sphere. Mekonne was its interstellar designation, but Sten preferred to think of it as the last outpost. There was no Rutan fleet left to defend the planet. The Battle Group had seen to that – at great cost: two War-Wheels and 117 capsules.

However, all they needed to do now was penetrate the planetary defences – laser cannon and missile batteries on the surface – and the last Rutan breeding world would be theirs for the taking.

'Reduce velocity,' Sten ordered. 'Estimate range of enemy weapons fire.'

'400 kilometres,' came the reply.

'Hold at 420 kilometres,' he said. 'Prepare capsules for launch.'

All around the equator of the Mothership's central core, klaxons sounded. Sontaran troopers and Commanders ran to their stations, clambering through the ports that led to their single-occupancy capsules.

'All capsules are combat ready,' a junior officer reported.

'Very good, Field Major!' Sten was enjoying this. He licked his grey lips, watching the orbital distance indicator slowly counting down to '420'.

The moment it reached that number, Group Marshal Sten issued the order to launch. He did not need a junior officer to tell him the information he could see with his own eyes.

Within minutes, the capsules had identified all planetary defences and the Mothership had destroyed them from orbit.

'Deploy transmat units and start landing!' Sten roared. He made for the door, eager to be one of the first to make planetfall. 'Field Major, you have the bridge!'

'Group Marshal!' The junior officer's voice seemed to rise in pitch, clearly nervous for some reason.

Sten turned back. 'Well?'

'Bio-scans, sir. Our instruments are not picking up any Rutan life signs.'

Sten managed a brief laugh. 'They are shielded! Re-scan. Full spectrum.'

The luckless Field Major turned to face his superior officer. 'I have, Group Marshal. Still negative. There aren't any Rutans here!'

Sten was across the bridge in seconds and struck the other Sontaran where he stood. This was a serious affront, and the Field Major would probably be assigned to the medical division as punishment. He crept away into the shadows.

'Would any *competent* officer like to replace the Field Major and take the readings again?'

A commander stepped forward. He saluted and took the station, his six fingers flowing across the controls.

'You're right, sir,' the Commander said.

'Ha! I knew it!' Sten nodded.

'The Rutan scum are blocking our scans. They have a dampening field. We are not close enough to the planet surface.'

Bring us in, then! Pilots, set optimum orbit at 100 kilometres.'

The Mothership moved forward smoothly, closing the distance to Mekonne in a less than a minute. It now loomed large on the main monitor.

'Scan again!'

An uncomfortable silence fell.

'*Well?*'

'Group Marshal, we have a larger problem,' the Commander said. He flicked a few buttons and a three-dimensional schematic of the planet appeared, showing the molten core and flow of magma beneath the surface in a volcanic network.

'What's this?' Sten demanded.

'We are picking up unnaturally high tectonic activity right across Mekonne,' the Commander reported.

'Unnatural?' Sten was frowning, his brows even more knotted than usual. 'As in artificial?'

'Yes, Group Marshal.'

Almost immediately, reports started coming in from Sontaran units already on the surface. Earthquakes were taking place – serious ones – and volcanic eruptions had been reported around the planet.

'It's a trap,' breathed the Group Marshal. 'Withdraw. There are no Rutans!'

'Full reverse,' squeaked a Sontaran pilot as the Mothership reversed its thrusters.

'Auxiliary power!' shouted Sten. 'We've been ensnared in the planet's gravitational pull.' He turned to another officer. 'Recall the capsules. Secure the War-Wheels!'

The Mothership strained to escape the planet below but managed to pull away. The War-Wheels were not so powerful and were taking longer to achieve escape velocity.

'Subterranean detonations detected,' the Commander said, his voice belying the calmness of his demeanour.

'Signal the fleet,' Sten said quietly. 'Assembly point Epsilon. Prepare for light speed.'

On the screen, one of the War-Wheels was almost away from the planet when a huge plume of lava erupted from the surface. It caught the ship on its port battle-pivot and sent the vessel into a downward spiral. The burning part of the War-Wheel detonated before it hit the ground, catching several dozen capsules as they attempted to flee. Then the War-Wheel collided with the liquid surface with a huge explosion.

The shockwave hit even them at such high altitude that the Commander had to yell over the noise to make himself heard. 'Coordinates locked!'

'Make the jump! Make it!' Sten screamed.

It was not just the 12th Sontaran Battle Group that was in shreds; the Group Marshal's reputation, his command and military standing – everything he had literally fought so hard to achieve was now burning along with his fleet.

There are many things a Sontaran mind does not like to contemplate. Chief among these is the concept of defeat. Sontarans are bred not only for war, but for winning. They are the finest soldiers in the galaxy and while they are willing – keen, even – for death in battle, it is only really what they would think of as glorious if that death ultimately results in a victory for their race.

This was the polar opposite of that and Sten had no idea at that moment how he was going to come back from it.

* * * * * * *

The hand that rose from the vat of green liquid was three-fingered. A powerful arm followed and a domed head of smooth, brown skin. Sontaran Science Squadron Leader Yarl watched as his new creation stood and looked at him.

'You are designated Commander Myre,' he said, a slight rasp to his voice.

The newly hatched clone nodded.

'How do you ... feel?' Yarl asked. He waved a white-gloved hand at his assistant, Science Squadron Officer Klym, who duly started taking notes on his datapad.

'I am ... strong. I am ... *Sontaran*!' barked the new-born.

'Very good,' Yarl said. 'You will find your armour there.' He pointed to a bench on which sat the black and silver suit of a Sontaran warrior, its heavy boots and dark helmet.

Myre stepped from the tank and moved slowly across the laboratory.

'Note his gait,' Yarl whispered to Klym. 'It is far more attuned for long-distance marches, endurance and combat.'

'Yes, Squadron Leader,' Klym replied. He, too, was wearing the white bodysuit of a Science Squadron officer.

'It is well known that science is not the most glorious of placements,' Yarl said, watching his new creation dress. 'But the weapons we in the Squadron create are crucial to victories of our military counterparts. Indeed, it could be said that we are responsible for far more deaths than any field trooper.'

'Yes, Squadron Leader.'

To the back of the laboratory a bulbous station housing a simple screen buzzed and a face identical to both Yarl's and Klym's appeared. It was Sten. Despite the orders from Sontaran High Command, his neck armour still bore the two pointed discs of a Group Marshal.

'Report!' he barked. 'Yarl! How did the experiment go?'

The Sontaran science officer moved across the brightly lit lab to the screen. He pressed a button to transmit his image back to his commanding officer.

'Group Marshal Sten,' Yarl purred, throwing an immaculate salute. 'I was about to contact you myself. The experiment is a success. Here, see for yourself!'

Yarl beckoned over Commander Myre who came to stand beside him. He threw his arm across his chest in salute but Sten pulled back from the screen.

'What is *that*?' he asked. 'The skin colour is markedly different! The facial structure changed. Is it ... *shorter*?'

Myre's light brown, smooth, shiny skin was very different to the other Sontarans. They all had greyish flesh tones and an almost matte finish to their skin.

'Improvements, Group Marshal,' Yarl said.

'Improvements for which I do not recall issuing the command,' Sten growled. 'You overstep your orders, Squadron Leader!'

'No, sir,' Yarl remained calm. In former days he might not have been so bold. 'They are side effects of the distinctive gene splicing we had to employ to bring about success in the experiment.'

Group Marshal Sten leaned forward, his face filling the screen; his voice even and hard. 'I want a full report from you *in person* in one hour. Bring the ... nonconformities with you!'

The viewer snapped off.

Yarl turned back to Klym. 'You heard him. Nonconformities. Plural. Proceed with the experiment!'

At the Sontaran Military Academy on the home world, the clone race had hatchings of a million cadets at each muster parade. To Yarl, that was nothing more than simple mass-production. What he was engaged in, much like the designers of the War-Wheel, could almost be considered *art*. The word felt alien and uncomfortable in his thoughts.

However, the analogy was a good one. The improvements he was trying to make to the Sontaran pattern were intricate and difficult. He was sure that in the sterile corridors of the Military Academy they would be considered heresy.

Klym was now bringing the second new Sontaran out from the cloning vat. This one looked slightly different to the first one. Klym voiced his concern that there had been an error in the process.

'Not at all, Klym,' Yarl said. 'Each one will be ... individual. That is the purpose of our mission. Individual thought, individual personalities, individual actions.'

Less than an hour later, all four of the new Sontarans lined up before Group Marshal Stem. They were standing in his personal quarters: a spartan room containing a simple, white chair; a single station of computer banks with a screen and behind the chair the diode bypass transformer used for feeding energy directly into his body via the probic vent at the base of his neck.

Stem moved down the rank of new recruits, inspecting them. Yarl introduced each of them to their new commanding officer.

'Commanders Myre and Promynx; Field Majors Atas and Epax.'

Stem sneered at them. 'They look like aliens dressed in our uniforms,' he said. 'Impostors!'

'With your permission, Group Marshal?' Myre spoke up. Stem eyed him suspiciously but gave a curt nod. 'I was going to ask for your consent to alter our uniforms, upgrade them.'

'Upgrade?' The Group Marshal smiled. 'You think you can improve the work of our scientists on the home world?'

Another of them answered. 'We do, sir.' It was Promynx. He seemed to have a gap in his teeth.

'Yarl, have you briefed them on the Mekonne campaign?'

'Yes, Group Marshal. They understand.'

Stem returned to his chair. 'You four have been bred for one reason: to think the thoughts normal Sontarans cannot or dare not,' he said. His voice sounded tired. 'Because of our code, we would never have thought of a cowardly attack like the one the Rutans carried out on Mekonne. And yet it would appear a valid military stratagem. So, you may do whatever is necessary to plot the downfall of the enemy. If you wish to alter your uniforms, do so. You will report directly to me. Is that understood?'

'Yes, Group Marshal,' the four new breeds all chorused.

Stem was above all a soldier and, while he liked nothing better than a frontal assault, he also knew the benefits of having
sound military intelligence gathered from reliable sources. So
he also saw each of the new Sontarans on their own at random
intervals following their initial meeting.

He sounded them out about how they felt towards the Empire
and the home world, towards the Rutan Host, towards their fellow Sontarans and – of course – towards him personally. Being
the individuals they had been gene-spliced to be, each gave
slightly different answers.

In the end, he selected the one he thought would see things
his way. He wanted the one who would be easily turned, who
would understand that the four of them could not have a completely free rein. Naturally, he told the target, you can discuss
anything within your unit, but he did not want just the edited
highlights when it came to their reports. He wanted – needed
– to know all that was going on. As an additional layer of security. His agent had agreed readily. After all, anything else would
have been mutiny.

So, while the Mothership limped around the far-flung
systems of the Empire, the group of four unique Sontarans
worked hard. They personalised their equipment, each building singular body armour in a slightly different colour. Myre
sprayed his a dark, blood green while Promynx favoured blue.
Atas adopted a sandy brown colour – almost the same tone
as his skin – and Epax went with a matte black. Even Myre
thought this made him look too much like a Judoon, but he
let it pass.

They did not move about the ship much because they drew
the bigoted stares of their fellow soldiers. Instead, they remained
in their quarters and let the world come to them. They went
through every Sontaran battle in the Mothership's database,

analysing what went right and how failures could have been avoided. Then they moved on to Rutan strategies. Epax seemed to have the best grasp of the enemy mind; he could see patterns in their movements the others could not.

After weeks of poring over all the data they could muster, the group of four – now assigned the designation G4 – believed that they had identified a pattern to the Rutan Host's movement around the galaxy. Even Mekonne had fitted in with this pattern, which was why it seemed plausible as a breeding planet.

Finally, they had something to report to the Group Marshal; something he would be very happy about. Myre, as their senior officer, made the report but they were all present.

'So my assault on the planet is vindicated,' Sten said. 'My actions were not rash and counter to Sontaran stratagem!' He now paced the floor of his personal quarters, becoming more confident with every footfall. It was as if the G4 had reinvigorated the Group Marshal.

'There is more, sir,' Myre said.

'We have identified a list of planets on which the Rutan Host might have settled instead of Mekonne,' Promynx added.

Sten stopped pacing and regarded the Commander with sparkling eyes. 'Vengeance?' he asked.

Epax confirmed this to be the case. 'Given time, I am confident we can narrow that list to a handful or even one specific target,' the Field Major said.

'And a chance to redeem myself to Sontaran High Command,' breathed Sten. 'No, more than that! A chance to join their ranks! Imagine being able to say that you were the Sontaran that finally wiped the Rutan scourge from the cosmos!'

Myre managed a thin smile. 'I believe that imagining was our purpose, Group Marshal. And we appreciate the glory such an outcome will give us.'

The hint of a frown flashed across Sten's burly features. 'Us?' he asked quietly. Then he smiled. 'Yes, of course. We shall all be heroes by Sontar! Ha!'

\*

The four Sontarans were examining the list they had come up with of possible Rutan Host breeding worlds. They worked in silence for a while, all making notes on datapads, cross-checking references, planetary conditions, distance from the ever-shifting battlefront.

Epax reached his conclusion fractionally before the others. He put down the datapad he was working on and announced the name of the planetary system. There had been one very good decoy, he said, but there was only one place the breeding planet could be. A minute later, Commander Myre concurred with his findings, followed by Atas and Promynx.

'I will double-check our findings,' Epax said and plucked the computer tablet from the surface once more.

As he worked the other Sontarans all regarded one another. There was a frisson of tension between them. Then Myre spoke. 'I will say what we are all feeling,' he said. 'The Group Marshal means to take the glory for himself. He is blinded by the need to rebuild his stature within the Sontaran High Command.'

Epax looked up from his calculations. 'He is ambitious. It is a Sontaran characteristic.'

'The Sontaran characteristic is for ambition in warfare,' Atas said. 'Not personal aggrandisement.'

'He is driven by a desire to correct a military miscalculation,' Promynx said. 'Who here would not want to do the same?'

The G4 considered this for a while before Myre spoke again. 'No matter what his ambition or what his actions will be in any post-battle situation, one thing is clear: he does not want us to be recognised for our part in the victory.'

Epax nodded and looked round the group. 'I agree. It seems obvious he would seek the plaudits solely for himself.'

'As is befitting a Group Marshal,' Promynx said, his brow deeply furrowed. He was clearly uncomfortable with the direction the conversation was following. 'Any senior officer will be credited with the actions of his men in a combat situation – especially a victory. I am sure we will be rewarded – promoted.'

'You are naive,' Atas said. 'You see how the others of our race look at us when we venture out of these quarters. The fear of the unlike is written in the faces as clearly as the information on these datapads!' He slammed his down on the table. 'I believe he knows that the High Command would see any victory achieved against the hated Rutan tainted by our very existence.'

Epax nodded again. 'Despite that victory coming due to our unique perspective.'

Promynx stared at the other three. 'What are you saying?'

'The Group Marshal will have us destroyed once the victory is achieved,' Myre said, standing up. 'It is ... a sound strategy.'

Atas and Epax made noises of agreement.

Promynx began to nod, too. 'What is *our* course of action, then?'

'The victory is ours by right,' Myre said as he walked around the table. 'We know that Sten made an error taking the fleet so close to the planet. Any one of us could have seen that the dampening field was a ruse.'

Myre came to a halt behind Promynx's chair.

'You believe him unfit for command?' Promynx asked, straining to look round at his commander.

'I do,' declared Myre.

'You should replace him, Commander Myre,' Atas said quietly.

'I agree,' Epax said. He tuned to Promynx. 'We must be unanimous.'

'It is clear you have been thinking about this in some depth,' the lower-ranking commander said. 'I have not. I would request a period of reflection to consider my response. Mutiny is not to be entered into lightly.'

'Very well,' Myre said. 'Reflect. But we need to act quickly. Sten will know we have identified the Rutan Host breeding world soon. He may have made mistakes but he is not stupid.'

※

'Commander Myre said all that, did he?'

Promynx was standing rigidly to attention in the Group Marshal's personal quarters. Sten felt the junior officer must feel he was both betrayer and devotee in equal measure – unfaithful to his own unit but loyal to the Sontaran military in its widest context.

'Yes, Group Marshal.'

Sten shook his head and made a clicking sound with his tongue. 'Mutiny,' he spat. 'Do you know the last time there was a Sontaran mutiny?'

Promynx quickly scanned his memory for all the data that he had assimilated in the past months. He could not cite one example. 'No, sir.'

'No. And I will tell you why not. Because there has never been a mutiny in the Sontaran ranks! Ever!'

He erupted from his chair and slammed his fist on the control panel in front of his viewscreen. Immediately a junior officer appeared, his tongue slightly protruding from his frog-like mouth. When he saw the Group Marshal he gave a salute and asked how he could serve.

'Commander Krent!' bellowed Sten. 'Take a detachment of your best troopers. Arrest the members of the G4 in their quarters. Escort them to the brig. Do it quietly. If they give you any cause, kill them.'

Promynx opened his mouth to protest, but then thought better of it.

'Also, please instigate my earlier order.' Sten stared at Krent until his eyes signified he recalled what the Group Marshal was talking about.

'At once,' Krent said and ended the communication.

Sten turned back to Promynx. 'You have done well, Commander,' he said. 'I knew, when I selected you for this mission, I could rely on your loyalty and devotion to duty.'

Before Promynx could reply the door opened and a squad of troopers entered, battle helmets on, their tubular rheon carbine weapons pointed at the blue-clad Sontaran.

'You understand, I hope, Commander. I cannot allow any of the G4 to remain uncontained while I carry out the last move in my plan.' He came right up to the different Sontaran and smiled. 'I just need one thing from you: the location of the Rutan Host breeding world.'

Promynx gave a curt nod. 'I understand, Group Marshal,' he said. 'The planet you need is in the Oceanid system.'

'Very good,' Sten said. 'Take him away!'

As the squad took Promynx to the cells, the Group Marshal gave orders for the fleet to get under way. They had a new destination now and a new mission.

❊

Promynx sat in the brig and waited. He had no idea what Sten planned to do with him and his fellow G4 members. But that was unimportant. What was crucial was that the squad sent to arrest the other three had not found the weapons concealed in the modified body armour of the new Sontarans. The one that arrived in the Group Marshal's quarters so abruptly had certainly not thought to search him.

As the ship passed from day watch to night watch status, Promynx watched as the locking mechanism on his cell door began to glow: dark orange at first, then light yellow, before becoming incandescent white and melting away to nothing. Powerful hands gripped the hole and wrenched the door open.

Atas stood there. He saluted Promynx and they moved together to the next cell. When all had been freed, they moved onto the detachment of Sontarans on brig guard duty, pummelling all five of the squad on their probic vents, thus rendering them unconscious.

'I assume the plan worked well,' Myre said.

'He believed I was loyal to the last – even as he was having me arrested!'

The Sontarans laughed quietly.

'Now, we must reach a capsule hangar before they find the brig breached,' Promynx reminded them.

They waited a few minutes for the changeover of shift to take full effect. Squads would routinely patrol their designated routes the moment they came on duty and then take up standard guard positions at intersections and outside doors. The G4 would encounter least resistance if they moved after the patrol passed their position, trailing them until they reached the closest companionway to a hangar bay.

Being stealthier and more alert, the new Sontarans managed to stay out of sight until they reached the hangar. By now, the first night-watch patrols had been completed and Sontaran troopers had taken up their positions around the ship.

Across from their hiding place behind some missile loaders, the G4 could see the perfect escape vessel: a four-seat assault shuttle capable of hyper-light travel. Now they just needed to wait for the trap to be sprung, for maximum chaos and the perfect diversion that would facilitate their escape.

Several decks above them, the Group Marshal was on the bridge in full battle armour, his crested helmet under his arm and a long energy-tipped baton in his right hand. On the screens before him, Sten could see the Mothership, one War-Wheel and several assault spheres – the remnants of the 12th Sontaran Battle Group – each craft hidden by an asteroid or dust cloud. Seven million miles ahead of them were the three planets of the Oceanid system.

He sneered at the image of the three worlds on the main screen. They were watery, lush environments and hundreds of parsecs away from the front line. Each one was ideal for the Rutan Host's need for binary fission, but together they represented a tantalising gift to the shape-shifting species.

It was typical of the Rutan to flee the battle; here the hated green race were cowering where they thought no one would find them. However, Group Marshal Sten had outwitted them. He was responsible for the creation of the G4 unit and therefore he had ultimately devised this perfect stratagem; the Rutans would never have guessed at its ingenuity, for not even the Sontaran High Command could have formulated such a plan.

With distinctive rings at an oblique angle, the three planets looked like some mischievous god had tilted them away from the norm, each one making the other seem more acute.

There seemed to be no Rutan shipping for light years around, but Sten had wanted to make sure. That was why the fleet had gone into stealth mode, masked by naturally occurring phenomena. The bridge crew had been monitoring the plants now for two watches and a third had just begun. Sten was convinced that if they were going to see any movement – any clue of a Rutan presence – they would have seen it by now.

'Alert the fleet,' Sten barked. 'Close on targets at full speed and hold arrow formation at 600 kilometres.' His orders were relayed and the Mothership led the charge, accelerating to full sub-light speed and firing retro-thrusters to bring it into perfect orbit around the largest of the three planets.

Almost immediately the Mothership was rocked by the first impact.

'Report!' Sten growled. 'Nothing can prevent our victory!'

A second shockwave hit, causing the floor to vibrate slightly.

Commander Krent turned from his screen. 'Sensors indicate a meteorite strike.'

'An asteroid shower that can penetrate Sontaran shielding?' Sten was livid. 'Check your report, Commander! You'll find it must be false.'

'Other ships are reporting meteor collision.'

'The readings check out, Group Marshal,' Krent said nervously. 'The impacts are natural in form. No energy weapons, no missiles.'

A third, more powerful collision made some of the Sontarans stumble across the bridge, grabbing at their colleagues or protruding sections of bulkhead to steady themselves.

'Analysis indicates some form of rock projectiles camouflaged by the planets' rings, Group Marshal,' reported a trooper at weapons control.

'What about life forms?' Sten shouted over the din. 'How many Rutan do we have?'

A double impact shook the Mothership and even Sten himself went sprawling now.

'None!' Krent sounded desperate now.

Sten propelled himself over the junior officer's command station and shoved the Sontaran out of his way.

'Again?' Sten shrieked, quickly checking to see if there was a Rutan dampening field blocking their scans. His check came back negative.

'How? How can this be?' he asked, staring blindly around the bridge as it shook repeatedly from the damaging impacts. His eyes lit on the internal communication system and he stumbled over and tried to raise the brig. But he knew, even before his call went unanswered, who had betrayed him.

＊

As the Mothership began to break up under the increasing number of anti-grav-propelled rock projectiles, Promynx led the G4 Sontarans across the hangar bay and into the assault shuttle. Not one of the pilots or troopers in the bay had stopped them. They had been too busy attempting to secure the ship and ask for orders.

The Assault Shuttle burst from its housing and launched out into space. This happened moments before the last remaining War-Wheel two hundred kilometres above them exploded as a meteor almost the same size hit it dead centre.

Myre was in the command seat; Epax was at the communications array. Promynx already had the ship's meson cannon firing on the projectiles homing on the Assault Shuttle, and Atas was monitoring the shields, drawing power from the diode bypass transformer to enhance their performance.

'Ready for light speed,' Myre said as he readied the warp drive.

'Listen!' Epax fed the message he was receiving through the ship's speaker system.

*This is Group Marshal Sten of the 12th Sontaran Battle Group. This is an Empire-wide warning. Four rogue Sontarans have stolen an assault shuttle and are now at large. They have caused the death of many of their fellow troops and the destruction of this entire fleet. They must be apprehended as they pose a vile and very real threat to the Sontaran Empire. I repeat: this is Group Marshal Sten...*

All four of the new Sontarans had to shield their eyes as the blast from the destruction of the Mothership blinded them.

'We must proceed with the mission with all haste now,' Myre said. 'Light speed. Now!'

He operated the controls and the Assault Shuttle vanished from the debris field that had once been a Sontaran fleet.

❋

On the Sontaran home world, the message from Group Marshal Sten had been received and processed before being relayed as an emergency alert bulletin to all fleets and outposts. Every ship, every last trooper would know to be on the lookout for a four-seat assault shuttle.

So that was why the G4 had identified a small repair shop and supply dump on a large asteroid that had been deserted in haste as the battlefront in the war with the Rutans had shifted. The war had moved far away, and the outpost had been forgotten.

The benefit of having every report the Empire had issued in recent times was that, if you were clever enough, you could see tiny tactical errors; breaches that could be leveraged to full advantage.

As per the last manifest schedule transmitted back to the home world, the auxiliary logistics station on asteroid H34

TH3r housed six Sontaran one-seat capsules – the backbone of the Empire. It also had a small amount of fuel, a small stockpile of weapons and a transformer the G4 could all feed on to sustain them for the next stage of their mission.

They each took a capsule and programmed the remaining pair as slaves to Myre's ship. In this way they travelled from system to system in formation, dropping out of light speed in a secluded area to check the military situation before moving on again. Each jump they made took them closer to the home world.

As the Sontaran security systems had been programmed to be on the very highest alert for a four-seat shuttle or – as a rational tactical precaution – four one-man ships, six capsules did not fall within the list of shipping that needed extra checks when they passed through the system cordons that surrounded Sontar.

The G4 were able to pass through these cordons by using security codes from Sontaran Special Space Service missions logged in the database. Their capsules were not boarded once, and indeed they were given special military honours on three occasions.

Security on the home world itself would be much tighter. The group knew this and planned accordingly.

As they neared the planet, several fleets were in position, defending the home world from any attacker. But as Sten had said himself, no Sontaran had ever mutinied. So they did not expect a threat to come from Sontaran ships, piloted by individuals with identifiable Sontaran DNA.

To ensure their approach was not detected too early, the capsules split up into two groups of three, intermingling with the capsules from the protective fleets. When they were close enough to the other capsules, the G4 cloned the ident-tags of the legitimate ships and then rotated them, using five or six to throw any combat computer off the scent. All this had been planned and agreed in advance so they could maintain communications blackout at all times during the operation.

The final phase came as they had to penetrate the atmosphere of Sontar itself. This was difficult as almost no ships ever returned to the home world. Although a million embryos were hatched every four minutes, growing to adulthood in ten more, they were all flown off-world as soon as each warrior had been assigned his rank and posting. Only the highest-ranking of the Sontaran Military High Command ever left the planet and returned. And they tended not to fly in small capsules.

So the G4's arrival on the home world had to appear like an accident.

As they skimmed the atmosphere, Commander Myre caused his two drone ships to collide with each other in close enough proximity to the other four that it might look like an impact wave had knocked out their main thrust engines temporarily, putting them in a 'sphere spin' in which the capsule was totally out of control.

So the planetary protection batteries on the surface and the satellite defence platform in orbit did not open fire. The four Sontarans simulated perfect re-ignition sequences and pulled their ships out of the seemingly fatal dive.

Myre immediately broke silence. 'Sontar Prime Control! We need emergency landing coordinates. Please advise!'

The four pilots were duly assigned to a hangar more used to departures than arrivals. A team were on standby when they landed, a green flash on their sleeves marking them as the lowliest of ranks: Sontaran nurses.

Myre and the others kept their helmets on as they stepped from their capsules. While different uniform might be excused, a different face would certainly raise the alarm. All around them, huge troop carriers were being loaded with the hundreds of thousands of fresh recruits off to fight the Rutan Host. The hangar most closely resembled an insect nest – activity everywhere and countless bodies moving in a well-orchestrated ritual.

Rank upon rank of troopers in their black padded jumpsuits awaited embarkation while technicians saw to the ships themselves, their cargo and payload. Officers shouted instructions, and the speaker system overhead gave a constant commentary on which units should board what craft.

Promynx quickly dismissed the medics and turned his attention to the security in the situation. Members of the Home World Guard stood at every entrance. They were dressed almost identically to their fellow troopers, save for the gold stripe around their neck armour and a matching one on their helmets. They were armed with the standard rheon carbine weapons, held pointing down in their right hands.

Fortunately, the G4 were armed with much more advanced weaponry: blaster rifles that could target and kill multiple hostiles with one pull of the trigger. The four retrieved these much bulkier, longer weapons from their capsules. They then turned and marched to the exit that was farthest from any other so that reaction to their presence would take longer. As they neared the Home World Guards, Myre brought the blaster to his shoulder and opened fire, dropping them where they stood. With the thousands of troops standing between them and the other Guards, there was no line of sight, so no other Sontarans noticed for a few moments. This was enough time for the G4 to slip through the huge hangar door and out into the main cloning complex.

The Complex itself was the size of a huge city. The cloning vats themselves took up several square miles, producing the vast number of Sontarans necessary to sustain the burgeoning Empire. Clones grew in a matter of hours, already clothed in a simple one-piece suit and white collar that marked them as new-borns.

When they were mature, they were extracted from the tanks and taken to the Quartermasters. Here they were given the black padded jumpsuit, boots, belt and helmet. They then passed to the Armoury, where each was issued with his personal carbine, communicator and the silver utility device that hung from every trooper's belt. Finally, they were processed by Logistics and assigned a unit, fleet or group before being despatched to the hangars.

The High Command was housed in a separate complex, but they were not the G4's target. At the centre of the Cloning Complex stood the Core Clone Tank of Sontar. These contained the pure building blocks of every Sontaran. Thick pipes led from the large pool and snaked through the complex, feeding each and every individual clone vat – ensuring the purity of the race. The closer to the core a Sontaran hatchling was, the more senior his rank as he was assigned more intelligence or strength.

It was this purity that Science Squadron Leader Yarl had dared to tamper with to create the four individual Sontarans. It was the opinion of these new Sontarans that this purity was the cause of all Sontaran defeats: the entire race had become sterile, unchanging and too rigid to adapt to the more complex military situations they found themselves facing. Change was what was needed, and the G4 intended to deliver that on a species-wide scale.

The G4 made their way successfully back down the process, bypassing the Armoury and the Quartermaster and arriving at the entrance to the cloning vats. The main doors were lightly guarded because the constant stream of freshly hatched

Sontarans never caused any trouble. But this made them a difficult method of entry. Instead, they followed a white-clad scientist and his group as they made their way along a high walkway
to an access door.

Here there was even less resistance, but each member of
the G4 knew that this area was carefully monitored. Even the
High Command recognised that in actuality it was here that the
most precious military asset lay – not in the War Councils and
Emperor's chambers.

They paused outside the small door and Atas produced a
scientific device he had taken from Yarl's laboratory. It was a
gene-material sampler. It looked not unlike the rheon carbines
but was smaller and fatter, with a squat hypodermic nozzle at
the top. Atas jabbed the device into his neck and extracted a
copy of his DNA. He then did the same to Myre, Promynx and
Epax.

'This will change the Sontaran race for ever,' he breathed.

'This will *improve* the Sontaran race for ever,' Promynx said.

The others smiled. 'For Sontar and the good of the Empire!'
Myre said and they all lifted their fists into the air, hitting the
others' hands with their own. Then Myre punched the door
control and it opened to reveal row upon row of clone vats.

The moment they stepped through an alarm sounded.
'Intruders in Clone Vats Section F1n. Home World Security to
all Clone Vats.'

Almost immediately, they could hear the sound of pound-
ing, booted feet coming in their direction along the walkway.
Promynx took point, climbing down a ladder to ground level
and moving forward at speed, scanning every nook and doorway with his weapon as he went. The others followed, making
up a diamond formation with Epax in the rear.

'Halt!' The cry came from behind them.

Without stopping, they looked back to see a squad of gold-ringed troopers bearing down on them. They were slower than the new Sontarans and more lumbering, but they were still good shots, and their weapons fire only missed them because of the zigzag pattern in which the G4 were now running.

But then the impossible happened. Epax was hit. He went down, and this time the group did stop. Promynx bent down and took the gene-material sampler from the matte-black-armoured hand of his dead comrade. Then he stood, roared in anger and removed his helmet.

'I will fight open-skinned,' he bellowed. 'To honour my fallen brother!'

He brought the blaster to his shoulder and fired at the approaching squad, cutting them down in seconds. He gave a satisfied grunt and turned to Myre. 'We cannot let anything stop us,' he said.

Myre removed his helmet and lofted his gun. 'Sontar-ha!' he shouted and the others took up the chant as they ran. Ahead a trooper and a Field Major stood, also without their helmets.

'You are the renegades!' the Field Major said in a low voice. He had the vestiges of some hair on his chin – a throwback to the earliest Sontarans. Promynx found this distasteful and shouted a Sontaran curse at him. The two raised their tubular side arms, but Promynx was quicker, and each one received his gift of deadly red laser fire before they could even aim.

Now the alarms were constant and overlapping across different districts as if the whole planet was crying out. Myre and Promynx and Atas fought on past the Home World Guard, who were ill equipped to deal with the new elite that they faced. The closer they came to the Core Clone Tank, the more troops they had to fight. Now even the new-borns were being thrown into the fray and, although they lacked finesse, their numbers were such that they would soon overwhelm the G4.

Atas suggested a plan. It amounted to a suicide mission, but it would save the other two and allow them to reach their objective. The three of them agreed and he departed, snatching up some gas grenades from the fallen troopers that lay scattered around them. Then he was gone.

Promynx and Myre moved to a service hatch in an alcove of section A1a of the Vat Tanks – the closest to the Core. They worked quickly, removing the panel and making the necessary adjustments. They could hear the approach of hundreds of Sontarans – all newly forged and freshly equipped.

'I hope Atas completes his mission before they find us,' Promynx said.

'Atas is one of us,' Myre replied. 'He will carry out the operation. Have no fear.'

As he spoke, the sounds of the Vat Tanks – the constant bubbling and gurgling – ceased. Even with the approach of so many Sontaran soldiers, it became eerily quiet. Never since the Clone Vats had first been switched on had the process been halted on a system-wide scale. But now no new Sontarans were being born.

Suddenly, a thin yellow gas began to issue from the ventilation ducts at the base of the corridor walls.

'Gas!' said Myre and they quickly donned their helmets once more. While other, older Sontarans were equipped with helmets that did little more than protect them from blunt instruments, the G4 had augmented theirs with a lot of useful equipment, including a respirator.

They stepped from the alcove to find the space between the rows of vats crowded with warriors, all stumbling forward, choking on the gas Atas had released. One managed to raise his weapon, but could not loose a shot, so weak had he become. He collapsed to the floor with the others.

Promynx glanced at Myre, and together they turned and made their way through a quarantine air-lock into the Core Clone Tank of Sontar. A dozen scientists were rushing around the control panels, trying to work out what had happened to their well-oiled cloning process. They didn't notice the two new arrivals at first, but when they did they proved that they were still Sontarans by rushing forward to engage the interlopers in hand-to-hand combat.

Myre was stronger than Promynx but both were better fighters than the scientific corps. In moments, the floor was strewn with unconscious or wounded Sontarans in white suits. As the final remaining members of the G4 moved to execute the last part of their plan, wall panels below them exploded and several squads of elite Sontaran Special Space Service burst through, weapons blazing.

Myre was caught by one shot to his shoulder and went spinning back against a control panel.

'Go!' he hissed. 'Do it!'

Promynx, produced the extractor from his armour and gripped it in his hand. There would be no time to take it down to the vats. That was the plan, to insert their DNA into the Core Clone Tank and irreversibly alter the Sontaran race forever. But that called for the introduction of the DNA to the tank via injection to the nutrient feed. Instead, Promynx would have to take more direct action.

He stepped up to the edge of the platform. Twenty levels down was the tank, a light mesh covering its surface, ensuring no dust or contaminants got in, but allowing the soup of deoxyribonucleic acid to breathe. Promynx allowed himself to fall, head first, executing a perfect swan dive.

Laser fire zipped past him as the Special Space Service troops opened fire at the moving target. The three seconds it took Promynx to fall seemed to stretch away into minutes. He saw the Sontarans shooting at him from ground level. He saw the mesh racing up to meet him, and he saw the DNA extractor in his hand. A shot from a carbine took him in the stomach, and he felt his life ebbing away. He exerted more pressure on the device as he closed on the tank. Then, with his last iota of strength, he gave it one final, powerful squeeze as he hit the surface, shattering the phial of genetic material and sending it dissipating into the rest of the liquid.

The Sontaran troops bounded up the stairways to the top of the vat but there was no need for haste. Promynx was dead. Above them, though, Myre still lived. Now Promynx had delivered their genetic material direct to the tank, he had to restart the cloning process.

Other troopers were already scaling the ladders to the control level and reached it as Myre rebooted the system. Weapons fire hit the control panel and it exploded in Myre's face but he died with the sound of the bubbling, gurgling Clone Vats in his ears. This sound ushered in a new era; a new race that would bear the likeness and heritage of four individualistic Sontarans.

# THE KINGDOM OF
# THE BLIND

The raiding party came in the dead of night. The refugee camp was small, and there was no defence against the soldiers. Almost eighty Dahensa had been taken: male, female and offspring. The terrified families had been ushered onto transport ships by troops wearing full uniform and helmets but each of their captives knew exactly who the aggressors were.

For some time, the scorpion-like Dahensa had been embroiled in a war with a vicious, callous, war-like race called the Jagaroth. They were more humanoid in form – a head of green, veiny strands with a central eye in their foreheads and large flaps either side of their face, beside their concealed mouths. They carried extremely nasty-looking, snub-nosed laser repeaters with a curved bayonet at the end, which was their preferred method of killing on the battlefield.

Krys'Mar, the female clutch-leader, had been telling the children a story in their shelter while Scaljei'Mar had been out foraging for food. Cur'Mar and his younger clutch-brother Ig'mar

– or Iggy, as they affectionately called him – were on the blanket that served as their bed. The plastic sheeting across the front of the shelter that kept the rain out was pulled aside violently, and a Jagaroth trooper came in and ordered the family outside.

Krys'Mar calmed the children as they were taken down the street of the shantytown and put aboard the transport ship. All the time, she was searching for her partner. As they stood in the bay of the ship, pressed closely together with other families as if on a crowded land-train, Krys spotted Scaljei and shouted to him. The Jagaroth nearest to her warned her to be quiet with a wave of his blade. But the male clutch-leader had heard his partner and, as he was shoved onto the transport, managed to manoeuvre himself over to embrace her.

'What's happening?' Krys asked.

Scaljei looked up from hugging his offspring. 'I don't know,' he said. 'Why would they want *us*?'

*

The answer lay several hundred thousand miles away, on the Jagaroth technical vessel T1R-1. Here, a photonic scientist called Phemoth was waiting to greet the refugees as soon as they were pushed down the landing planks of the transport ships.

Unlike the soldiers, Phemoth wore a grey robe with the traditional beading down the front. This told any other Jagaroth his rank and experience, his family history and any distinctions he had earned. In Phemoth's case he had earned many and displayed the green beads with pride.

'Welcome,' he said. He had long since learned the unusual tongue of his enemies. He let his eye pass over the huddled masses. Like their species, the aliens were bulky and although they were humanoid – walking upright – they had two sets of arms, one that ended in finger-like appendages and one that had thick pincers.

They were also glowing slightly, as if they had been dipped in phosphorous. They wore no armour for they had no need. They had a thick exoskeleton and what looked like a tail protruded from the backs of their necks and over their heads, ending in a bulbous growth that Phemoth knew very well hid an unpleasant-looking sting.

'You, the Dahensa,' he said, stretching out each syllable: Dar-Hen-Sah. 'You are the guests of the mighty Jagaroth.'

Krys looked down at Ig'Mar, who was clutching her leg. 'Don't worry, Iggy,' she whispered. 'We'll be OK.'

'Let me explain what is going to happen to you,' Phemoth was saying. 'As I say, you will be our guests. And I promise you will be well treated. In return we wish you to help us.'

His voice echoed across the hangar bay in which they stood, only the occasional coughing from a Dahensa interrupting the speech.

'I am conducting a series of tests on our technology – nothing to be scared of. We don't want to cut you up!' A couple of the soldiers laughed. 'No. We are not barbarians. We simply cannot spare Jagaroth from the front line to participate in scientific experiments.

'I am sure, being civilians, you will not give us any trouble,' Phemoth concluded, marching down the line of scared and hungry Dahensa. 'You will now be escorted to your new living quarters, which I am sure you will find of a much higher standard than your little settlement of scrappy lean-tos.'

It never occurred to him that the refugee camp, however basic, had been their home for almost a year.

❉

The spacecraft that stood in the side hangar was round and green with three jointed legs that pivoted out from the sphere's equator. This was a single-occupancy version of the much larger ships that comprised most of the Jagaroth fleet. In the hexagonal cockpit sat Scaljei'Mar. The Dahensa were generally larger than the Jagaroth so it was an uncomfortable squeeze. The scorpion-man also knew that he was, in effect, helping the enemies of his people. However, he could also see his family through a narrow window of a viewing gallery, a trooper behind them with the unpleasant bayonet ever at the ready should he decide not to cooperate.

Every morning now for the past three weeks, the males had been selected for basic pilot training. This had been given in a computer simulator. In a way, it had been like playing the holo-games that Scaljei used to design before the war came to their planet. While he wasn't sure he could pilot a real ship, the Jagaroth scientists thought that Scaljei now knew enough about the basic controls to be moved on to the genuine article.

The Dahensa was coached by a duo of Jagaroth technicians who were working under Phemoth. Scaljei could not tell if they were the male or female of their species. To him, they looked identical in skin tone and body form, although one was taller than the other.

As the experiment began, a thick, transparent wall was lowered over the three-legged ship, shutting Scaljei off from the rest of the world. Once that had been locked into place, the technicians asked him to initiate the engine start sequence. With that done, they immediately moved to channelling power from the warp drive to create what, to the untrained Dahensa, appeared to be a form of shield or cloaking device.

Before the field could be generated, he felt the ship vibrate and a high-pitched screech filled the hangar. The shorter technician who, Scaljei now saw, had a larger eye told him to power down and stand by. Phemoth came running into the hangar.

'You've terminated,' he said to the other two Jagaroth. 'Good. There's been an implosion in bay four.'

It was only later that the Mar clutch saw what had happened. Bay four was cordoned off, and Jagaroth in both technical and military uniforms were standing before it, examining or guarding respectively. Through the barriers of red tape, he saw the hole that had been blown in the scientific vessel's hull. There was a small debris field strewn across the floor from a ship identical to the one he was using.

Back in the cell, Krys confronted Scaljei.

'You saw that mess,' she whispered urgently, trying not to attract her offspring's attention. 'That ship was the same type as yours.'

'I know,' the male replied. 'They said they couldn't afford to use Jagaroth pilots. I think we can see why now!' He shook his head.

'This isn't a joke, Scaljei!'

'You don't have to tell me that,' he said. He slumped onto his blanket on the floor.

'We need to figure something out. We need to escape,' Krys said.

Ig'Mar came over and grabbed his mother's leg. 'I made up a story!' he said.

'Not now, Iggy,' Krys said. 'I'm talking to your father.'

'It's a good one!' the youngster replied. 'It won't take long! Promise!'

Krys smiled down at him. 'Sure,' she said. 'Of course.'

She sat and took the little scorpion-boy onto her lap, her hands entwined with his, her pincers gripping his. Iggy's story was about a farmyard and a bad farmer who kept his animals in the barn, except his sheep, who had to go out in the field in the morning. The other animals really wanted to go and play outside so, one day, they hid under the sheep's woolly coats and, when the farmer let his flock go out, the animals escaped.

It was a good story. Clever. But then, Iggy was very clever. Krys told him so as she kissed his head.

'Hey!' said Cur'Mar who had been listening in. 'We made up that story. Together!'

'You're both clever,' Scaljei said.

'Yeah,' said Krys'Mar. But she was thinking about the sheep and a plan was beginning to form. 'You are.' She smiled and beckoned Scaljei over to her. 'I think I know how we can get out of here ...'

*

Over the next few days, the technicians analysed what had happened with the experiment in bay four. Computer modelling that recreated the accident showed there was a problem with the warp core. Even though it should have been possible to form chronon particles by manipulating the warp field, it had caused a feedback loop that had detonated at the engine core, creating an implosion that had crushed the ship.

The Jagaroth were only concerned that the implosion had damaged the T1R-1; they did not care it had cost the life of a Dahensa. As Phemoth said to his team, that is why they had taken the aliens. They were expendable. Jagaroth pilots were extremely valuable. So, they had increased the strength of the shielding and begun the experiments once more.

Every time something went wrong, the test ship imploded, taking a Dahensa with it. What none of the scorpion-people saw was that, when this happened, the dead Dahensa's family were executed. The Jagaroth would halt the trials, examine the data from their computer models and then try again.

Phemoth was coming under intense pressure to deliver the results he had promised Jagaroth High Command. For some months now, the two mighty fleets of the Jagaroth and the Dahensa had been deadlocked. With both species employing the best computer intelligences to model their strategy, it had become like a children's game of circle and cross: no matter which side made the first move, the outcome was mutually assured destruction. There was no advantage to be had.

With resources low and both races close to exhaustion in every sense, Phemoth had come up with a plan he hoped wold give them the military advantage by fooling the Dahensa into making a move. His audacious idea was not to fool them with false intelligence but instead let them believe the evidence of their own eyes.

Although they had not been able to master time travel, they had a rudimentary understanding of it. Using this theory, Phemoth was attempting to project an image of the Jagaroth fleet into the future. When real time caught up with the projection, it would look to the Dahensa like the Jagaroth fleet had doubled in size. This would cause their computer intelligence to make a strategic move based on this information and any move at that point would be an error, and that was the very thing that would allow the Jagaroth to win.

Phemoth was acutely aware that he was running out of Dahensa pilots. Only a handful of families remained. He could feel he was close to the solution, and he had found one enemy pilot in particular to be very helpful and insightful.

'Scaljei'Mar!' Phemoth greeted the Dahensa as he entered the bay. Scaljei waved a pincer in return. 'How are we getting along?'

'He has suggested a new warp field setting,' the technician with the larger eye said.

'Really? How interesting.'

The Dahensa's proposal was a false one. Due to his work in the holo-game industry during peacetime, Scaljei could programme the ship's shield to take the form of the ship itself. Then it was a relatively simple matter of programming the emitters to project the shield as a mirror image, sitting beside the original.

The key was not taking the power from the warp drive, which was what was causing the deaths of his fellow Dahensa. Instead he drew the energy from the atmospheric thrust motors. Scaljei wanted to make the Jagaroth think that their time-shifting project had worked because if they did, he – and the other remaining members of his species – would not be killed.

He made the final adjustments to the emitter and brought the warp-drive power online. The Jagaroth technicians alongside Phemoth himself stood in awe as the duplicate ship appeared in the hangar. The scientist then left the room in a hurry. Scaljei asked where he was going.

'To tell High Command!' one of the technicians said.

'You can power down the ship,' the other added. 'Then you can join your family.'

Scaljei clambered from the little ship as quickly as he could and was escorted by a guard up to the viewing room. Krys flung all four of her arms around him.

'Good job!' she said.

He smiled at her, and together they hugged the offspring.

A little later the door to the antechamber opened, and Phemoth came in. He seemed very happy, although with no facial expressions to go by, it was difficult to tell.

'Thank you, Scaljei,' he said, and his strange, trilling voice sounded light. 'You have served the Jagaroth very well.' Then his voice changed. 'And you have betrayed your entire species. How does it feel?'

Phemoth put a hand on the Dahensa's shoulder. 'Terrible, I imagine. But do not fear. I would never deprive you of witnessing the fruits of your infidelity.'

The Jagaroth scientist explained that he had sent urgent instructions to the entire fleet to replicate the experiment on their ships. Only Phemoth's vessel would be immune as they would watch the destruction of the enemy ships from a safe distance. Indeed, everyone would watch it in the main hangar including all the remaining Dahensa.

They were then escorted down to the hangar and the Mar clutch saw now that there were just four families left – eight adults and six offspring. They were lined up before the bay doors which were used as a screen to display the space battle.

Of course, there was no battle. The order was issued by the Jagaroth flagship and the entire fleet powered up their warp engines exactly as Phemoth had directed. Just one reported a fault in the engines that would need to be investigated, but the effect would work just as well without one ship. So, they proceeded with the plan.

Phemoth came up to Scaljei one more. He gave a short, controlled laugh and whispered in the Dahensa's ear. 'And afterwards, in a few soneds, we will kill you.'

Scaljei regarded the Jagaroth coolly. 'You have always been monsters,' he said.

The scientist went to hit him, but on the screen the ships of the Jagaroth fleet began to explode in twos and threes. Phemoth just stood there, rooted to the spot, his hand lifted to strike his captive.

'You have tricked me?'

Scaljei scanned the hangar. There were only half a dozen troopers on duty. Because of the threat of death that hung over their families the adult Dahensa had never even shown their stings. Until now.

Krys gave the prearranged signal, and the Dahensa who had edged close to the guards all attacked them at once, taking the enemy completely by surprise.

Within moments, the guards lay dead on the floor, poisoned. Krys ushered the offspring aboard the transport ship. Now the males had been trained to fly the small Jagaroth fighters, a transport should be easy.

Scaljei advanced on Phemoth, who now held his arms up in useless defence.

Later, on the transport ship, he was reunited with Krys, Iggy and Cur.

'We did it,' Krys said. 'And all because of that great story from you two!' She beamed a radiant smile at her two offspring.

The four of them embraced as the vessel left the hangar of the penultimate Jagaroth ship in the universe just as Dahensa battle craft moved in to destroy it.

*

The only warship of the Jagaroth fleet limped away from the battle. It hid in a magnetic cloud and then cruised to a nearby planet that was barely formed, dry and dead. It was the third planet in its solar system.

The large, round vessel fired its retro rockets as it touched down with its three spider-like legs. The operator, Scaroth, cut the power and examined his instruments. Their atmospheric thrust motors were damaged. He double-checked: inoperable.

They would not be able to take off. He knew full well that the ship was the last surviving ship of the fleet; the Jagaroth on board were the last of the species. But he was determined to survive.

As he sat in the warp-field pit, the voice of his superior officer came over the speaker system. He was suggesting that, as the atmospheric thrust motors were impaired, they might be able to use the warp drive to give them enough power for escape velocity. Scaroth checked his instruments once more. He shook his head. That would never work. They were stranded there and if the Jagaroth ship's captain ordered him to use the warp thrust, they'd be killed. Or worse ...

# THE LABYRINTHINE WEB

It was a web of traps: a horrifying network of angular turns. This way. That way. Doubling back. Twisting around. Some corridors sloped upwards, others ended abruptly in a gaping hole and ladder. Once inside, there was only one solution for reaching the centre. Some said that there was also no way of getting out again as the Cob-Commander sealed up corridors as you passed. Whether this was true no one knew because no one had come out alive.

Trakkiney was a dust ball of a planet: dry and hot all year round and with no mineral wealth to speak of. However, it was one of Gallifrey's first colony worlds and, as such, a strategic outpost for the new members of the Fledgling Empires. These reasons made it an attractive target for the dreaded Racnoss.

Fysusoidengeus – Fysus to his friends– was a relatively new arrival on the planet when the Racnoss had invaded. Although to use the term 'invaded' was to exaggerate what had taken place when the spider-like alien arrived.

Being a new colony, Trakkiney had no planetary defences to speak of. It certainly had nothing like the transduction barriers that Rassilon had recently installed on Gallifrey. In fact, the only protection it had was a satellite that was meant to detect stray asteroids and meteors that might pose a threat to this on the planet's surface.

That was the first warning the settlers had. In the lab block of the shelter, a technician had received a signal from the satellite. All it told him was that a new spatial body had been detected and it seemed to be on a collision course with the planet. It also gave an estimate until impact: 32 hours – less than a day.

This news had naturally sent the colonists into panic. Governor Gathen had ordered everyone to the stores – the only subterranean part of the prefabricated shelter complex. Everyone sat in the semi-darkness of the ad hoc shelter, gazing upwards even though all they could see was the laser-cut ceiling.

No impact explosion ripped the planet – or even their settlement – apart, so the small contingent of guards was sent above ground to see what had happened. They never reported back, so the majority had taken a decision that everyone should go and look.

When they did, they found a Racnoss spacecraft hovering above them. It was grey-white and its eight points twinkled in the sunlight. Fysus knew it was a Webstar. Like everyone else, he'd been briefed before he came that any Time Lord colony could expect assault by any of the myriad enemies the novice race had already made.

'This is Cob-Commander Messothel,' a voice boomed from the ship. 'This planet is now under Racnoss control.' A laugh filled the air that was deep and nasal. It would have been ridiculous had it not been for the bright bolts of energy that shot with no warning from the points of the Webstar. Eight Time

Lords lay on the floor. As they began to regenerate, the bolts hit them again, and this time the bodies did not start to glow. They simply lay there, dead, their lives snuffed out. Again, the laugh echoed around the shelter complex.

There was nothing they could do against such a superior force. Gathen surrendered and ordered the colonists to do whatever the Cob-Commander said. Secretly, the Governor attempted to get messages to Gallifrey but, both times he tried, the Racnoss executed eight more colonists. He stopped after that.

It did not take long for them to learn that Cob-Commander Messothel was a vicious and ruthless being, even by the standards of his own race. The Webstar planted itself in the soil not far from the shelter, and the colonists were forced to build new structures: the corridors of his labyrinthine web.

When this was complete, the first consignments arrived from the Empress. Messothel let it be known this would be a day of celebration. He ordered Gathen to make available extra rations and even wine. A feast did take place that day, but it was a sullen affair. None of the Time Lords liked hard, manual labour, and they liked being torn away from their scientific endeavours even less.

Fysus was a skilled biochemist, although he had no qualification to show. When he'd first arrived and met his superior, Aria, she had questioned him about this. Running a nervous hand through his blond locks, he'd told her that he was a fervent believer that the Time Lords' destiny was out among the stars, not entrenched on an ever-more isolationist Gallifrey. That's why he'd jumped at the chance to help start a new world.

Aria had laughed, and even her normally immaculate long, auburn hair had jumped around. She called him an idealist. She could not have been more than 75 years his senior, so Fysus took little notice. Despite not getting off to the most auspicious of starts, their relationship had become one of mutual admiration. Aria was the cautious one. She not only got results, she recorded and analysed them. She had what the Academy would have deemed 'good scientific rigour'. Fysus was not like that. He still got results, but he cut certain corners that he saw as unnecessary. He made leaps of intuition and, to make matters worse, he was usually right.

Now he and Aria were nothing more than glorified drones, building whatever the Cob-Commander said, bowing to his will. Existing. Not living. And, that night at the feast, they discovered that this existence was actually even worse than they had thought. For days, everyone had been speculating as to what consignments the Empress of the Racnoss was sending to this backwater. As they ate their rations and sipped at the beakers of wine, the nasal voice boomed out across the shelter.

'You are privileged, my little lords and ladies of time,' Messothel said. 'For the Empress has chosen you to help increase our number. She has sent me eight precious eggs and eight of you will help them grow to adulthood.' The laugh again. 'From now on, all Time Lords will be given a special bedtime drink. Huon particle shakes! Enjoy your feast!'

Fysus looked across the table at Aria. They had both heard of Huon particles, but only in relation to the experiments being conducted on Gallifrey into time travel. One of the few things they knew about them was that that they were highly poisonous. Any long-term exposure to even the amount needed to make a beverage would be fatal.

They discussed this later that night as the wine took hold and caution became less of a barrier to truth. Aria had concluded that not only were Huon particles not poisonous to the Racnoss, they were in fact necessary to the hatching somehow. Fysus saw the logic. Why else would the Time Lords be dosed with it? But that brought with it an ugly realisation. The Racnoss were voracious feeders. All the Time Lords Messothel had killed had been taken away and spun into cocoons to be kept in his food store at the apex of the grounded Webstar. Whichever eight were chosen to go into the web would be used by the hatchling Racnoss as their first meal.

'And!' said Aria, brushing a stray auburn strand from her eye. She was sitting on an upturned water drum. 'We can't do a thing about it.'

Fysus was on the floor, cross-legged. He looked up at her. 'Not yet,' he said mysteriously.

'What does that mean?' asked Aria. Some of the words had become meshed together as she spoke. 'You and your "not yet". You think you're so cryptic, mister idealist!' She sat back and took another gulp of wine.

'I'm not!' Fysus said, in a false whisper. 'But what if *he's* listening!' He pointed behind him at the Webstar. The gesture was meant to be subtle but failed.

'He doesn't need to listen!' Aria said loudly. 'Oooh-oh! Messothel!' She waved her beaker at the Racnoss ship. Nothing happened. 'See?'

Fysus hushed her and scuttled across to sit at her feet. 'Do you think we could engineer the particles?'

She tried to repeat the last part of his sentence, failed and laughed. 'Why?' she asked.

'I think we could,' Fysus said. His tone was now so serious that Aria seemed to sober up in a matter of seconds, suddenly sitting up straighter. 'I think we could reverse their poisonous effect.'

'But we'd still die when the spiders ate us!' Aria shook her head.

'Not necessarily,' Fysus said and winked. Then he gave a broad smile as Aria stared at him. 'OK, that was a bit mysterious, I'll admit.' He stood up with a little help from Aria. 'Let's talk tomorrow at the lab.'

'We don't work at the lab any more,' she said. 'Remember?'

'First rest period,' Fysus replied. And he sloped off into the night to find his bunk.

※

They met in the laboratory the next day for the first time in many months. Fysus presented his theory to Aria and she checked it for factual errors or leaps of logic. She could find none. It seemed a sound plan to her, she said. It still meant they could not help the first eight victims; the 'tributes' Messothel was calling them. Nor even the second, but soon they would be able to act.

At noon, the Cob-Commander gathered all his subjects in the area directly before the Webstar and its newly finished maze. Just under ninety Time Lords remained. They stood in the blistering heat while Messothel made a manic speech about the greatness of the Racnoss Empire and how its children would destroy the Fledgling Empires. It was tedious and long, with the only respite being the prolonged periods of grating laughter that came after every colourful phrase. At the end the Cob-Commander said that he would now take eight Time Lords as tribute.

They all just stood there. Who should go? How did they decide? They had assumed that Messothel would make the choice for them. Instead it was quickly agreed they should draw lots. Those who occupied certain positions in the colony were to be ruled out as being vital – physicians, hydroponics experts, geo-survey and the like. Gathen put himself into that category, too, although Fysus wondered if that were strictly necessary.

Soon enough the eight Time Lords – five male and three female – stood apart from the others near the ground-level entrance to Messothel's evil web. Hods, the Time Lord whose job it was to add the Huon particles to the shakes and give them to the tribute, approached with a tray of the drinks. Each one took a beaker and drank them down. Some were fast, chugging the liquid in defiance; some were slower, more cautious, as if the liquid would poison them then and there. When all the beakers were empty, a round door slid aside at the base of the Webstar.

Fysus craned to see inside. He would need to know everything he could if his plan was to work. All he could see were cobwebs covering the walls of a metallic corridor. The tributes went inside and the door closed. Most of the colonists waited for some time before realising that there was nothing else to the ceremony. That was it; they would never see their friends again. They began to drift away in small groups.

✻

Whenever they could, Fysus and Arial stole away to the lab. They also recruited the help of several other colonists. The first was Hods. He was vital. Luckily he had no love of the Racnoss and was not the type to keep his head down; he wanted to help by doing more than just providing samples for the biochemists to work on. Fysus was all for it. Aria refused. She reasoned that if Hods went around stirring up trouble and was discovered, Messothel would suspect that the Huon particles were being tampered with. Fysus saw her point. As ever, her logic was safer than his gut instinct.

Another lunar cycle passed before a second Webstar arrived in orbit. Fysus presumed it was taking the hatchlings away and delivering more eggs. He was soon proven correct on the second point, as Messothel announced he would need another eight tributes. Aria was actually more frustrated by this news than Fysus. They had been working hard and were almost ready, but they would need another month for the escape strategy to have any chance of success.

Following the second eight's departure into the maze of a web Messothel had created, Fysus and Arial met every night to toast their mission and every day they made small preparations. As the next lunar cycle loomed, they told Gathen about their plan. He was a politician and afraid of losing his position more than anything. But he was also a realist. He knew that unless something happened to prevent the whole colony being eaten by the Racnoss he would have no head, let alone a position of power. So he acquiesced, reluctantly. He was actually vital, too, as it was he who could organise the repurposing of some buildings they would need.

The day before the new consignment of eggs was due to arrive, Aria took Fysus to one side. She said she had been trying to build a computer model of the Webstar and its labyrinth. She couldn't be sure, but she thought that if one followed the straightforward path, not deviating left or right – or especially down – it should prove the most direct path to the heart of the Webstar where Messothel would have his lair.

As the noonday sun reached its apex on the third lunar cycle, the remaining colonists gathered before the Webstar as they had twice before. Again, those in reserved positions were separated from the rest and then the lots were drawn. This was a simple process. A large container was hefted into the middle of the group. It contained small, metal nuts harvested from the construction supplies and painted red or green.

The first colonist moved forward and thrust his hand into a small hole on top of the container. There was no way to see the contents and no way of telling what colour the nuts were. He searched around for a short while and then made his choice. He pulled his arm out and held up the hexagonal nut so that everyone could see it. It was bright, metallic green and glinted in the sunlight. The fortunate man moved over to join the reserved members of the colony. So it would continue until eight red nuts had been drawn.

The initial drawing of the lots had been an ordered affair with a queue, but none liked this. Instead, it became a bit of a scramble with those who wanted to get it over and done with, pushing to the front while those scared of their fate hung back. It really made no difference. There were only eight red nuts and the laws of probability dictated although the odds of finding one diminished each time another was found, it could easily be the last nut drawn that sent you into the Webstar.

However, that had never happened; all the red nuts had been found long before all the colonists had drawn. This was the flaw in the system that Fysus was about to exploit. He had positioned himself close to the container and did not force his way through those keener to choose. Already one red nut had been found by the time he got to make his selection. Except, his was not a selection – it was a foregone conclusion. He held in his fist a nut that had been painted red to match those in the container. He thrust his closed fit through the hole and made a show of moving his hand about before drawing it out and showing everyone the colour of his fate.

Red.

Fysus moved over to join the other colonist standing by the entrance to the Webstar. Presently, they were joined by six more and the container was carried away once more. All the other

Time Lords then lined up behind them. Fysus saw Gathen staring at him with both pride and fear – possibly more of the latter. And then there was Aria. She smiled at him. It was a brave smile. If she was afraid, she certainly wasn't going to show him.

As they all stood in silence, Hods approached. He carried his usual tray of eight beakers. He, too, was eyeing Fysus with a mixed look. But his seemed to be that of an amused conspirator, rather than a concerned friend or a fearful politician. As he held out the tray to Fysus he even managed the slightest hint of a wink. Fysus tried not to show any reaction in his face. Messothel would be watching all this on his surveillance system. If anything seemed out of the ordinary, he was bound to investigate.

He didn't, and instead the doors at the base of the Webstar opened as they had in the past. The eight tributes walked forward as everyone watched in silence. Some faltered in their steps. And then potential disaster struck. One of the tributes, a younger Time Lord, started running away from the door, heading for the far side of the settlement compound.

A jagged bolt of energy struck him down. Fysus thought the mad spider had killed the man, but he was still alive, rolling around on the ground.

'Retrieve him!' Messothel ordered over the loudspeakers. The seven remaining tributes looked at each other, and then Fysus set off along with another called Phaedra. Together, they plucked the errant tribute from the sandy earth and dragged him towards the door. He was sobbing, and dragging his feet.

'Just get inside,' hissed Fysus. 'Then we'll be OK.'

The man shook his head vigorously, but they were soon inside the Webstar with the other five and the door closed behind them. Fysus and Phaedra left the man on the floor, hugging himself.

'Welcome!' Messothel announced. 'Now you are inside I can reveal what your purpose is and why I have made you drink a delicious Huon shake!' He laughed annoyingly.

The seven tributes who were standing looked at one another.

'We Racnoss use Huon particles in the revival of our new-born – especially when they have been in hypersleep. They like to get their dose of Huon particles as part of their first meal. That's you, my tasty time snacks!' The laugh again, even more maniacal this time. 'Now, I would advise you to keep moving through the corridors. There are motivational tools hidden within their construction. See you soon!'

Fysus turned to the others. 'Listen,' he whispered. 'Some of us have been working on a plan. You need to come with me. We need to act as a team, but don't worry, the Racnoss hatchlings won't kill us. Not this time.' He turned and faced the long, dark corridor that twisted away before him.

'What about Messothel?' asked Phaedra.

'I'm going to deal with him. Come on!'

Naturally the man who had run away was not keen on the idea of going further into the maze, but Phaedra proved adept at persuasion. He told them that he worked in the sanitation farm and kept himself to himself. His name was Hellner.

A burly cook called Drandell also helped them. He encouraged the younger man, and eventually they were all ready to move forward.

'We must stay together,' Fysus told them. 'I hope we can find our way to the centre quickly, but that may not be the case.'

They moved forward, always trying not to turn unless the main shaft did. They ignored side corridors and kept to the path that led upwards. As Aria had suggested, this seemed to work for a while, but they soon found themselves walking downhill. The corridor ended in a round hole that led to a sloping tunnel almost like a chute. Other than doubling back, they had no alternative than to follow it. Fysus made Hellner go first. He seemed to have lost some of his fear but had found a whining negativity in its absence. Only Drandell seemed to be able to control him, so he went second. The others followed before finally Phaedra and Fysus himself jumped down the slide.

They were now in a narrowed section of the maze. Fysus tried to climb back up the chute, but it was too well polished and he just slipped down again before he reached even two metres.

'No way back,' he said. 'Not that way, at least.'

He estimated the chute had brought them halfway back to ground level, but he couldn't be sure. The drop certainly didn't feel as high as he thought they were. Phaedra and the others agreed. Hellner did not seem to hold an opinion. They continued, following the same plan as before: straight on, always upward.

They had been wandering the maze for hours when Hellner suddenly stopped. 'What's the point?' he asked and slumped to the ground. 'I won't go on!' he shouted at the walls. 'I won't, you hear?'

Drandell tried to get him on his feet, but Hellner was afraid and behaving like a tired child. Fysus tried to convince him that he had to if they were all going to make it out of Messothel's labyrinthine web. He just looked up at the biochemist with red eyes.

'We're not going to *make it out*,' he said. 'We're lunch! For the Racnoss.' Fysus touched his arm, but Hellner yanked it away. 'No! You go on. You try your *plan*,' he sneered. 'Good luck to you! I'm not going to march to my death like a blind sheep.'

Phaedra stepped up to him and slapped him hard across the face. 'Just get up,' she shouted. 'Get up!

Even then he didn't move; he just looked at her in total shock before starting to cry.

'We'll have to leave you,' Fysus said. Hellner ignored him.

'Come on,' Phaedra said. 'Leave him.'

However, as they started to move off up the corridor, Hellner leapt up with a shriek. The others all turned to face him. 'Electric shock,' he cried by way of explanation.

Phaedra grinned at Fysus. 'Well, Messothel did say he had methods of persuading us to keep moving!'

Fysus smiled back, nodding. 'Good old Messothel.'

After that, although he hung back from the rest of the group, Hellner did not complain again or sit down.

When they had been travelling through the impossible maze of corridors and chutes for almost twelve hours, they stopped. Would Messothel permit them a rest? Fysus doubted it. Not a long one, at least. They gave themselves fifteen minutes and then got moving again. Almost immediately they found a ladder.

'I wonder if this is it,' Fysus said.

'Let's see!' Drandell moved forward to take the first rung. Then he stopped. 'Where's that rat, Hellner?' Sure enough the cowardly Time Lord was lurking further down the corridor, almost in darkness. 'Get over here,' bellowed Drandell. Reluctantly, Hellner came forward. 'Start climbing!'

This time Phaedra went last and, as Fysus helped her up the last few feet to the top, they saw that they had indeed completed their journey.

In front of them was a huge, dark red spider form at least eight metres across. Its legs twitched on control panels ranged before it that in turn operated the wall of screens that showed images from the maze and the settlement compound.

'You made it!' Messothel said. 'Although one of you needed a little persuasion!' He turned to face them now, and they got their first proper look at a Racnoss.

He was indeed mostly spider in appearance: blood red in colour with eight legs and one pair of arms or even mandibles, it was impossible to tell. His face was humanoid with six eyes on a crested head. They were all black except one, which was white and had an old war scar on it. His mouth was constantly open, his head turning from side to side as if to catch the air.

'Behold your young charges!' He laughed as he pointed one of his razor-tipped arms at a row of eight roundish, yellow balls the size of boulders. They were lined up between where Messothel was standing on his raised command platform and the eight Time Lords. 'The maze was the hard part,' he continued, eyeing each of the tributes in turn. 'Dying will be easy because our young are born starving! Now, get into position: one in front of each egg.'

As they took their positions by the yellowy eggs, they saw that the young within them were starting to wriggle slowly, becoming more agitated by the second. Suddenly, the egg nearest to Drandell burst with a plume of tiny white filaments that filled the air and covered the tribute. A small, red leg appeared over the side of the broken casing. Then another, and another, until the Racnoss hatchling was balanced on the remains of its egg.

Straight away Drandell began to glow – almost as if he were regenerating – but this was a different, more sparkling effect. Fysus realised this was the Huon particles being drawn from the tribute by the Racnoss. His own egg then shattered and a third and then two at once until all the eggs were broken and all the hatchlings were drawing the Huon feast from those who had carried it to them.

Cob-Commander Messothel cackled away as this happened. He thought his mission for another month was done. But Fysus knew he was very wrong. One by one, starting with the hatchling feeding from Drandell, the baby Racnoss vanished.

'What's going on?' Messothel asked, coming closer, dabbing with his forelegs at where the nearest hatchling had been moments before. 'How have you don't this? Where are the hatchlings?'

Messothel rounded on the eight Time Lords now, bearing his pointed teeth and dribbling with saliva. It stopped before Hellner and roared in his face. 'Tell me!'

'He said it would be OK,' Hellner whined, pointing at Fysus.

The Cob-Commander rounded on his new target and bore down on him. Fysus stood his ground.

'You are the ringleader, my little Time Lord?' Messothel demanded.

'I am,' Fysus said. 'Shall I tell you what I've done?' He didn't wait for the giant spider creature to give him leave; he just ploughed straight on. 'We re-engineered the Huon particles you yourself wanted to feed us.'

'Re-engineered?'

'They're poisonous to Time Lords,' Fysus said. 'Well, most living beings really. They should be destroyed. But we re-engineered them to reverse the poisoning effects.'

'Reverse ... So you are not dying?' He reared up on his back four legs and went to strike Fysus with the razor tips of his forelegs. The Time Lord quickly rolled away to one side, knocking into Phaedra. She helped him up as the Racnoss scuttled across the chamber to attack again. But then Messothel faltered. Now he, too, was glowing. He reared up, bellowing in anger.

But then Messothel laughed: a gurgling sound more than a cackle. 'A brave move, Time Lord,' he said. 'But ultimately …

a foolish one ...' He gasped for breath as he faded in and out of view. 'You will never ... be able escape my web.' The warbling laugh again. 'You will be ... trapped here ... and starve to death.'

Fysus smiled. 'Huon particles attract each other – even over large distances,' he told the Racnoss. 'Don't you know?' Of course, Messothel knew. Fysus was goading him. 'My friend, Aria, has been dosing herself with the re-engineered particles. That is where the hatchlings have been sent. She is waiting in a specially built cell. That is where you're being sent!'

'Noooo!' The Racnoss roared and moved to kill Fysus but, before he could reach the Time Lord, he disappeared. Deep in the complex of the colony, the holding facilities that Gathen had okayed now contained nine Racnoss: prisoners who would be handed over to the Gallifreyan authorities as soon as the rescue ship arrived.

Hellner was the first to speak. He seemed a different person. 'Did you say we can get out of here easily?'

'Yes,' Fysus said with a smile of relief. 'All I need to do is activate this.' He fished in the pocket of his robe and produced a pen-like metallic rod. 'A sonic control device ... We'll be back wherever Aria is in a matter of seconds. Might be best to wait a moment for her to leave the cells otherwise we'll simply be facing Messothel once more!'

'Although I'm sure he's tempted to leave you to find your own way out,' Phaedra said. But she patted Hellner's shoulder to confirm it was a joke.

'Ready?' Fysus asked and they all gathered around him. He pressed the operating switch on the sonic rod and they vanished from the Webstar's control chamber just as their captors had done minutes before. The only difference being that the Time Lords would now be free.

# THE ANGELS
# OF VENGEANCE

When Lectyno opened the door to be confronted by his mother, he was shocked to see how much she had aged since she had been executed seven years previously. There was an uncomfortable silence as he stood, staring at her.

Nestyra had been quite the beauty back in the day. A few times he had even seen her image in the chatter bulletins on the arm of his father, Memyno. She was always demure yet glamorous, the perfect companion to an Evaluator – one of the judges who were untouchable by the law other than in their own courts. Lectyno had seen his father depicted on the page as the guest of honour at legal balls or the headline speaker at law symposiums many times.

Lectyno remembered how his mother always came to say goodnight to him when she was going out. Her dark blue hair always looked amazing and her amber eyes twinkled with such allure. But it was her jet-black skin that he always reached for. It had such lustre in the glow from this bedside light, she almost looked like a holy herald.

Then there had been the other images, the ones
on the information bulletins. Lectyno recalled one in
particular: the body of his father on a hover-stretcher
covered in a white shroud. Behind this his mother,
in nightclothes – not demure at all – having her arms
pulled behind her back by two Proctors.

The awkward silence ended as his once beautiful
mother – now a gaunt old hag – spoke to him.

'Lex,' she said.

Lectyno flinched as if she had slapped him. How dare she speak his name? How dare she come to his threshold? Rage swelled in his chest and made his body shake.

'Murderer,' he said. Slow and deliberate. Then again: 'Murderer!' Louder now, the unbridled aggression spilling into his voice.

Now it was Nestyra who recoiled. 'So many years have passed ...' She trailed off as her voice cracked.

'For you, Mother. Not for me.'

Lectyno was becoming angrier, but now with himself. He should just slam the door but something made him hesitate. She was his mother, his 'Mitty'.

'I need your help,' she said.

That was the impetus he needed.

'I am a Guardian of the Rock! How can you do this? You kill my father – your husband – and now you backslide your family?'

He shoved the door back at her with all his might, and the crash of the door in its frame reverberated through the house.

❋

The courtroom was triangular, stark and white with the defendant at the centre. At one point of the triangle, elevated above proceedings was the Evaluator. Behind him were the Advisory – the 15 members of the junior judiciary whose job it was to counsel him. To the left and right of the Evaluator, elevated but on a lower level to him, sat the Advocate and the Indictor – defence and prosecution – the former to the left, the latter to the right.

Lectyno strained to see who was sitting on the bench. They were all watching him; twelve men and three women. One of the women was watching him very intently. And with good reason. She was Lectyno's sister, Rosytra.

The Evaluator stood. 'Was this an accurate account of what took place outside your domicile three days ago, citizen?' he asked.

Lectyno bristled. This was a slur. He did not answer the Evaluator, and the Advisory began to mutter amongst themselves. Rosytra detached herself from the line and came up behind the man evaluating the case. The man they usually called Uncle. The man who had never liked Lectyno.

Evaluator Gistyho smiled as Rosytra whispered something in his ear. He cleared his throat and spoke once more.

'I apologise if I have offended the defendant. If I have, let the record show it was not meant.' At this he glanced upwards for a brief moment at the cameras recording events. 'Please, Guardian, answer the question.'

Lectyno gave a mirthless smile. 'Thank you, Evaluator. That looked to me like what happened. Yes.'

'Good.' Evaluator Gistyho flicked at his bald temple as if an insect were aggravating him. But Lectyno knew this was just a show of his irritation with his nephew. 'So, in the common tongue, your mother was "backsliding" you.'

'She was also backsliding my sister,' added Lectyno bitterly.

Gistyho gave a snort. 'Your sister is not on trial here!'

He turned and looked down the Bench to where Rosytra sat. She bobbed her head in recognition of the clarification.

'Your mother was "backsliding" you. And you wanted ... What? Revenge?'

'I am sure I do not have to tell you the law,' Lectyno said.

Another round of mutterings from the Advisory and this time a different person stood up, but he was positioned in the Advocate's balcony. He had dirty-green hair, braided around his ears, and held himself as if he found himself the most important person in the room. Which he no doubt did. This was Portyn.

'Your eminence,' he began. 'I am certain the defendant means no disrespect in his statement.' Portyn wrung his hands together in an appalling display of obsequiousness. Lectyno almost smiled. 'It must be a difficult undertaking for him to detach avuncular familiarity from the decorum that these procedures demand.'

'Indeed,' Gistyho said, staring at his nephew with steely eyes. 'But as a Guardian who hails from a family with a long tradition of legal service, I doubt it was unintentional.'

Portyn squirmed for a moment and then looked helplessly at his defendant. 'I just wanted to point out that it is the duty of all citizens to deal with the problem of backsliders as quickly and efficiently as possible.'

The Evaluator smiled condescendingly. 'This,' he said, 'is not the law.'

Lectyno frowned. 'But it is our way. It is "common" law.'

One of the Advisory came forward and passed a handwritten note to Gistyho. He looked down at it and then shook his head.

'I understand the issue well enough. The Yumyni judicial system deals in absolutes. It has to. Since we became the fifteenth broken moon of the Medusa Cascade, ours has been a harsh existence. We demand blood for blood. No leniency. But once justice is served, there will always be the possibility of the condemned returning and backsliding.'

Murmurs and nods from the Advisory greeted the Evaluator's little speech.

'As the defendant agrees on the veracity of the previous video testimony, let us move to the homicide itself.'

Lectyno turned to stare at the white wall behind him as it once more became a huge screen.

❋

It was dark and the roadway was slick with a recent rain shower. A vehicle pulled up, humming. The electric engine was cut and a man got out. It was Lectyno. He had a raincover over his Guardian's uniform.

The buildings that lined the road were clearly deserted, their windows broken and doors smashed. Through their broken façades, graffiti could be glimpsed. It was daubed on all the buildings' internal walls.

The figure of an old woman detached itself from the shadow of one doorway and approached Lectyno, hobbling.

'Lex,' she said.

'I agreed to meet you here for one reason, Mother,' Lectyno said. He had a small case in his right hand.

'I know Rosytra told you I wanted money,' she said. 'And that is what I told her. But it's not true. I want to ... come home.'

'Home?' Lectyno stared at his old mother. Then he gave a short laugh. 'That's never going to happen, old woman.'

'I am still imprinted on the system,' she said, a slight tone of peevishness about her. 'I could just come whenever I please.'

Her son crossed the ground between them very quickly but stopped short of actually touching Nestyra. 'If you try that,' Lectyno hissed, 'I will *kill* you!'

*

'Your eminence.' Portyn was on his feet again. 'I'm sure we can all agree that is merely a turn of phrase, a common colloquialism.' He smiled.

'I am not sure that we *can* all agree,' Evaluator Gistyho said, taking in the Advisory bench with a sweep of his arm. 'For the fact is that, one day later, the victim was seen entering the Guardian's property in the manner she described and is now dead.'

'Ah, I think the official verdict is *missing* presumed dead,' Portyn said and quickly sat down.

'Duly noted,' the Evaluator said.

Lectyno looked at the floor. The case was progressing almost exactly as he had guessed it might. He let his gaze linger as he thought about what lurked beneath the polished surface he was staring at. For here was what served as the tools of justice on the fifteenth broken moon: the three Angels of vengeance.

When the planet had been devastated, the government of the time had used every technology at their disposal to ensure that anyone and anything coming near was transported to an underground bunker. Many officials had been killed when they caught the Weeping Angels. Now they were kept in a round chamber: constantly lit with no doors or windows. Each one was positioned at 60 degrees to the others, so that they were all looking at each other – quantum-locked – and therefore could not move or pose a threat. Until they were used by the court as the ultimate sanction.

This is why the 'executed' sometimes came back. The Angels fed on the temporal energy given off when they touched victims and sent them back in time. However, they also displaced them in space. Because the fifteenth broken moon was little bigger than a city, the majority of those they touched found themselves in the void of space with nanoseconds to live before they boiled to death in the radiation of the void.

A few were 'lucky' and found themselves back on the streets, but many years prior to their previous lives. It was forbidden for them to meet their future selves and it was a serious taboo for them to seek their families again. In most cases the first thing these backsliders did was seek retribution. The judicial system's blindness to this had led to a cycle of killings and revenge. It had become an almost inescapable loop.

'My mother was punished by this system,' Lectyno said aloud. 'She was sent back in time by the Lonely Assassins and lived on the streets for forty years.'

'What is your point?' the Evaluator asked, clearly irritated by this unnecessary statement.

'I am merely making an observation,' Lectyno said. 'How we think of these poor unfortunates as "lucky" ...'

'I believe the accused is feeling remorse for his mother now, yes?' The skinny grey man that was serving as his prosecutor finally made himself known to the court. Fualik. 'A typical response, your eminence, of a guilty man.'

'At least one member of the family upholds the law,' the Evaluator said, nodding his head at Rosytra. His stare returned to Lectyno. 'I believe it was she that alerted the authorities to her mother's disappearance.'

'Just as you did all those years ago,' Lectyno replied, holding his uncle's gaze.

Gistyho flushed red with anger for a moment and then coughed to hide his anger. 'Quite so, my nephew,' he said. 'Quite so. But I am sure no one is impinging *my* record when it comes to upholding the law.'

This brought polite laughter from the bench.

'And you are right, even with siblings, the rule of law is absolute. And now you face the same punishment as your mother. It is apt, do you not think so?'

One of the Advisory rose and passed the Evaluator a note.

'Yes. "The defendant is wasting time," it says here,' Gistyho said. 'As Evaluator I am inclined to agree. Shall we press on?'

✤

The next footage to be shown to the court depicted Nestyra entering the house using her eye-scan on the security system. The security camera had a time stamp in the bottom right-hand corner. The front door opened and she went inside.

The scene froze and Fualik rose to give the prosecution notes. 'As you can see the camera stamp bears the time of 25:89, late in the evening.'

He snapped his fingers, and the woman sitting next to him quickly passed him a remote-control device. He pressed a button. Beneath where the Evaluator was seated, a small hatch opened and something floated out, propelled by a tiny tractor beam. It was a gun.

'This is the defendant's sidearm,' said the greyer than grey Fualik. 'Can you confirm that, Lectyno?'

Lectyno made no effort to look at the gun. 'All our weapons are standard issue. They all look identical.'

'But each one is coded upon issue.'

'Yes.'

'And you have not mislaid your sidearm?' Fualik leant forward, a nasty slug of a tongue moistening his lips. He knew full well that for a Guardian to lose his sidearm was a serious offence.

'I have not,' Lectyno said. 'That is ...' He coughed and took a drink from the beaker beside him.

'Well?' asked the Evaluator.

'That is, until it was taken from me by Proctors of the Court.' Lectyno smiled sweetly.

'This is not a performance dome!' roared Gistyho. He was so animated that his Evaluator's collar almost flew off. He had to refasten it hurriedly.

Fualik moved on quickly. 'Let the record show: the accused identified his sidearm,' he said. 'And we have this!'

The gun floated down to a shelf that protruded from the same lectern the Evaluator sat behind. The tractor beam disengaged and almost immediately another one started up, producing a computer printout from the same hatch.

'This is the weapon's usage report from Guardian Headquarters. It shows a discharge on the same day as the victim entered the house and only three minutes later.'

Now there were gasps from the bench.

'Can you explain why you discharged the weapon, Guardian Lectyno?' Gistyho asked. He wasn't even trying to conceal the slight smile that gave his lips a slight upturn to them.

'It was in the execution of my duty,' Lectyno said.

'The *execution* of your duty,' the Evaluator said. 'And do we have an incident report to verify the Guardian's version of events?'

Fualik made a large show of holding his hands out – empty. 'No, your eminence.'

'Well,' said Lectyno. 'I believe it is better not to have one than to falsify one.'

The court went silent. What could he be talking about? The bench all exchanged nonplussed expressions. Except Rosytra.

She produced a piece of paper and passed it to the Evaluator, who was looking very uncomfortable suddenly. He took it from her, looked down at it and then looked up again, frowning. 'What is this?' he asked.

'A similar report, your eminence,' Rosytra said. 'From forty years ago.'

Now the Advisors were all speaking very loudly.

'Silence in this court!' screamed Gistyho. 'I will have silence!' As the prattling from the bench subsided, he turned back to his niece. 'What is the meaning of this?'

'It is the record of your own sidearm, is it not?' she asked. 'From the night my father was killed. Sorry, *murdered*.'

'This is preposterous!' the Evaluator said. 'I have no case to answer. You are confused, my dear. Stricken with grief. I suggest you remove yourself from the court.'

Lectyno spoke up. 'It was falsified. Do you recall?'

'I do not, because it did not happen,' Gistyho said reasonably. 'I am going to call a recess,' he added. 'I feel this whole unpleasant business is putting a great strain on the family bonds in this court.'

'You don't, do you?' Lectyno said. 'Truly. Or, at least, your forget the name or the face of the junior technical who was just starting out in the legal system back then.'

The Evaluator jerked his head this and way and that, passing his gaze over the court.

Lectyno laughed. 'And if you did not do it, who are you looking for now?'

'No one.'

Rosytra was on her feet now. 'He doesn't recognise you. Sorry.' She gave a humourless laugh.

Portyn rose so he was standing, facing the Evaluator. 'That is a shame.'

Gistyho stared at the Advocate in disbelief. 'Recess,' he said and hit his fist on the lectern. But no one moved.

'Not yet,' Lectyno said. 'Let us hear from this key witness shall we, *Uncle*?'

'He approached me,' Portyn said, nodding. 'I am ashamed. But I had no inkling why he wanted it done. He promised me he would help my career.' There was a tear in Portyn's eye now, but he chuckled nonetheless. 'Of course, he didn't. But he did pay me. And then he became a judge. So I said nothing. You cannot challenge a judge.'

'Except,' said Rosytra, 'in open court!'

Gistyho rose now as well and smashed his hand on the lectern again. 'No recess,' he hissed. 'I have my verdict. This man is guilty! Let sentence be carried out forthwith!'

'Summon the Proctors!' shouted Rosytra as the cameras fell dormant. Everyone knew what this meant.

Suddenly the floor around Lectyno folded away, and three figures rose slowly from beneath. Lectyno stood, the man condemned now surrounded by the Weeping Angels. Gistyho looked very solemn as he pointed his finger at his nephew. His other hand was moving toward the lighting control. It would extinguish the lights in the court for the slightest millisecond, but in that blink of an eye justice would be served. This was enough time for the prisoner to be displaced and to give the Angels sustenance to keep them alive, but not enough for the Angels to feast and escape.

'Wait!' The cry came from the gallery, where the Proctors had arrived with a very unexpected addition. Nestyra was pointing down at the courtroom. 'That man killed my husband!'

Before Gistyho could react, Lectyno was moving. He ducked between two of the Angels and snatched up his sidearm from the evidence shelf. He quickly checked the battery pack and then loosed a laser bolt, and the Evaluator spun back against the wall of the court.

'Do not be alarmed,' Lectyno shouted, scaling the lectern and clambering over the top. 'I am a Guardian, and I arrest this man for the murder of my father!'

Gistyho was slumped against the wall nursing the power-burn on his arm. 'You did not believe I would kill you?' he asked. 'That would be against the law ...' The Evaluator looked at his nephew with a glimmer of hope in his eyes.

'No!' laughed Lectyno.

'Not when there is sentence to be carried out,' said Rosytra. 'Who in this court finds my brother innocent of his mother's murder?'

Everyone called out 'Nay!'

Rosytra grabbed her uncle and thrust him towards the approaching Proctors. 'And who in this court finds my uncle guilty of my father's murder?'

This time the court rang with the call of 'Aye' from all sides. Even Fualik.

Gistyho walked fitfully down the steps to the waiting Angels. 'You had better hope I do not backslide, boy, for I will visit on you a—'

'Quiet,' spat Lectyno as his uncle was pinioned in place between the Angels. 'Clear the court! Seal the doors!'

The Advisors and Proctors, the Advocate and Indictor all moved from the chamber, leaving just the family: Lectyno, Rosytra and their mother, Nestyra. They all stood by the door, looking back at Gistyho. 'We planned this for my beloved Memyno,' Nestyra said. 'I hope it's painful!'

Lectyno ushered his mother and sister out before following them with never a backward glance. Gistyho heard his nephew call out: 'Kill the lights!' Everything went black and the last thing he heard was a terrible rasping of stone teeth ...

# THE JEOPARDY OF SOLAR PROXIMITY

The ship was a thing of beauty. It was round but not so much a saucer, more an elegant bowl. The silvery-white metal hull was lit from within by the palest of blue lights. Three nacelles protruded from the circular vessel at precisely 120 degrees around its circumference. A soft violet glow described each thruster and manoeuvring jet – even the main engine.

Its stunning design made it all the more difficult for the Grand Marshal to watch its demise. But watch he did.

A huge explosion tore through the battlecruiser, sending green bodies and blackened debris floating out into space. More missiles sped towards the stricken target. They spun almost uncontrollably, dodging the ship's defensive sonic cannons, before closing on the vessel and smashing into its hull. The detonation of these two rockets all but ripped the silvery craft apart and sent what was left hurtling at an ugly angle towards the planet Knossos below.

Skaldak growled and ordered the viewscreen changed to show the enemy fleet. At least, it had once been a fleet. As had his. The mighty *Xix-Thassis* fleet of the Ice Warriors had been

all but destroyed in this galactic battle with a flotilla of Dalek ships.

By contrast to Martian elegance, a Dalek command ship was truly saucer-shaped. Only one remained: a dirty-bronzed golden colour with a central, rounded hump on the upper surfaces and several similar-shaped bulges on the undersides. Around their edges were lines of elongated lights that rotated as the ships moved. There were also three smaller Dalek Councillor-class assault craft, far more utilitarian in design: gunmetal grey with two distinct levels and no adornment.

Daleks. Skaldak found himself wanting to spit. Even the fearsome warriors of Mars feared these creatures. The Grand Marshal knew there was no shame in fear. Fear kept a warrior sharp. Complacency and stupidity were as much his enemies as the motorised cones from Skaro.

The sacrifice of the cruiser *Saavid* was a military calculation. By commanding it to separate from battle formation and head for the far side of the nearest planet, it had appeared to the Daleks as if the ship were fleeing, deserting. Indeed, Skaldak had sent a blanket of sub-space transmissions cursing them for abandoning their posts and threats of vengeance and punishment. They were encoded, but not so strongly that the Dalek cypher computers could not decode them.

The Dalek strategy was always for overkill. They had sent two assault ships where one would have done. They wanted to ensure the strategic advantage and in so doing had thrown it away. For now, as the two Dalek vessels moved in to completely destroy the *Saavid*, it jettisoned its hyper-drive core right between the two enemy ships.

'Do it,' said Skaldak, his teeth clenched in a grim smile.

A wave of energy bolts from the impulse cannon streaked across the heavens. One impacted the core and there was a blinding flash that took a few moments to clear from the screen. Then the shockwave hit the *Thassis* itself, causing the command deck to quiver slightly despite its shielding. The effect on the Daleks' assault ships was devastating. They had almost literally been atomised. The explosion of the core had obliterated the ships and their crew, leaving nothing larger than a Dalek dome floating in space.

'Confirm enemy numberss,' he said, sitting back in his command chair.

'The Dalekss have only two shhipss remaining, Grand Marshal,' replied a warrior. 'A command ssaucer and one asssssault shhip.'

'We sstill have three,' another added. 'Oursselves and two desstroyerss.'

Skaldak smiled in the semi-darkness. He dressed like his warriors. He eschewed the jewelled helmets and sleeker, more flexible armour worn by some Ice Lords. It might have been more comfortable, but the protection it afforded was meagre. No good for actual combat. And Skaldak lived for combat.

Like his warriors, his armour was sturdy: a solid main body with flexible leg and arm pieces; a sonic blaster mounted on his forearm; and all in dark green colour, and covered in thick scales to mimic their reptilian nature. Even the helmet had this pattern and housed a heads-up display unit in its red eyepieces. The augmented reality feed was telling him everything about the warriors he could see on the command deck: vital signs, combat performance, military history, and mental health. Every one of them was functioning at nothing less than 82 per cent.

'I wishh to sspeak to my daughter,' Skaldak said.

'Connecting to the desstroyer *Hathaar*,' the communications warrior confirmed.

The image of a true Warrior of the Ice appeared on the round screen, filling it. She was magnificent. Marginally more slender than her male counterparts, Iclar had also taken to wearing the breastplate of an Ice Lady – as was befitting her station. This might have upset her father, but much to Skaldak's delight she had ordered the Chief Armourer to enhance its inadequate combat protection and had even added a few modifications of her own devising. She wore at her waist the ceremonial sword of a ship's commander and a lavender cloak billowed behind her as she turned.

'Father!' she smiled. 'We have the sstrategic advantage now.'

'We do,' he replied. 'And we musst usse it well, for the Dalekss are a cunning and powerful adverssary.'

She inclined her head. 'Of coursse, Grand Marshal.'

Skaldak laughed. Of course it was right she should address him by his rank, but it sounded odd. He never thought to use hers. To him, she would always be his *shsurrin*: his little lady.

'What iss your plan?' she asked, still beaming at her father.

The warriors on the command deck of the *Thassis* couldn't help but smile too. Of course, they concealed it for none wanted to incur their Grand Marshal's wrath. What they did not know was that he would never reprimand them for it. After all, if Martians could not recognise familial bonds and celebrate them, how were they better than the evil cones of hatred they were fighting?

'We musst not losse our hard-won numerical advantage,' Skaldak began. 'We musst act cautioussly now. Rashh action that appearss brave in the moment would only sserve to light the way to our certain doom.'

'You are quite the poet, when the fancy takess you, Father.'

Skaldak laughed again. 'You know I am fond of the ssongss of the old time,' he said.

Just then, an alarm sounded, lyrical but urgent.

'Unknown Dalek activity,' reported a warrior.

'We will sspeak later,' Iclar said. She cut the communications; she knew an emergency when she heard it.

'What do you mean, "unknown"?' Skaldak said. 'What are they doing? Shhow me!'

The screen changed to show the Dalek command saucer. It was still a long way off, way outside effective weapons range, but strange beams were coming from the domes on its underside: faint and greenish-white, almost like searchlights. They were illuminating the hull of both the *Hathaar* and the other destroyer, the *Azax*.

'The beamss are alsso on our shhip, Grand Marshal.'

'What iss their effect?' Skaldak was leaning forward now, urgent. He didn't like the unknown. And anything unknown to do with the Daleks meant trouble. They were as devious as they were ruthless, and if they could gain an advantage by a dishonourable act, they wouldn't think twice.

'It iss unkn ...'

'Yess, yess, yessss,' Skaldak hissed. 'Unknown. I know.' He turned round to the science station. 'I am expecting an analyssiss from you.'

The Scientific Officer was peering at his screen. 'The wavelength iss unusual,' he said. 'It iss not a sscan.' Now he turned. 'I think it iss an attempt to hack our ssysstemss, Grand Marshal.'

'Move uss out of range. Now!' shouted Skaldak. 'Relay thiss information to the fleet. I want additional perssonnel on cyberattack duty. Nothing getss through. Nothing!'

The Martian ships hastened away from the Dalek saucer, heading toward the system's twin stars. As they did so, the *Azax* started to veer off course. Its engines spluttered for a moment, and then died. As the other two ships kept moving, it was left behind. Clearly the cyber-attack on the destroyer's systems had been successful.

Seeing this, Skaldak ordered his own ship about, but it was too late. The last Dalek assault ship had nipped in behind them, strafing the unprotected *Azax* with laser fire, cutting off one of the nacelles and leaving deep scars on the hull of the stricken craft.

It may have crippled the Martian vehicle, but the Dalek assault ship was now itself within firing range of the *Thassis*.

'Open fire!' Skaldak ordered. 'All weaponss!'

Missiles, sonic cannon fire and impulse lasers raked across the starry void, inflicting multiple impacts on the Dalek ship. But instead of limping away, the small round craft accelerated towards the listing bulk of the Martian destroyer. Daleks were spilling from the access ports – abandoning ship!

Skaldak took a deep intake of breath as he watched it smashing into the deepest scar on the Azax's outer skin. A moment later an explosion blossomed in hues of orange and yellow, slitting the destroyer in two.

'Target individual Dalekss,' he said flatly. 'Make ssure none ssurvive.'

As the weapons crew hunted for the live Daleks hiding amongst the wreckage of the destroyer, Skaldak ordered a report from his other departments. The Scientific Officer confirmed that all three of the Martian ships had been affected by the Dalek cyber-attack. This had weakened their firewalls and allowed the enemy to implant a computer virus in all three warships. As the nearest one to the Dalek saucer, it had been the *Azax* that had fallen first. However, due to Skaldak's quick thinking this had allowed the other scientific and computer crews to analyse the virus and combat it.

'I feel ass if you are about to give me bad newss,' Skaldak said.

The Scientific Officer bowed his head. 'Yess, Grand Marshal.'
'Well?'

'Before it wass taken offline, the Dalek viruss did manage to damage the control functionss of hyper-drive and shhields on both the *Thassis* and the *Hathaar*.'

Skaldak was on his feet. 'Iclar?'

'We sstill have life-ssupport, communicationss, ssub-light enginess and shhort-range weaponss,' the Officer concluded. 'We both do. Your daughter is ssafe, Grand Marshal.'

'It iss well that it iss sso ...' growled the old warrior. He had terrible visions of what lengths he would go to if the Daleks harmed his beloved offspring. He was certain it would not end well for either side. Then it hit him. 'We only have shhort-range weaponss?'

The Scientific Officer confirmed this was so and Skaldak smashed one of his armoured green fists into the palm of his other hand. 'Then we are sssand-rats in a rock fissssure!' If the Daleks ships could move faster and had longer-range weapons, there was little the Martians could do to defend themselves. 'We musst concentrate on one thing: Dalek firepower musst be nullified.'

'We have never been able to do that in the passst, Grand Marshal,' the Scientific Officer said.

'Obligation iss the parent of development,' Skaldak said. 'You will find a way. I am certain. But it will take time. We need to give oursselves what advantage we can.' He gazed at the viewscreen. It showed the binary stars looking ever larger as they travelled towards them. 'And they may be the answer,' he said pointing at the viewer.

He explained that they could use the gravity fields of the double stars as a means of escaping the Daleks. However fast the remaining command saucer could go, the Martians would be able to outpace them and escape using the suns as a slingshot.

Skaldak grinned. 'The Dalekss may have clipped our wingss,' he said. 'But we shhall sstill fly!'

He quickly relayed his plan to Iclar. As he did so, he felt himself experiencing anxiety. He tried to repress it, but the sensation was alien to him; it was the first time in his adult life that he had such a feeling.

'You have no shhieldss,' he said. 'The danger of ssolar proximity is acute. If our coursse putss uss too closse to the twin sstarss, the radiation levelss will fry everyone aboard.'

It would require precision, and Skaldak would not normally have hesitated in pursuing the plan. But his daughter, Iclar, had given him pause for thought. She nodded. 'I know, Father.' She was calm, and he felt pride swell within him, vanquishing the nerves.

'That iss why we are making the mosst accurate calculationss we can before we reach the binary ssunss,' she assured him, smiling. 'I can do thiss, Father,' she said. 'Becausse I am your daughter.'

'You are your own being,' Skaldak replied. 'And I am more proud of you than anything in my entire life.'

A moment of silence passed and it seemed as if there was no one else on either ship as they stared at one another.

'Sso be it!' Skaldak said triumphantly. 'Let us vanquishh the Dalekss and return home heroess!'

He turned then to address the command deck, sending his words ship-wide through the address system. 'I did not vanquishh the Phoboss Heressy to have my fleet torn apart by metal coness of hate!' He pointed to the communications officer. 'Make ssure the Dalekss can hear thissss . . .'

The Warrior at comms altered the array and then nodded to the Grand Marshal.

'Hear me, Daleks. Harm one of uss and you harm uss all. By the moonss, this I sswear.'

A grating voice came back in reply. 'Oaths-mean-nothing. Daleks-conquer-and-destroy. You-will-be-exterminated! This-is-your-fate.'

'We shhall ssee!' Skaldak gestured to cut the signal.

He knew the Daleks would be scheming to counter the Martian plan. He also knew that they would not leave their ship to try and board the *Thassis*. They could not simply leave their ships and fly over. They were susceptible to sonic weaponry – as Skaldak had proved when they tried to flee their earlier kamikaze attack.

The two Martian ships were now closing on the twin stars of Samox and Delox. Although they were described as twins, Samox was redder and smaller than its bigger sister, Delox. But size did not count here. It was density. And the denser of the two was Samox. It was that star they needed to give them the biggest boost, catapulting them to near light speeds and allowing them to escape the Daleks and head back to Martian space where the lone saucer dare not follow.

'Grand Marshal, we believe we have a plan.'

Both science and weapons teams had been working together. They believed they could modify the ship's deflector array to make a macrotransmission, aimed at the Dalek ship. Using it in such a way would burn out the Martian device but, if they used the correct wavelength filter, the effect would be to disable all Dalek weaponry on the saucer's hull.

Skaldak smiled. 'You have done well,' he said to the two warriors.

'There are a number of variablesss that we cannot guarantee,' replied the more senior officer.

'Do it.'

The officers saluted and moved away to take up position at their stations.

'Macrotranssmissssion of K-filter wavelength in five, four, three ...'

Skaldak watched the screen as the huge dish on the ship's hull sent a targeted pulse at the Dalek saucer. It had no visible effect, but Skaldak wanted to test the outcome. He ordered his ship to slow. A pilot questioned whether he wished the *Hathaar* to do the same.

'No, let my daughter fly,' he said. 'I want to ssee how tooth-lessss these Dalekss have become.'

Sure enough, as the saucer closed to weapons range they did not fire.

'Ha! They are dissarmed!'

Skaldak was tempted to turn on the Daleks then and there, but he knew how many Daleks the ship contained. They would send patrol ships or hoverbouts. Too many for the reduced armaments his ship now had. But at least they could flee in safety.

With Iclar's ship already ahead of his, Skaldak ordered her to go first. She would need to command her ship carefully: keeping the exact distance from the star so as not to become overwhelmed by radiation, but close enough to maximise the effect of the stellar gravity well on the ship's velocity.

As the *Hathaar* went into solar orbit, it accelerated away from Skaldak's battlecruiser. This was to be expected. It would take them only a few minutes to circle the sun, picking up speed exponentially until they shot from the star like a well-aimed bolt from a bow.

'Grand Marshal!' the Science Officer squealed.

'What?' Skaldak did not like the sound of this.

'The Dalekss, they have been transsmitting!'

'Transsmitting what?'

'Falsse readingss. To the *Hathaar*.'

'Get Iclar! Now!' he bellowed, rising from his seat to approach the screen.

The face of Skaldak's daughter filled the huge viewscreen. She looked sullen.

'We have been fooled,' she said. 'I have failed you.'

Skaldak stumbled forward. 'Never,' he said. 'Correct your coursse!'

She shook her head and Skaldak felt his stomach drop as he saw a tear on his daughter's cheek. 'We cannot,' she said. 'They have transsmitted falsse readingss to our array. We are too closse to the ssun. Our orbit of Ssamox will ... decay. There iss ... nothing ...'

She could not finish the sentence and Skaldak reached out a hand to her image on the screen. 'Iclar. My *shsurrin* ...'

She was crying now. Fear and loss of pride filled her. Skaldak felt every emotion with her.

'Tractor beamsss!' he roared. Despite the technicians' claims that they would be no use, they tried anyway. Iclar begged him to stop; not to come too close. If the readings from her ship had been tampered with, then so could Skaldak's be.

'I'm ssorry, father,' Iclar said.

'Clear the command deck,' Skaldak said quietly.

Without a murmur, the warriors left their stations, silently processing through the doors, which then closed behind them.

'Just uss now, *shsurrin*,' Skaldak allowed himself to feel the wave of emotion and let it wash over him. As the tears fell form his own eyes, he managed to speak 'Let uss ssing the old ssongss together, Iclar. My ssweet, ssssweet girl.'

And that is what they did. As they had done when she was little and he had held her in his arms. The songs of the old time, her favourites. The songs of the red snow ...

✻

The Warriors trooped back onto the command deck to find the Grand Marshal slumped in his chair and the screen showing just static. He looked up as the senior Deck Officer approached him.

'Make it known to the crew,' Skaldak said. 'I do not intend to allow the Dalekss to ssurvive thiss. Thosse who do not wishh to sstand with me can usse the lifepodss to leave.'

The Deck Officer saluted. 'I sspeak for the entire crew, Grand Marshal. We are all with you.'

Skaldak closed his eyes. 'Thank you,' he said. Then his eyes snapped open and he gritted his teeth. 'Then let uss begin.'

He urgently issued several snap commands, telling the pilots and navigators his plan. They would not slingshot away using the star's gravity. This was what the Daleks expected – indeed hoped – they would do. As it was entirely possible they would try to fool their instruments and take them into the sun's radiation aura, as they had the *Hathaar*, the Martian strategy would be to make the Daleks think they were doing this while actually performing a different manoeuvre.

'We will be further out from the sstar,' Skaldak explained. 'Thiss will appear ass caution to the Dalekss. In fact it iss becausse we do not wishh to esscape. We wishh to attack!'

The *Thassis* fell into its solar orbit, and the ship began to move faster with every second. Skaldak gripped his command chair and ordered the saucer to be shown on the screen. He snarled when he saw it rotating slowly in space, smugly, as if nothing could touch it.

'Esscape velocity achieved,' called one of the pilots.

'Hold,' ordered Skaldak. 'I want ramming sspeed! All Warriorss prepare for boarding!'

'Grand Marshal, if we ram them we will ssimply be thrown off their hull,' the science officer said. 'We won't be able to board.'

'We will if we manoeuvre the nacelless to act ass grappling hooksss!' Skaldak said. He sounded slightly crazed now and every Warrior knew he would taste blood that day, be it his own or the enemy's.

'Ramming sspeed,' confirmed the pilot.

'Now!' Skaldak shouted and the battlecruiser lurched from the solar gravity well, hurtling towards the Dalek command ship at terrifying speed. Skaldak watched the screen unblinkingly as the saucer swelled in his sights. 'All Warriorss prepare for boarding on the main assssault deck! And set autodestruct at ten minutess.' Then the Grand Marshal stood and walked from his chair for the last time.

❋

On the bridge of the command saucer, a Gold Dalek was being fed new streams of information by the second. Around it the dark – almost black – shapes of the other Daleks glided to and fro, making adjustments, fine-tuning the engines, trying to bring the external weapons arrays back online. When the battlecruiser suddenly appeared from the far side of the star, Samox, it was a totally unexpected scenario, and the battle computers struggled to counteract it.

As it was, the Gold Dalek had no time to issue a command to retreat or to avoid the oncoming Martian ship. The idea that the Ice Warriors would ram them had never been contemplated. This was something the Gold Dalek was determined to rectify upon his return to Skaro. As the two ships collided, many Daleks went careering across the deck, smashing into computer banks or bulkheads and sustaining damage.

'Hull-breach. Levels-nine-to-seventeen,' intoned a deep voiced Dalek.

'Intruder-alert!' screeched another. 'Aliens-entering-air-locks: nine-delta, thirteen-lamda, sixteen-epsilon.'

'All-Daleks-to-defensive-positions,' ordered the Gold Dalek. Its voice was pitched slightly higher than the others. 'Defend! Defend!'

All over the ship, Daleks broke off from their secondary jobs to converge on the section where the Ice Warriors had entered.

At the airlock, it was carnage. As Skaldak had suspected, the Daleks had not been prepared for such an unorthodox move. His Warriors had taken the Daleks already stationed there by surprise and were able to establish a bridgehead between the two craft. There were two entrances that gave onto the airlock entrance – both round and studded with a circular Dalek design. As the metal monsters poured through, so the Ice Warriors tore into them, the sonic blasters fitted to their forearms vibrating the Dalekanium skins and exploding the mutants housed within.

Skaldak was part of the vanguard in this battle, killing Daleks to his left and right, ploughing forward, taking more of the ship. Naturally the Daleks were fighting back hard, their battle cries of '*Ex-ter-min-ate*' ringing throughout the saucer. Officers and Warriors fell as Dalek gun sticks bathed them in their negative radiation.

At one point, the Daleks withdrew and tried to use one of their chemical weapons on the Martians, but Skaldak was too canny for that. The moment the Daleks stopped trying to kill, the Ice Lord knew something wasn't right and issued an order to all his Warriors to engage their faceplates. This was a special section of the Martian helmet that closed across the open mouth section, acting as both a space helmet and a respirator.

The Warriors penetrating the other airlocks lacked his battle experience and did not think to do this, which cost them dearly. One of the assault forces had been all-but wiped out. This allowed the Daleks to counterattack and board the Martian battlecruiser.

'Penetrating-enemy-ship,' reported one of the grey Daleks, his voice transmitted to the bridge of the saucer.

'Find-the-command-deck,' ordered the Gold Dalek. 'Exterminate-all-resistance.'

'I-obey!'

But there was no resistance. All the Martians had left to board the Dalek ship or to run interference as Skaldak called it. This involved selected units taking the mobile sonic cannons from the hold and floating them down to the saucer, magnetising the weapons to the Dalek hull and opening fire on any target that looked crucial: power nodes, communications relays and the like. The Gold Dalek had already dispatched hoverbout units to deal with them.

When the Daleks reached the Ice Warrior command deck, they found a large countdown on the viewscreen. The slightly panicked squad leader reported back.

'Enemy-have-activated-cruiser-self-destruct! We-must-withdraw. Withdraw!'

By now, Skaldak had led his force through the core section of the saucer, directly beneath the bridge, which was housed in the dome on the upper surface. It was then that the *Thassis* exploded, taking a huge wedge of the saucer with it. The Dalek ship now hung in space like a round delicacy that had been bitten through by a hungry predator.

With the Dalek ship now falling into the twin stars, too, Skaldak led his Warriors to the bridge. They massacred all the enemies they found in the corridors. For every score of Daleks they killed, one Warrior was lost. Even with those odds, it was an uneven battle and there always seemed to be more Daleks, flooding in from every corridor, replacing those that had already fallen.

Finally, though, Skaldak and his troops reached the heart of the ship. They blew up the two Dalek guards stationed either side of the arched entrance and marched calmly onto the bridge. The Gold Dalek turned to face them as they entered. Two other dark grey Daleks opened fire on Skaldak's two flanking warriors. The four enemies killed one another, leaving just the two leaders.

'You-have-not-won,' the Gold Dalek said, exaggerating every syllable, satisfaction evident in its voice despite the electronic filter.

'Win?' Skaldak strutted forward. 'Thiss iss not about uss winning!'

'The-ship-is-out-of-control. Soon-we-will-enter-the-radiation-field-of-the-star.'

Skaldak came right up to the Dalek's eyestalk. 'It iss about *you* losssing!'

'Your-statement-is-illogical,' the Gold Dalek said. 'We-will-escape-using-temporal-technology-beyond-the-comprehension-of-Ice-Warriors.'

'Whatever you call uss, we won't let you esscape!'

'You-have-no-choice.' The Gold Dalek glided away. Its arrogance in the face of a Martian Ice Lord warrior was staggering.

Skaldak growled. 'You murdered my daughter. Killed her right before my eyess. Thiss will mean nothing to you, I know. But you underesstimate uss, Dalek. We know about your bridge dessignss!' Still the Dalek ignored him. 'We know there iss a masster control for maximissing Dalekanium power feedss!'

Now the Gold Dalek swung back to face him, its gun stick raised. 'Ext—'

But it was too late. Skaldak was already firing his own weapon. The Gold Dalek froze before beginning to vibrate, shaking from side to side as smoke poured from the vents above its weapon and manipulator arm. Finally its dome exploded and it lay still.

Skaldak came across the bridge and kicked the shell of the golden Dalek across the floor. Then he moved to the mechanism

that controlled the Dalekanium power feeds. He could feel the temperature rising. They must be falling into the sun.

With a grimace and kiss of his fist in honour of Iclar, he turned them to maximum. Although every Martian had fallen by this point, there were a still a large number of Daleks throughout the ship. But each one now exploded as the power they fed on was overloaded.

Now there was no one else on the entire ship. The deck started tilting as the gyroscopic dampeners failed. Skaldak stood, watching the Dalek screen and on it the blazing surface of Samox. He would be happy to die the same way as his daughter. It was fitting.

As the Grand Marshal prepared for death, a message flashed on the screen informing him that the Time transmitter was prepared. A prompt followed, asking for space time coordinates.

Skaldak looked around at the bridge. The raised platform for the Gold Dalek, the computer banks and control stations. The rounded door leading from it and to the left, a smaller, sealed door. A bright lift was coming from underneath it. Escape, the Dalek had said, using temporal technology. But the Dalek had been right: Skaldak had no idea how to operate it. He turned back to the message on the screen. It was now flashing.

The Grand Marshal found some controls beside the door and punched randomly at the keypad. A string of numbers and letters appeared on the main screen. Skaldak swayed slightly now, the heat was so intense he could barely concentrate. The door opened and Skaldak stepped inside.

He would live. For now. For her.

He just hoped that wherever this thing was sending him it was cold there . . .

# THE MULTI-FACETED WAR

Skellis had been there when her friend died. She had seen the monster take Gith's head, and there had been nothing she could do about it. The planet Lerna was a damp world of marshes and muddy rivers that were prone to tidal flooding. Poisonous gasses belched from the mudflats in great bubbles that burst to free the acrid dirty brown mists. The two of them were simple soldiers, drafted in the war with the Great Vampires.

They had only met on Military Training Squad at a barracks outside Arcadia. They'd been at the Academy at separate times and came from different houses. They even lived on opposite sides of the world from each other. But they had become fast friends. They looked out for each other, had each other's back.

Everyone knew the war against the Vampires was dragging on – an ever-burgeoning conflict. For every Vampire nest they destroyed, two seemed to spring up in its stead. The Public Register Video only covered the battles and skirmishes in light detail. It had once been headline news. Soldiers returned to Gallifrey traumatised by what they had experienced – what they had seen and done – but no one at home seemed to care.

Those who were lucky enough to stay on Gallifrey pretended the war wasn't happening, or at least wasn't their problem. The academics buried their heads in their books, while the politicians buried their heads in the sand. Only a very few of the lower-ranking Time Lords protested that the war had to stop; that veterans needed to be better cared for upon their return.

With Rassilon away, leading from the front as he always did, a power vacuum had formed. The High Council became a pantheon of the inadequate and self-serving. Naturally, whenever the President returned from the war he was given a hero's welcome – parades, banquets – but he was never given a true picture of the situation or the sentiment of the Gallifreyan people.

Perhaps Rassilon *was* aware of the unrest and the political lethargy. Skellis didn't know, but it might have explained why he never stayed long in the Capitol, why he rushed off again as soon as he could. It looked like heroism and bravery but it might just as easily have been an unwillingness to face facts.

Skellis and Gith had been posted to Lerna with the rest of their battalion to take the planet from a nest of Vampires, ruled over by a Great One. It was difficult. The locals were broad-footed and well versed at 'bog-hopping', as they called it. They had snout-like noses and dug around in the weed beds, searching for their diet of simple roots and grasses.

The Lernans were sentient but undeveloped. They lived in scattered simple villages of bamboo. Their grass huts were elevated off the damp surface and meant they were not swept away by the tidal floods that occurred whenever one of the planet's three moons circled too close. Their simplicity made them an easy target for the Vampires.

The Time Lord squad knew that a Great One had made its nest on the driest part of the planet, in a place called the Long Kahn Hills. Of course a huge proportion of the hog-like

Lernans had been bitten and turned into the Great One's servants. They ruled the plant and brought sacrifices to the Hilltop shrines with their feeding pipes that took the slaughtered creatures' blood down into the Vampire's lair.

While it was true that the Long Kahn Hills represented high ground, militarily the Gallifreyan troops were better armed and better organised. Skellis and Gith – like the rest of their unit – believed themselves to be the better fighters, too. This would be an easy victory. And so it might have proved, had not the Vampires brought in help.

It was not a Vampire – not a Great One – that had beheaded Gith. It was a Macra – a crab-like being that fed on the poisonous gasses the planet offered up in bountiful supply. How the creatures had been brought there, no one knew. They had only discovered the alliance when they had killed the Vampires and villagers protecting the hills and breached the lair.

The Macra had made tunnels that led from the lair all the way out to the marshes. This also explained why an unusually high number of troops were going missing. Senior officers and those minor politicians on the ground blamed desertion or the sinking sand that peppered the landscape.

Gith and Skellis had been sent down one of the tunnels to flush out the Macra. The memories of that battle still kept Skellis awake at night. She tried not to think of them, to bury the images, but they came unbidden – especially at night.

They had crawled along the tunnel, but it did not go straight out into the marshes, it curved round and sloped downwards, taking them lower into the Vampire's lair. They found nothing in the tunnel itself. It was only when the burrow opened up into a large chamber that they found the enemy.

*

'General?'

Skellis woke from the dream of his former regeneration. An orderly was standing in the doorway, a dark figure against the light. Skellis mumbled. He could feel he had been sweating; the sheets were slightly damp and his skin was clammy.

'You wanted waking early, sir.'

Skellis nodded. 'Thank you,' he said.

'Breakfast in your ready room, sir,' the orderly added and then left, shutting the door once again.

General Skellis closed his eyes. The memories of that day were truly etched on his subconscious. But then, if they had not been, he would not be waking to a ceremony that might see the end of the Vampires once and for all.

Skellis took a sonic shower and dressed quickly in the red and gold uniform that marked him as a General. How far he had come since those days as a woman in the trenches.

After his breakfast, Skellis was collected by air car and taken to the secret facility out on the Argolid plain. The Time Lords had set up facility on the hollow world of Phonida because it was suitably removed from the fighting, but still far from Gallifrey.

After his service on Lerna, Skellis had returned to Gallifrey and gone back to the Academy. He had been determined that Gith's death – and those of so many other of his fellow soldiers – would not be in vain. He kept a close eye on Rassilon's military campaign, but it was not going well. No matter how many fronts they fought on or how successful their operations were, the Time Lords never seemed to be able to eliminate the Vampire scourge from the galaxy.

By that stage of the war, even Rassilon himself was battle weary and it seemed to Skellis that everyone involved in the planning of the war had fallen back on tired strategies that only kept the beast at bay; it never dealt it the killing blow.

After what Skellis had witnessed in the lair on Lerna, he had glimpsed the solution to the problem. He had worked hard on his ideas, first in theoretical study at the Academy and now at the military's 'Golden Sword' facility on Phonida.

It had taken Skellis almost twenty years to get there and, although some frowned on his experiments, they saw that he was the most driven of all the scientists there. Eventually Rassilon himself came to hear of his work.

He studied Vampires and their deaths and, ironically, for that he needed 'live' subjects. A special commando unit was set up with the sole purpose of capturing Vampires alive. At this point, no one imagined they could ever capture a Great One for experimentation. None had ever been captured. They either fled or died; their remains placed in dispersal chambers to ensure they could never be brought back to life.

Then the commandos started to capture victims. One or two at first, but over the years more than a hundred were brought to the Golden Sword – to Skellis himself. By that stage, he had cast off the arcane titles of academia and embraced the military once more. But such an important contributor to the Time Lord war against the Vampires could not be a lowly trooper. Even Commander seemed beneath him. Instead he was given the rank of General and proudly had his armour adorned with the badge of honour that marked his campaigns across Amymone, Iolaus, Bashmu, Alluttu – and yes, Lerna.

Back then, though, Skellis was still clad in simple black and white robes. He had just finished setting up the dispersal chamber when the first Vampire POW was captured. It was a female Saturnyne – an amphibious creature that had been caught up in the crossfire and infected along with its entire species.

Unlike most Vampires, her eyes were not dark and sunken. Its former dark skin was however now pale blue and it certainly had the characteristic fangs. To weaken the subject, she had been kept in constant artificial sunlight and dosed with an allyl methyl sulphide. She did look listless when two guards brought her in.

The lab had been set up to exact specifications. It was a circular chamber, two storeys high, with an array of computers and monitoring equipment around the walls alongside extraction and filtration mechanisms. All these were linked to a molecular dispersal chamber that stood at the centre of the lab.

Time Lords had long used this process to execute those rare individuals who had tried to bring Gallifrey to its knees, to usurp their power or in some other way threaten the wellbeing of Time Lord society by their continued existence alone. The chamber was sealed, and powerful particle disseminators were used to break up the subject's body into components no bigger than molecules. These were then dispersed across time and space using Time Lord temporal engineering. In this way it was ensured that the body and consciousness of the target could not be retrieved, reformed or in any other way brought back to life.

This particular dispersal chamber had been modified. It did not use the temporal aspects that the ones used on the Vampires did. Instead, the molecules were collected from the chamber by extraction and then filtered into specially sealed chambers from which they could not escape. Here they would be tested and analysed.

As the Saturnyne test subject was moved forward at gunpoint, it turned and, in its drugged state, fell to its knees before Skellis.

'Please,' it begged him. 'Help me.'

Skellis froze. It was as if the Vampire had read his mind. Perhaps it had – for they were known to possess psychic abilities. Whether a coincidence or not, it had used exactly the same words his friend had used all those years – and a regeneration – ago when Gith had been killed by the Macra.

Although he had seen action on many planets, Skellis was not used to being in a position of total power over a living thing. He chided himself. This was no living thing. It was dead. The Vampirism was like a parasitic disease that killed the host and simply used its body. He shook his head.

'Get it up,' he said. 'Put it in the chamber.'

As the Vampire was dragged to its feet, it gave a soul-wrenching wail. Skellis had to turn away. He climbed the ladder to a walkway that ran around the second level of the lab. He walked round to an airlock door and moved through to the control room. Here a reinforced window gave onto the lab below and monitors crowded a control panel that operated the dispersal chamber itself.

Skellis watched as the guards half-dropped, half-threw the subject into the round chamber. He pressed a button and a bright pink cover came down, sealing the Saturnyne inside. Then he leaned forward and spoke into a microphone. His voice cracked and he had to clear his throat before trying again,

'Clear the laboratory,' he said. 'Quarantine lockdown procedures.'

The two guards saluted and left the lab via the lower airlock. Skellis hesitated. His hypothesis. It all came down to this. Right or wrong. He would know very soon.

Behind him, the control room began to fill with junior researchers and even the guards. Everyone on the base had heard about the importance of the work even if they did not know the details of it. Skellis moved his hand across the panel, his index finger poised above the button that would kill the subject. He imagined he could hear it screaming but that was impossible: the chamber was sealed and so was the lab. He closed his eyes and slowly activated the dispersal system.

Afterwards they applauded him. Skellis did not feel like accepting plaudits so he went to the one place he was bound to be alone. At that stage, he lived in cramped quarters on the facility, but it wasn't there. It was outside. There was an emergency exit crawlspace that led up to a door. This opened onto the desert plains of the Argolid expanse.

There was nothing living for a thousand miles in any direction. No water flowed here and no dust blew up in the winds that constantly whipped the solid stone ground. The wind made little noise for there was nothing for it to vibrate or move, and so it was as close to silence as you could get without entering a vacuum.

Skellis leant back against the low wall and exhaled deeply. Then inhaled. Each breath felt almost painful, but it was good to get the fresh air of Phonida into his lungs after the constant recycled atmosphere of the Golden Sword facility.

He was right. The way in which the Time Lords had been going about the war was completely flawed. Tens of thousands of Time Lords had died; millions of regenerations had been given. And it all counted for nothing because of a flaw no one thought was there, let alone thought to look for.

The data collected from the filtration chambers proved that by dispersing the Vampires' molecules the Time Lords had actually spread the menace of the Vampire infection exponentially across time and space. They needed to find a different way of killing them.

Skellis cried then, for his friend's death had been worthless after all.

Naturally, the data would have to be checked, the experiment replicated – probably many times over with different species.

Eventually, they would need to test it on a Great One, but this was the first step on the journey to true victory. And, of course, Rassilon would have to be told.

✳

Rassilon stood on the deck of the lead Bowship. It was an elegant craft with curved wings. These swept back from a blunt nose in which was housed a sharpened length of steel, pointed at the end – almost like a huge sword. The bolt itself was the same length as the main part of the ship. The Time Lord President was a man reborn – quite literally, as he had recently regenerated. In this form, he was strong and athletic, if older and with a full beard. He was pleased with his new appearance. It suited the triumphant leader returned from battle very well.

His fleet was returning from the war victorious; bloodied but the eventual winners. He and his forces had driven the Vampire blight from the galaxy for good. Of course, there would always be vampire-type creatures, he suspected. The old dispersal chambers had seen to that. Yes. But the Great Ones. They were the ones that mattered. They had been wiped out.

It had taken almost a hundred years since Rassilon had first been told of the experiment on Phonida. New weapons had been needed and they took time to build. Then they had needed to find the Vampires and flush them out. And they had spread far and wide.

Information on enemy movements had become key. That was when the Celestial Intelligence Agency had been set up. Agents were recruited covertly from the Academies and trained in every aspect of espionage and the gathering of data. The network of Gallifreyan spies was huge now and it would be difficult to dismantle it. But that was a problem for another day.

Rassilon smiled as he recalled the first time they had forced a Great One from its nest and out into space. He couldn't even recall what the planet had been called. It made little difference now, as the planet no longer existed. But the Vampire had tried to flee. It was fast, but the Bowships were faster. They caught up with the creature easily and, despite its laughable attempt to mesmerise the entire fleet, it had been cornered.

He was on board the lead ship when it approached the being. The Great One was a huge humanoid beast with sickly-looking grey-green skin and slightly pointed ears. Beady black eyes stared unfeelingly at the Gallifreyan vessel as it moved in for the kill. Rassilon gave every command, positioning the front of the ship just so. The weapon it was armed with was crude. It had no guidance system. Once fired, it only needed to strike home accurately. So Rassilon had manoeuvred the ship carefully. The Great One had no idea what was happening. It could not have known the Time Lords now knew how to kill it in one move.

It was still staring – almost straight at Rassilon – when the Bowship shot its bolt. The huge, iron stake sailed across the silent void and struck the Great One exactly where its heart was. There was just time for it to open its mouth in a silent scream before it crumbled away to nothingness. Using the equipment developed and refined in the Golden Sword facility, the Bowships had scanned a square astronomical unit for any trace of the Vampire. There was none.

The Great Ones soon became aware of the new weapon being used against them. They soon became more fearful of the Time Lords – the whole cosmos did. As they became more terrified, the Vampires became more desperate and far more ruthless. They thought nothing of using entire races as conscious shields against the Gallifreyans. But Rassilon knew that the price paid would never be too high to rid the universe of the Vampires. He loathed them with a pure, unsullied hate. In some cases it blinded him to things: what others called atrocities.

As the Bowships fulfilled their task in space, the Gallifreyan ground forces were now able to truly take the battle to those the Vampires had possessed. All thanks to the Skellis Gun. Named after its inventor, the weapon was multi-barrelled, firing four, eight or even twenty elongated metal shafts simultaneously, depending on whether the gun was handheld or mounted. What they did was ensure that when soldiers came across a Vampire, they could be assured of a kill as long as they aimed at the chest. Triumph followed triumph, and fewer soldiers were required because fewer were dying.

As Rassilon sped home to Gallifrey, he knew that from then on everyone would know how to kill a Vampire: use a simple weapon to penetrate the creature's body and pierce its heart. He would make sure that every one of the new time ships he planned would have such information in its systems.

It would also carry an instruction, for Rassilon was not totally victorious. He had let the King Vampire escape. It was a tactical error, all due to hubris. He had had the chance to destroy the King Vampire or corner four of the Great Ones. He chose the latter because he thought it would strike fear into the King Vampire to know that he was the last of his species and that the whole Bowfleet was now coming from him. The battle with the other Vampires had given their monarch the chance to escape. This had meant that the 'war' had not ended because all the troops and all the CIA operatives and all the Bowships were engaged in the hunt for it.

After decades of searching and new time-space scanner development, Rassilon was at last convinced the King Vampire had disappeared; either it had died or it had fled somewhere beyond the reach of the Time Lords. Whichever the case, it was pointless to continue the search, so Rassilon had declared final victory and given the longed-for order that all forces should return home.

The war was over. All thanks to one man.

Of course, most historians would say that one man was he, Rassilon, President of the Time Lords, defender of Gallifrey. And he was happy for that to be the acknowledged version of events. Deep down, though, he knew the credit belonged to Skellis. He was a genius. Of that there could be no doubt. Without him, the Time Lords might even have succumbed to the Vampires themselves.

General Skellis now lived in splendour in Arcadia. He had even become friends with Rassilon, and they dined whenever the President retuned to Gallifrey. Of course, the breakthrough with the dispersal chamber and the knowledge it was spreading the Vampire curse rather than destroying it was well documented – even if it wasn't public knowledge. But in all the hundreds of years the two of them had now known each other, Skellis had never told Rassilon how he discovered the Vampire's fatal weakness.

*

Gith had gone first. She was like that. It was not bravado. Not as far as Skellis was concerned. It was a confidence that was needed to get the job done: a soldier's self-assurance. Skellis had to admit she looked up to Gith. There was no way she would have gone in first. No way.

Gith had entered the chamber and checked the corners with the torch mounted on her staser rifle – just as they had been taught on Squad. She gave a curt nod, and Skellis clambered through the tunnel exit herself, sweeping her weapon ahead as she did, covering Gith's flanks and rear. Then she moved past her, shining her own flashlight further into the gloom. She could see a ledge ahead of her about 60 metres. Her torch did not reach that far. The reason she could see it was because of a flickering light from beneath the ledge that cast odd shadows on the wall.

'Do you see that?' she hissed to Gith. As she turned to see if her partner had heard, she saw the thing on the ceiling above them. A huge, black crab: a Macra. It was already reaching down to Gith with one vast pincered claw.

Skellis opened fire and time seemed to slow, so that what must have taken milliseconds seemed to take a minute. Her staser bolts raked the ceiling and hit the Macra across its armoured exoskeleton. These hardly seemed to affect the monster at all. Its claw was already around Gith's neck. She was staring, terrified up at the beast, her face illuminated by the flash-flash-flash of staser fire from Skellis's rifle.

Gith looked back at her sister in arms. 'Please,' she said. 'Help me.'

With sickening slowness, the Macra squeezed its pincers together and Gith stiffened in its grip. Skellis was still firing and screaming now, although her ears were so full of her own double heartbeat she could hear nothing else.

In the next flash she saw Gith's head fall to the ground. Skellis actually stopped firing for a moment and her torch found her friend's face on the darkened floor. Her expression was too terrible, too agonised, too despondent for Skellis to take. The Macra was now on the ground, coming towards her.

Then Skellis heard a low otherworldly moan from behind her, where the ledge was. Something was stirring in the depth of the nest and she knew what it was. She had to get out of there. Fast. To do that she had to deal with the Macra and only one target seemed apt.

The monster crab lunged for her, but Skellis ducked out of the way, watching the claw intensely as it hit the earth wall where she had been standing a second before. Then, with a banshee scream of anger and sorrow, she plunged the jagged combat knife she carried on her leg deep into the soft joint between the Macra's pincer and the main part of its claw.

The Macra let out a high-pitched scream and backed away. It thrashed against the sides of the chamber in a desperate attempt to dislodge the knife but Skellis held on, driving the blade deeper, gouging as she went. Blood pumped from the wound and Skellis could feel it on her face, hot and thick and smelling like a sewer. Now she let go and stood back, taking careful aim with the staser rifle. But this time she did not strafe the Macra; she made each shot count, hitting the wound right on target. She kept firing until the power pack was exhausted and the Macra lay still.

Now Skellis could run. But she didn't. She heard the moan again, and turned to face the flickering lights. She walked steadily to the ledge and looked down. Some ten feet below her was a Great One. It was on its back as if lying in state. It was unconscious although the sounds of the battle did seem to be rousing it. Skellis raised her weapon. She would kill it. For Gith. For every Gallifreyan who had been fighting in this bloody and bitter war far too long.

She aimed at the creature's head and pulled the trigger. Nothing happened. Skellis cursed. She had expended the power pack. She looked around for the combat knife and found it with her torch. It looked too meagre to do any damage to the Great One. But, lying beside it was the Macra's pincer. It had been severed by her weapon's repéated fire.

It was almost as big as Skellis herself, razor sharp along one edge and pointed – albeit bluntly – at the end. She grimaced. It would do. She hefted it into her hands and walked back to the ledge. Now she saw the tubes that fed the horrific being lying beneath her. They were delivering fresh blood to the creature – both via its mouth and intravenously. Skellis looked at the Great One as it began to wake. She could see raised veins on its body and see the blood all pulsing one way . . .

Suddenly she knew what she needed to do. She lifted the Macra's severed pincer above her head and leapt forward into mid air, screaming as she came down on the Great One's chest and plunged the sharpened limb in the Vampire's sluggishly beating heart . . .

# THE ENIGMA OF
# SISTERHOOD

I wept when he destroyed Phaester Osiris. My sister also, for she loved our home world as I did. We comforted each other for a period. And then we sought revenge. Sutekh had killed many of the court and numerous members of our family. Yet Horus, our noble leader, told us that we would not seek revenge; we would seek justice. At that point, I did not care what he called it, I just wanted to see the foul creature drowned in the same annihilation he had poured on our home. How could I have guessed at that juncture that this desire for his death would lead to my own destruction?

Horus led the remaining 740 Osirans on a quest to pursue the coward across the galaxy and punish him. We were all related, and as such we were a family fuelled by anger and remorse. Our one huge ship combed the stars, seeking the bringer of darkness and his footprints were not hard to find. He fashioned a path of mayhem and death across half the cosmos, leaving nothing but dust and darkness in his wake.

We could have captured Sutekh several times, but it would have meant the loss of sapient life. Horus would not allow it. He thought the small creatures to be not only our responsibility but also – somehow – our kith. He was determined to show himself

better than his brother. We, too, had to be seen in that light. There were many, however, who would have gladly sacrificed entire systems to face the one who had put Phaester Osiris to the torch.

After many years' pursuit, the gathered forces of the Osirans at last came close to capturing Sutekh. He was cornered on a distant world where the natives had mastered geodesic principles and had become adept at manipulating space-time into singularities. We did not know what had drawn the evil one there, but when we found him he had manipulated their science to serve his own purposes and absconded.

Due to the proximity of our pursuit we were able to follow him closely and despite using a lodestone to travel forward in the time-space continuum again we tracked his movement to a vast, blue giant with clouds of swirling poisons. The so-called Cubil Terriors – a local species of dog-faced warriors that occupied the system's outer rim – had dubbed the world Zuliter. This was to be the last resting place of Sutekh. Or so my sister and I believed.

'Hathor! Khonsu!' boomed Horus in greeting.

All the Osirans had been summoned to his audience chamber in the fore part of the ship. It was a palatial triangle of floor, lined with cushioned seats. Already many of our noble cousins were there, each one wearing a different visage to the next and each bearing the robes of physiognomy; clothing that belied our true nature and powers. Horus the falcon-headed naturally wore white robes trimmed in gold, for his power was like that of the sun and stars combined. Only Sutekh matched him.

My sister, Hathor, wore a beautiful dress the colour of ancient red stars that clung to her figure, exaggerating every curve. Her domed head was a golden yellow and today she wore a humanoid face with long, flowing hair of deep blue and her eyes glowed a deep, garnet red. She had dressed for the occasion for she and Horus had once been lovers.

For myself, I had selected a similarly cut outfit of darkest cobalt silk with white piping at the wrist, shoulder and around the plunging neckline. Like my sister, I had chosen a human face, too, but green not yellow and instead of hair, my dome was the same deep blue as my robe. Hathor and Horus might have been lovers, but I knew the fascination I held for him.

'Lord Horus,' we said in unison. We liked doing that.

We took our seats and waited for the late-comers to arrive. The last was of course Bastet. Being a cat-goddess made her ever capricious: fickle and bending to no one's law but her own. If she had not been the last Osiran to enter, she would have been annoyed and might have taken herself to the back of the seating to sulk.

As it was she came to sit beside us in the front pew, moving with that sinewy grace she had, dressed very tightly in black and gold with the face of a lioness. There was no doubting her poise and beauty, but she was not at all interested in Horus. She preferred Anubis. This of course only served to make Horus want her more. Hathor and I greeted her with broad smiles that faded as she looked away.

'We gather,' Horus intoned.

Everyone sat up. This was the common call for attention and even Bastet seemed alert.

'The Eye is complete!' Horus announced.

A procession of servitors entered behind Horus. Our robots might seem odd to alien eyes. They do not appear mechanical at all. For they were not machines. They were controlled by cytronics – a type of psychic projection – that allowed them to be constructed as a simple wire frame emulating a human-oid shape. This was covered in bindings that were chemically impregnated to protect them against damage and decay. When new, these straps of cloth were the purest white – dazzling even. Over time, though, they become distressed and took on a creamier appearance.

These particular robots all bore a diagonal golden cross of silk on their chest that marked them as the servants of Horus. The first batch numbered nine, and four further servitors followed. These ones wore gold bindings from head to toe, something we had never seen before and which drew murmurs from the crowd. Horus was nothing if not the showman.

Between them, the four golden robots carried a giant red gem, totally smooth and gently pulsing as if it had a heartbeat. This was the instrument Horus had been constructing to carry out his will to hold Sutekh without destroying him. Personally, I would have liked to see the jackal-headed monster thrown in a decadron crucible and obliterated. But it was not to be, so I stamped my feet along with Horus's other adoring subjects.

The four special servitors reached a point towards the apex of the triangular floor and stopped. A segment of the floor vanished and was replaced by a golden stand that looked like a tree or flower. At the top was an indentation. Now Horus moved forward. He plucked the large gem from its transport and placed it on the tree so that it fitted snugly into the cavity.

'All is prepared,' shouted Horus. 'For my brother is at our mercy!'

Above our heads, the ceiling seemed to fall away like a waterfall, and a canopy of stars replaced it. At the centre of this was Zuliter, the many hues of blue cloud swirling around its almost tar-sized surface. Somewhere up there was Sutekh. Hiding. Or, more likely, preparing ...

Horus turned back to the Eye and made a sign with his hands. The pulse quickened now until the oversized jewel glowed a constant bright crimson. Just as I had suspected, things went wrong then. The gemstone faltered and a huge shadow fell upon us, cast from the sky above. We all looked up and saw a terrible sight. We could not make out its form because it just appeared as a colossal area of blackness between Zuliter and us. Size did not usually afflict an Osiran with fear, but we could all feel it in our core that the figure was not a natural being.

*You shall not pass*, it said and its voice felt like semi-frozen acid poured directly into our minds.

'I am Horus,' our noble leader growled. 'Who are you to deny me passage?'

*We are the Sivin*, it replied. *We are the singularity*.

This brought an exchange of looks between Hathor and me. Several others were also signalling their lack of understanding at this apparent oxymoron. Then I recalled that Sutekh's previous refuge had been a world that engineered such temporal-spatial events. I stood and said as much to Horus.

'That type of singularity?' he asked, agog. 'Conscious?'

'That is what those people did,' I said, walking towards him. I let a hand trail over one of his service robots. It did not move, but Horus started at me with inscrutable, falcon's eyes.

*We are aware*, the Sivin said. *We know you. All of you*.

'What is your purpose?' Bastet asked. She, too, had left her comfortable seat and was striding across the polished floor to join us beside the Eye.

*We protect the master. Sutekh is supreme*.

Horus made a sign with his hands and the ceiling re-formed, blocking the Sivin from view.

'If it is an event in space-time, we can surely bypass it,' Horus said. 'We have the lodestone technology. A time-corridor would take us back to a point before it existed. We could simply wait for Sutekh.'

The huge congregation of Osirans began speaking all at once, some stamping their feet in approval of Horus's plan. Some of them lacked the intellect to formulate their own opinions. I ignored the hubbub and summoned a sarcophagus with my mind.

Two of my servitors now entered. Their bindings were not as white as they might be but they bore the cobalt cross on their chests that told the assembled deities that whatever was about to take place was due to my actions. It was a mistake I would regret until the moment I died. Fortunately, I would not have to wait long.

The ornately carved sarcophagus was duly set up and a lodestone was brought forward. My service robot placed it in the side of the casket and activated the requisite cartouche on the casing. Immediately a colourful tunnel leading into the time vortex appeared.

Horus stepped forward. Naturally, he meant to lead the way; he meant to steal my glory. That was when there was a feedback explosion from the sarcophagus. It threw Horus, Bastet and me across the floor and left my robot missing its head and torso. The time winds had scarred us, but we would heal. What was more damaged was our pride. Before Horus could rise to his feet, the ceiling was ripped apart and the dark form of the Sivin loomed over us once more.

*We told you. You shall not pass.*

Horus now rose. His falcon beak was actually smiling. 'What would you have of us?' he asked. 'We can offer you much.'

At that moment, the Sivin revealed its true form to us. At least, a form that it wanted to project. It was now humanoid in shape with wings on its back and cat-like features to its face. If anything, it resembled a hybrid of formidable panther and mighty eagle. And then, it yawned as if bored by our existence.

Horus bristled, his feathers separating on his head. Bastet was walking in circles, staring up at the creature that so closely resembled her.

*We tire of your efforts to deter us*, the Sivin said. *But you may amuse my master by solving a conundrum.*

Horus smiled. 'A riddle?' he asked. 'You truly are the creation of my brother, for there is nothing we like better.'

I smiled too, although I was thinking that I would prefer the head of Sutekh as my plaything.

*Very well.*

'Wait!' Horus held his arms up to the singularity. 'What will our reward be for delivering you a solution?'

*The Great Sutekh will allow you to pass.*

I looked across at my sister who was leaning back, examining her nails. She did not care for politics and hated this manner of posturing and power play. I smiled at her and she rolled her eyes at me as if to say: *Play your games; I am over here if you need me.*

'In so far as we can ever trust the word of Sutekh, we accept the terms,' Horus said haughtily.

He did not really have a choice but he made it sound as if we were in control, which was all that mattered.

*The answer must not only be given as a verbal response*, the Sivin announced. *We also require a physical manifestation of the solution.*

Horus nodded. 'So if the key is an old man, an old man must be produced; if it is a river, we must bring you a river.'

*That is so. If you deliver an incorrect answer, the offer shall not be made again.*

'We understand.'

*There are two sisters: one gives birth to the other and she, in turn, gives birth to the first.*

Sisters. I looked back at Hathor. She was interested now, staring at me in return. Her expression was one of concern and I had not the slightest idea why.

*You have the time it takes the planet to make one revolution on its axis*, the Sivin said and it waved a mighty paw across the sky, reinstating the ceiling of our ship.

Horus silenced the legions of Osirans that started speaking all at once and despatched them in small groups that could debate the meaning of the enigma more easily. He kept Bastet and me to hand, and I insisted that Hathor join us.

'It is a stand-off,' Horus said. 'No matter what happens, Sutekh cannot leave. We will out wait eternity if needs be.'

'Your brother has more guile and cunning than all of us,' Hathor said. 'This puzzle of his will have consequences and if we are allowed to pass by this Sivin *thing* then it will be to his advantage somehow.'

Bastet agreed but said that we needed to solve the puzzle first. It was a statement of ludicrous obviousness. However, it did serve to bring our focus back to the task at hand.

We began by separating the riddle out into its constituent elements. The use of the word 'sisters' meant that there would be two aspects or parts to the answers that the Sivin would require of us. The 'giving birth' part was the thing that vexed us the most. We argued over whether the statement was literal or not. While Hathor and I were convinced it was allegorical – as, we thought, was the entire thing – Bastet wondered if we were meant to think that. I voiced the opinion that a singularity might lack the experience to employ a double bluff. Horus snapped that it was not the singularity we were dealing with, but Sutekh.

We sat in different parts of the chamber, each on a different row. Riddles were the primary entertainment in Osiran culture. Well, certainly the more intellectual one. We also loved dancing. I moved across to Hathor and whispered that of the two, it would have been amusing if Sutekh had chosen dance as his method rather than enigmas. She laughed a little too loudly and drew irritated glares from the other two. But I laughed with her. We were like that: sisters against the cosmos.

That is when it hit me.

The solution actually came in waves: first the answer itself and then the implications. My sister saw the change in expression on my face.

'What is it, Khonsu?' she reached out and took my hand. I looked up at her. She could read me very well and knew that I had bad news to impart. She pulled me close and embraced me. 'What?' she whispered. 'Tell me.'

'It is us,' I said, my voice a grating whisper.

Hathor pulled away and frowned at me. 'What are you talking about?'

Bastet heard us and came over, Horus plodding along behind. They could see in my eyes that I had an answer and that it tasted bitter to me.

'The answer is us,' I said, putting a hand on my sister's shoulder. 'Day.' And then I pointed to myself. 'Night.'

Horus was stony-faced. 'One gives birth to the other ...' he said.

Bastet looked own. 'And she, in turn, gives birth to the first.'

Now my sister saw it. She was a goddess of the sun, I of the moon. We were sisters, representatives of the day and the night. Her head slumped and her shoulders fell.

Horus shook his head. 'It makes no sense,' he said angrily. 'Why ask for your deaths? How is that going to stop us bringing him to justice?'

I cocked my head. That was true.

'That's the obvious part,' my sister said quietly. She was still looking down, her hands slowly wringing each other in her lap. 'He wants time to escape.'

We all looked at her.

'Of course,' Horus said, almost marvelling.

'We could have given him that easily,' Bastet said. 'There was no need for ...' She trailed off, unable to bring herself to say it.

'This is Sutekh, remember?' I said.

Bastet looked at me. 'And his gift of death must follow him wherever he treads.'

Horus asked if we wanted to be left alone, but I did not want to creep off into some private chamber with my sister to wallow in what was about to happen. Of course, I wanted to see her privately, but to scuttle off now seemed too pathetic.

So we stayed and together we worked out exactly what must happen when we confronted the Sivin. First, the creature would need to see us die. Then Horus would give an order that could not be countermanded, telling the ship to put all the Osirans and itself into suspended animation for the duration of one Zuliter day.

The Osirans were gathered again, and Hathor and I stood before our brothers and sisters, willing to make the ultimate sacrifice.

'Promise me this will be the last,' I said to Horus so no one else could hear. 'Promise me that you will use the Eye as soon as you find him. No "my brother deserves a trial" or any nonsense like that.' I knew Horus and knew that was going through his mind.

He nodded. 'I swear it,' he said and put his hands on my shoulder. 'Your sacrifice will not be in vain. My brother's crimes will find their punishment. He will be made to suffer.' He sounded so calm that I could tell he was on the verge of exploding. 'The evil Osiran has ensured he will have time to flee, but we both know this is but a short stay of sentence.'

We demanded that there be no ceremony, no speeches. Horus was not to use this event to grandstand. We just wanted it to be fast and with no suffering – much as anyone does about their own death. To this end a large decadron crucible had been placed in the centre of the triangular floor, just beyond where the Eye stood ready.

Horus opened the ceiling to the stars and called to Sivin. But the creature was already there.

*What is your answer?*

'Day and night,' Horus called. He made no attempt to disguise the anger and hate in his voice. 'To which end our sisters Hathor and Khonsu offer themselves to death.'

*Is this the totality of your solution?*

'No. We further swear to place the Osiran host in suspended animation for one day.'

The huge panther-like being flapped its wings.

*You speak the correct response*, it said.

Horus lifted his arm to give the signal to the servitor that stood beside the crucible that would obliterate my sister and me. Hathor reached out and took my hand. I looked at her and tried to smile, She just nodded.

'I know,' she said.

*Hold.*

Everyone looked up at the Sivin.

*The solution may be interpreted in contrasting conclusions.*

'What do you mean?' Horus asked. 'Is our answer incorrect?'

*We would have the goddesses Hathor and Khonsu join us*, the Sivin said.

I looked at Hathor. She mouthed the word 'join' to me, a spark of hope in her eyes.

*We asked for a physical manifestation. They should not die. We shall link with them* ...

In the blink of an eye, the Sivin was standing on the floor of the chamber. He looked about at the astounded Osirans and walked towards the crucible. He crackled with some form of extraordinary energy as he moved. He waved a paw and the mechanism of our destruction vanished. Then he split into two identical parts, one simply walking out of the other and both manifestations stood before us. Much to my amazement, the two Sivin then held hands, mirroring the pose in which my sister and I stood.

*Join*, the creatures said in unison.

So my sister and I stepped forward. We became Sivin. And they became us, in a way. The initial conjunction was strange and I could feel the driving desire to pursue Sutekh slipping away. I turned to Horus. I don't know what I looked like by then, but his expression was one I will treasure for a long time.

*'We are well,'* I said. *'Carry out the order and then find your brother.'*

What had already been joined now combined with my sister and her Sivin. As one, we left the Osiran ship and removed ourselves from space-time. We observed the universe as it spun and then we returned to Zuliter. What amount of time had passed, I had no inkling. Times merged together a little to me then. All I knew was that the Osirans had gone. They had pursued Sutekh.

I scrutinised the time wake and saw a desert. He had fled to a place called Egypt. Horus and the others had followed him, imprisoned him. I felt this was right. Then I reached out to Hathor and she embraced me with her being. Or was it Khonsu that embraced Hathor? It mattered not. We were together and free of such burdens in every single fashion imaginable.

# PANDORIC'S BOX

The situation on the ground was not good. The enemy was too strong. They did not need to regenerate. They were not flesh and blood. They were not *alive* in the sense that the troops fighting them understood the term.

Wearing the off-white tunic and armour of a Pathfinder, Commander Naxil usually cut a dashing figure. Not today. Today he looked old and beaten, tired from the constant need to be alert, dirty from the sodden battlefield.

He was squatting down, pressed against a low wall that had clearly once been part of a larger structure. The staser rifle he clutched had personal modifications made to it that allowed him to differentiate organic from plastic. Not something the regular Gallifreyan troops had.

Naxil looked behind him at the three other members of his team. Their mission was to establish a power-boosted, open-ended transmat zone deep in hostile territory.

The enemy had become adept at detecting TARDISes and either warp-shunted them to far-flung destinations or sealed them in plastic film that those inside could not break through. So good old-fashioned matter transmitters were being used.

This was the turning point. If the Time Lords could secure this planet, Lord President Rassilon believed they could push the enemy back to their planet of origin and maybe even time-loop it with newly acquired technology.

Low chance of resistance, General Brissilan had said. Get in, get out. He had almost made it sound easy. But then the Pathfinders had entered the town. A few survivors remained – mostly in rags – flitting between the piles of debris, trying to keep a low profile. That had played havoc with the motion sensors.

So, they just had to rely on their eyes and ears – as well as the feed of information through their earpieces and helmet visors. Naxil led his team through the ruined buildings, sweeping their weapons to and fro, desperate to cover for any surprise attack.

When it came, the attack was no surprise.

They heard the bombardment creeping towards them: explosion after explosion of high-impact plasti-shrapnel mortar shells. Naxil and his troops kept their heads down. They knew they couldn't move. And yet, this was exactly what the enemy wanted.

As the barrage died away, the enemy came, moving though the smoke with their uncannily fitful movements; their genderless, dead faces turning this way and that, trying to get a lock on the Gallifreyans. Clad in the blue boiler suits, guns protruding from where their fingers had fallen away – there was no mistaking them.

Autons.

Naxil didn't need his instruments to tell him what they were. He signalled his squad and they all opened fire. Their weapons had minimal effect, melting the plastic from face or torso, but never stopping them.

'Concentrate your fire!' he yelled.

Before the troops could regroup, the Autons attacked. Nasty, sulphurous smoke blossomed from their blunt metal weapons and two of Naxil's team fell. The brown smoke billowed around their bodies where the shots had hit and then retreated again as if time was being reversed. The two Gallifreyans vanished with an unnatural swooping sound. Total destruction.

'Get us out of here!' Naxil roared into his helmet mike.

But then more Autons appeared. He witnessed the last member of his squad killed before him. And then multiple Auton impacts cut down the dashing Commander himself. As he vanished from existence, his visor camera stopped transmitting.

❈

The young Rassilon stared at the static image projected into mid air for a second and then turned to face General Brissilan.

They were standing in the War Council room on Gallifrey. Several other high-ranking soldiers, the Castellan and the head of the CIA were in attendance. The table they were standing at was indented in places as if a huge mouse had taken bites from an oval biscuit.

'It is clear to me that this strategy is not going to work,' Rassilon said.

The General – resplendent in red and gold armour – looked stern but determined. 'Lord President, our strategists have deduced that only this place – here, now – can be the turning point. Even the Visionary concurs.'

Rassilon placed his gauntleted gloves on the table before him. 'How many squads have you sent in? Five?'

'Nine, my Lord.'

'Nine!' The President of the Time Lords rose and patrolled the table, pointing at the static that still hung at its centre. 'You've sent nine of our best Pathfinder squads in there! And none of them have been able to set up the transmat.'

The General lowered his head. 'If we are to win this war before the Nestene reach our galaxy …'

'If we are to win this war, *at all*,' Rassilon said calmly, 'we will need a new strategy.'

'My Lord President?'

'Pull your troops, back, General. We are retreating. Contain the Nestene threat as best you can.'

The General went to protest, but Rassilon already had his back to him and was leaving the War Council room.

As he left the chamber, Rassilon was joined by his most trusted aide, Sektay. She had tied her auburn hair in a tight bun and wore the simple, black robes of a technician. Rassilon knew she was anything but.

'What will you do?' she asked, casting a sideways look at his face. He had recently lost the full beard and looked younger now, handsome even with a jocularity to his face that did not sit well with his office.

He smiled. 'There is always another solution.' But then he stopped and sighed. 'I don't know. Ever since Omega's accident …' He trailed off. 'No matter.'

He started walking again, heading for his personal chambers. Two junior councillors passed them in the corridor, bowing and casting a suspicious eye at Sektay. She smiled sweetly at them.

As they reached the entrance to Rassilon's chambers, two Chancellery Guards snapped to attention. They passed inside, and immediately Sektay offered the President her solution.

'You could consider Roppen, Lord President,' she said.

Rassilon turned. 'The idealist?'

'The scientist. The renowned creator of the Eye of Discord ...'

Rassilon raised an ample eyebrow. 'You would have me force him to re-engineer his device?'

'It is another *solution* ...' Sektay offered.

'I will consider it, as I do all options for dealing with the Nestene High Command.' And he swept away before pausing in the doorway. Then, without looking back he said: 'Thank you, Sektay. Your counsel is always appreciated.'

Sektay inclined her head. 'Of course, Lord President.'

She'd never heard him quite so tired.

*

Sektay returned to her quarters and went to her personal Matrix Access point. She quickly brought up all the files relating to Roppentheomjer. Her vidscreen filled with images of the man and details of his career.

He was a handsome man, if a little gaunt. He had slick, black hair swept back from his high, intelligent brow and dazzling green eyes that seemed somehow haunted despite their glint. As Sektay had reminded Rassilon, Roppen was a renowned scientist. He had served with Omega on the initial attempts at black hole manipulation.

After Omega's disappearance, he should have become the natural successor to the legendary stellar manipulator. Instead, Roppen had taken up the position as Lead Scientist at the

Academy's so-called Lost Laboratory – its name a reflection of the brilliant minds to be found hiding there.

Every member had been a great Time Lord thinker, engineer or scientist once. Now they simply wanted to hide away from the glare of unwanted attention – as well as the realities of the wars their race found themselves fighting: the Racnoss and the Vampires.

Roppen played no part in politics. He never attended council meetings – even though he was permitted to do so. He avoided the media at all costs and never appeared on the Public Register Video telecast about the lives and deaths of Omega.

So he fitted right in to the Lost Laboratory: collaborating with other top minds, competing to outthink each other. This created a hothouse for scientific breakthroughs – perhaps driven by pure ability alone.

He took his studies in a different direction, applying what he had learnt about the forces controlling the Eye of Harmony and reversing them. Roppen had applied the effect of retrogressive solicitation used in early TARDISes to these forces and created a device both astounding and terrible.

No one at the Lost Laboratory had seen the military application of his new discovery. However, per the edict of the High Council, all such breakthroughs had to be submitted to the War Council for assessment. It did not take them long to see that Roppen's discovery would make an awesome weapon. If the destructive gravitational forces of a thousand black holes were to burst at once into life, that would be unlike the splendour of any weapon before it.

At first he dubbed the device the Eye of Discord. It was a scientific witticism; a Time Lord in-joke for the intelligentsia of the Academy. Later, the War Council called it the Galaxy Eater. No matter what its name, the device was timely, for war had just erupted between Gallifrey and the Nestene High Command in the constellation of Sephin in the nearby Illia galaxy.

That was when Roppen had truly become lost. He dismantled his device and used a sentient computer virus of his own creation to destroy all record of his research. Soon after, he left the Academy and travelled to the Mountains of Solace and Solitude to take up a life of contemplation and simplicity.

The War Council had been livid. They had demanded that he be arrested. Rassilon himself had interceded and told them no such warrant would be issued while he was still President.

Sektay smiled as she looked at the Executive Order granting Roppen clemency for any perceived crime the scientist had committed in destroying both the research and the device. Rassilon was truly a great man.

This was exactly what she was thinking the next morning as he informed her of his decision.

'I believe you are correct,' Rassilon said. He was slowly pacing the gardens of his residence, his robes replaced with attire more fitting to an outsider from beyond the Citadel.

'Thank you, Lord President.' Sektay was genuinely thrilled to hear these words.

'It would take too long to develop the sort of weapon we need. Roppen must be convinced to return to the fold. The Galaxy Eater will deal with this threat, and Gallifrey can concentrate on more compassionate undertakings.'

'That sounds most reasonable,' Sektay said.

'That is why I have decided to leave straight away,' Rassilon said. 'Alone.'

He waved an arm at a hover car standing on the gravelled driveway beyond an ornately trimmed hedge.

'You cannot go alone!' Sektay was aghast.

'It is a simple journey into the Mountains, Sektay, not an irresponsible mission to a Racnoss Webstar.' Rassilon was already walking towards the vehicle. 'Roppen is not a man who would respond well to us sending gunships or even the whole High Council! I must go.'

'But, *alone*, Lord President?'

'Yes.' Rassilon smiled and took her hand in his. 'Thank you for your help. I think you may have saved Gallifrey.'

Sektay smiled back. She wished no part in history. How could she, beside such a figure as Rassilon? He climbed into the driver's seat of the hover car and started the engine.

'Hurry back,' she said.

Rassilon nodded, gave a characteristic grin and was gone.

❈

The two Time Lords sat at a plain wooden table, drinking wine from the vineyards on the lower slopes. Roppen's home was not quite as simple as rumour had it. The building was more like a villa than a hovel and lacked for no technology, although its trappings were not opulent.

'I thought the War Council would try again,' Roppen said. His face had more lines these days and his eyes were a little hooded. His voice remained steady and slow, however. 'I did not think you would come in person.'

'How could I not?' Rassilon said. 'You should be ruling beside me. Like Omega. Not skulking in the dusty corners of academia – or worse: stuck out here like a Shobogan!'

'Shobogan!' Roppen laughed. 'You always had a colourful turn of phrase. I am hardly an outsider!'

Rassilon smiled. 'Maybe not. But you are hiding out here.'

'I am retired.'

'A Time Lord does not retire,' the President replied. 'To spend an eternity watching sunsets and drinking wine is no life for the greatest mind in the galaxy.'

Roppen raised a glass. 'It sounds good enough to me!'

'Will you be happy to indulge yourself while Gallifrey is over-run by the Nestene?'

'That will not happen.'

'Don't be so sure,' Rassilon said, He leaned forward and stared evenly at his friend. 'They have us beaten in Illia. They have almost that entire galaxy in their grip. All their protein planets and Auton factory worlds … if we do not stop them now, our galaxy will be next – maybe the entire universe.'

'When I showed the Wider War Council my research, some of them laughed, one or two cried. Most people were silent. I just stood there and recalled the line from the ancient Pythia texts: In my duty to defend existence I became mortality itself, the slayer of spheres.'

'I know your feelings on the use of the Galaxy Eater.'

Roppen winced. 'Please do not call it that.'

'Whatever its name, we need it,' Rassilon said. 'Please. It will save countless worlds. It will save us.'

'It will not save Illia.'

'The Illia galaxy has no real civilisation to speak of now. Any races or cultures that once existed there are lost; all the planets and races endure only to serve the Nestene.'

Roppen gazed at the orange sunset, slowly turning blue as twilight fell. He closed his eyes and felt the warmth of the sun. 'If I do this,' he said. 'The device will be built exactly to my specifications.'

'Of course.'

'It will be only used once.'

'Agreed.'

Roppen let out a long, low breath. 'And we should start at once.'

Rassilon raised his glass. 'I think we have time to finish these first.'

*

While Gallifreyan warships kept the Auton assault ships and Nestene Swarms contained within the Illia galaxy, Roppen returned to the Lost Laboratory. He worked in seclusion and almost entirely alone. Rassilon and a team of technicians worked on a specially fitted TARDIS that would allow him to operate the weapon and still escape its destructive force.

When the day came, Roppen walked into the War Council room and placed his cuboid device on the table, right in the middle. It looked very different to the Eye of Discord. That had looked cold and functional; prosaic. This looked almost lyrical.

Instead of brushed metal, this device was made of dark wood with what looked like brass cogs and gears visible on some of its panels. Their circular designs seemed to mimic the Gallifreyan language that was carved into its edges.

On other facia were maze-like patterns, as if some outward appearance of the complex computer programmes running within. Although instead of electronic circuit boards or any other higher technology, Roppen had favoured clockwork for the device's control mechanism, which whirred and ticked as if almost alive.

'How is it operated?' asked Rassilon.

'Simply turn the wheel on top,' Roppen replied. He looked pleased with himself for some reason. 'Then give it your instructions.'

'It's voice activated?' asked General Brissilan.

'The operating mechanism is sentient.'

Rassilon raised an eyebrow. 'Is that wise?'

'Exactly to my specifications,' Roppen replied. 'Remember?'

Rassilon smiled. 'Of course.'

The echo of their conversation faded and Rassilon ordered the device taken to the specially equipped TARDIS.

Rassilon looked round the room. Sektay smiled at him from a dark corner.

'Well then. Let us end this war!'

*

A line of Chancellery Guards led to the TARDIS door. Rassilon sighed. But he understood better than most how ceremony was used to reinforce and to some extent control a society.

Wearing the deep red armour of a soldier, he marched between the guards dressed in their sunnier, scarlet and white uniforms. Rassilon turned as he reached the TT-capsule. Unlike Roppen, he did not avoid the Public Register Video, and this was being transmitted across Gallifrey and its colony worlds. He gave a heroic smile, waved and stepped inside.

At the six-sided central console were half a dozen science techs, all in white overalls. Rassilon gave the order for dematerialisation and passed through the vast chamber to another door, leading deeper inside the spaceship.

The room he found himself in now was unfurnished save for a grey-white plinth on which stood the wooden frame of Roppen's device. The walls surrounding it were indented with circular craters, echoing the quiet ticking of the machine they housed.

Rassilon positioned himself over the device and carefully turned the golden wheel on top. The whirring of the mechanism intensified for a brief moment and then died away once more. But nothing else happened. The Lord President of Gallifrey frowned.

'Well?' he said.

'Well what?' asked a deep but slightly croaky voice behind him. Rassilon turned slowly. He expected to see one of the white-clad pilots form the console room.

Instead, an old man stood before him. He had a lined but kind face, a white-grey goatee beard and unruly hair of the same colour, swept up into the merest suggestion of a crest at the centre. His clothing looked alien: an animal skin jacket and woven scarf. Across his chest he had a bandolier.

'Who are you?' Rassilon shouted, angry at the intrusion. He began to approach the stranger. 'You shouldn't be here.'

'Neither of us should,' the old man replied, then he smiled. 'Ha!'

Rassilon gazed at the man. 'You're an artificial intelligence?'

'Artificial?' the old man scoffed. 'I am the interface. Well, a representation of it. Chosen especially for you so that you'd feel at home.'

'Feel ... at *home*?'

Just then, the door opened behind the old man and a fresh-faced pilot stood there looking slightly foolish.

'Excuse me, Lord President, but is everything all right?'

Rassilon glared at the intruder. 'Of course! Why?'

'We ... heard you call out.'

'I was talking to this man!' Rassilon said.

The pilot stared at him and then slowly looked around the room. 'Man?'

'You can call me Pandoric,' the bearded man said. 'But he can't. He can't see me.'

'Ah,' Rassilon said. 'The device has a sentient operating system. The interface is only visible to the operator. You may leave us.'

The pilot bobbed his head and darted from the room, closing the door firmly behind him. Mad old Rassilon. That was what he'd be thinking. The Time Lord smiled and turned back to this OS that called itself . . .

'Pandoric?'

'Yes. After the Pandorica. Another mythical box that was supposed to harbour something very dangerous; the prison of a warrior or a goblin that fell from the sky and tore the world apart. Sound familiar?'

'Not at all.'

The old man looked crestfallen. 'Oh,' he said. 'Ah. Hang on. I'm a bit confused. That's the future. They're so easy to confuse, aren't they? Don't you find?'

'No.'

'Oh. Well, I do.' He walked across the room and looked at the wooden box. 'Still. Let's just stick with Pandoric, shall we? It's a good enough name.'

'I'm sure you've chosen wisely,' Rassilon humoured the old man.

'Now that *is* funny!' Pandoric smiled. 'So, I've heard what your intentions are.'

'Really?'

'Gallifrey stands.'

'In essence. Yes.'

'Your whole life: that is what drives you.'

'Really? So you can read minds, too?'

'You wish to destroy the Nestene? Set fire to a whole galaxy?'

'To save Gallifrey, yes.'

'Then your Moment has come!'

'We haven't arrived yet,' Rassilon said. 'I'm sure the pilots will alert us when we do. And then you can carry out your function.'

The old man sat upon the floor, cross-legged and toyed with his bandolier. 'You want to kill some time?'

Rassilon sighed. The operating system was certainly using some very parochial speech patterns.

'You know that along with what you think of as the Nestene infection, your actions will wipe out countless billions of innocent lives.'

'Enslaved lives. Lives that only exist to serve the Nestene war machine: slaves. Nothing more.'

'Slaves are still innocent. Take it from me.'

'Nonetheless ...'

'Gallifrey must stand.' The old man suddenly grabbed his leg. 'And so must I!' He got up and hobbled around the room. 'Cramp!'

'Did Roppen really programme you to be like this?'

Pandoric rubbed his calf vigorously and then looked up, smiling. 'I'm supposed to manifest the interface that best suits both the situation and the operator.'

'So why you?'

'I think because we're similar.'

Rassilon laughed. 'Really?'

'You're in a pickle. A fix. And the situation you find yourself in now is like one I will find myself in one day. Well, not me. The image I am using.'

'Very soon, you won't exist.'

'You're a great man, a leader of your people. Prepared to make the tough decisions. The ones no one else has the stomach for. But while you can be a hard man, you don't need to become a murderer on a galactic scale. You don't need to abandon decency and compassion. That way lies disaster.'

'I have fought the Great Vampires. As part of the Fledgling Empires, I have brought an end to the voracious Racnoss. An even bigger disaster will come if the Nestene sweep across this galaxy and destroy Gallifrey.'

'I tell you what: I'll show you!'

'What?'

The room became a swirling white treacle of temporal energies and Rassilon felt himself falling through time.

※

Suddenly, Rassilon was cold. The air was saturated with a fine mist of freezing droplets. Despite the padded armour, he shivered. He was alone. There was no sign of Pandoric and no indication what he should do. The ground underfoot was almost spongy and the sky overhead a monochrome palette of grey and whites.

He turned around and found himself facing a tower less than a mile away. It jutted into the dreary scudding clouds like an ancient place of worship and was topped by a large sphere bisected by a crescent. This seemed to be his destination.

As Rassilon made his way across the depressing landscape his gaze wandered to the horizon. He thought he recognised the shapes of the hills and mountains that seemed to ring the moor on which the tower was built. Could it be? Why would Pandoric send him to the Death Zone? Or was this an era before he'd put a stop to the Games?

At the foot of the tower he could see several figures, definitely Time Lords by the robes. They were engineers – his kind of people – and Rassilon found himself greeting them as if they were not just compatriots but friends.

They all regarded him suspiciously but they recognised his military uniform and said nothing as he approached. Rassilon thought this for the best. He passed them and went through a vast door into a room with a chequered floor.

'It's all right. We haven't activated the ceiling lasers,' said a voice. Rassilon peered into the gloom and out stepped a technician. He was dressed in similar robes to Sektay, but had short, dark blond hair and a slight moustache.

'Ceiling lasers?'

'All part of the Game of Rassilon!' said the man.

Rassilon laughed. A game! Well, that was interesting.

'The President is down there.' The man pointed down a corridor lit with flaming torches. 'Guessing that's why you're here.'

'Yes. Thank you.'

Rassilon soon reached a much larger chamber. There was a pyramidal structure at its centre and there seemed to be galleries running round the hexagonal space. At the foot of this structure was a group of men. Most were dressed in simple robes and skullcaps of black. One wore white.

The last figure wore magnificent golden robes with a pointed headdress that was kept in place by a coronet of gold inset with large purple crystals. He had the most astounding-looking facial hair Rassilon had ever seen: mutton-chop sideburns that became a bushy moustache and elongated, wispy eyebrows. That arched up at the outer edges.

'Who are you?' the man in gold boomed. His voice was rich and deep.

Rassilon stared at his future self.

'Well?'

'He's so much more ... avuncular than you, wouldn't you say?'

Rassilon turned his head to see Pandoric leaning on a stone pillar.

'Has the sense of foreboding affected your speech?' the older Rassilon said.

'No,' Rassilon said at last. 'What sense of foreboding?'

'It's a mechanism I have installed in the Dark Tower. It will help deter those whose will is not set upon the prize.'

'This is your last incarnation,' Pandoric commented, the rasp in his voice quite pronounced now. 'He's preparing for eternal sleep.'

'How poetic,' Rassilon said quietly.

The older Time Lord examined the new arrival carefully. Then his mouth fell open. 'No,' he said. 'This cannot happen. You are in contravention of the Laws of Time!'

'The laws I decreed,' Rassilon replied evenly.

'*We* decreed,' the older Rassilon said. He circled the younger man. 'Why are you here?'

'Why am *I* here?' another deep voice answered. This one was edged with steel.

A man in red and gold robes appeared from the shadows. He had grey-black hair closely cropped to his head and he wore some form of cybernetic glove on his right hand. It glowed slightly with time energy.

'Answer!'

'I think I prefer old Mutton-chops to Mr Crewcut here,' Pandoric said. 'Tell him you need to make a decision.'

'Who are you?' Mutton-chops asked, staring imperiously at the new arrival.

Crewcut shook his head, a thin sneer on his face. 'You!' He walked right up to Mutton-chops and growled in his face. 'The last thing we need right now is you, a pompous old windbag.'

Rassilon stared at the new arrival. Was this really him, too? He seemed so ... rigid, so humourless. At least the incarnation with the funny hat and the coronet smiled.

'You are addressing the Lord President of Gallifrey!' Mutton-chops said haughtily, proving his future self's appraisal of him.

'So. Are. You,' said Crewcut, spitting each word as if it was poison.

'I thought this was my last incarnation?' Rassilon waved a hand at Mutton-chops.

'He is,' Pandoric said.

'I am,' the older man confirmed.

Crewcut looked slightly lost for words. 'I was ... resurrected,' he said.

'Since when do Time Lords resurrect the dead?' Rassilon was aghast.

'There's a war coming,' Crewcut said. 'One you cannot even begin to imagine.'

Pandoric walked between the three Rassilons. He glanced at the youngest incarnation. 'He might be able to help you with your decision,' he said.

'I need your counsel,' Rassilon said.

'Have you time-scooped me?' Crewcut said. He was a very angry man.

'Not exactly.'

'Why do I not recall this?' asked Mutton-chops.

'Tell him the time streams are out of sync,' Pandoric said.

Rassilon relayed the information.

'I am very busy ...' Crewcut said.

'With your war,' Rassilon said.

'Yes. What do you need us for?'

'I have a war of my own.'

Crewcut laughed. 'Which little skirmish are you talking about?'

'Nestenes.'

'I destroyed them!' Mutton-chops said.

'You did?' Rassilon was surprised.

'Even he had the resolve to do what was necessary. Is this why you're here? Because you do not?' Crewcut spat the question at his original self.

'I was told I had a choice.'

'You do.' A fourth man appeared before them. He was very old – even more so than Pandoric. He had a worn face, lined with sorrow and bitterness. He was bald and wearing a

Gallifreyan shouldered headdress and crest, marked with his seal. 'You always have a choice.'

'Another one?' asked Mutton-chops.

'You are me?' Crewcut asked with a grimace. 'But that means …'

'You lose,' said the bald man looking evenly at Crewcut.

'What happened?' the young Rassilon asked.

'He got into a fight with a real maniac,' Pandoric said. 'One of his own making, in fact. But then the maniac regenerated into a female and Crewcut regenerated into Baldy.'

'But Gallifrey …' Crewcut was suddenly deflated. His purpose was gone.

'Still stands,' Baldy said. 'But not as it once did.'

'How is this meant to help me?' Rassilon grimaced. This was a waste of his time.

'These men are your future. Bright in the short term, but look at the final result.'

'Gallifrey stands!' Crewcut said, his bravado regained. 'That is all I ever wanted.'

'No matter the cost?' Rassilon asked. He knew the answer.

'Of course.'

All three Time Lords nodded. Rassilon smiled.

'And you have had much longer to think about this than I.'

Crewcut came up to him. 'Gallifrey must remain constant, though it cost the entire universe.'

Rassilon felt a chill run through him. Crewcut vanished.

The oldest incarnation approached him now. 'One day, you will reflect on all this and wonder if it was worth it,' he said. Then he, too, faded from sight.

'Well,' said Mutton-chops. 'That was an education. And not the most pleasant one.'

'No,' agreed Rassilon.

A moment later, he was back in the room aboard his TARDIS. Pandoric was leaning against the wall now and in the centre of the room, the wooden box had transformed into a primitive explosive detonator, complete with a plunger shaft.

'That was your tomb, you know,' Pandoric said.

'What? The tower?'

Pandoric nodded. 'I hoped it might give you a sense of mortality.' He laughed. 'The irony of trying to show that to someone who discovers immortality is not lost on me.'

'These things you have shown me, what you are telling me now ... all because you want to change my mind?'

'Hope. Not want.'

'I fail to see the difference.'

The door opened and one of the pilots stood in its frame, not daring to enter. 'We have arrived, Lord President. General Brissilan reports all forces ready to return to Gallifrey on your command.'

Rassilon moved towards the plunger handle on the detonator. 'Give the order. Prepare for weapon discharge.'

The pilot bowed and left.

'Nothing will alter your decision.'

'As my future self said, Gallifrey must remain.'

'You know you won't even destroy all the Nestene with this action. Some will survive.'

'A few survivors will never be able to pose the same threat that this galactic infestation does.'

Rassilon placed his hand on the wooden handle. So simple. So ... physical. He closed his eyes.

'Gallifrey stands!'

He pushed the plunger down hard and everything froze.

The President saw beyond the TT-Capsule, beyond its outer plasmic hull. A galaxy of stars whirled around him: clusters, nebulae, planets, moons, and creatures – life in all its different dimensions and varieties.

Then he felt the power of Roppen's terrifying weapon. It was like a frost creeping across creation, turning everything to a lifeless snapshot. Then it became a wave receding from the beach pulling all matter, space and time with it.

Whether it was his imagination of whether the sentient operating system was affording him a view of the destruction, Rassilon could not tell. But he could feel the loss of all that life. Each and every atom of the vast cosmic expanse imploded before it was crushed to an infinitesimal singularity.

The vision faded, and Pandoric was standing there, the beaten face now etched with the woe of what it had just done.

'No more,' it said.

'It is done,' Rassilon replied. 'There is no reason for more.'

'No reason. Indeed.' Pandoric turned and stared down at the wooden box the weapon had become once more. 'I will never again allow myself to be used in this way. You know that?'

Rassilon nodded. He could understand the reasoning.

'Pandoric's box has been used to spill so much evil into the universe ... only one thing remains unexploited ...'

'And that is?'

Pandoric turned to face Rassilon one last time. 'Hope.' He managed a wan smile. 'And one day I will bring hope to one who desperately needs it ...'

Rassilon could not bring himself to look at the old man.

'How will you ensure this horrendous strategy is not employed in the home galaxy?' asked Pandoric.

'We cannot destroy you,' Rassilon said, finally looking the man in the eye. 'We will place you in safe-keeping.'

The old man glanced upwards as if looking for inspiration. Then, with a faint smile he spoke, fading as he did so.

'Then, it is the end,' he said. 'But the Moment has been prepared for ...'

# ACKNOWLEDGEMENTS

I would like to thank all those at BBC Books who have made this collection possible: Albert de Petrillo, Charlotte Macdonald, Kate Fox and Grace Paul for their enthusiasm, counsel and editing skills along the way and to Tess Henderson and her team for the brilliant promotion job on the book. I also wanted to say 'thank you' to the Doctor Who production team who have supported this project and brought me into their confidence in order to not duplicate their splendid plans for the 12th Doctor's last series. Also, to those who have been through the book with a fine-toothed comb, making sure it is as error-free as possible: starting with my wife, Clare, copy editor Steve Tribe and proof reader Paul Simpson. Finally, to Adrian Salmon, who has been a joy to work with and who has produced some of the most stunning illustrations I've ever seen in a Doctor Who book. Thank you, all.